P9-DDQ-900

7/26/01

great book.
Believable
Characters.

An
Unexpected
Love

An Unexpected Love

a novel

Michele Ashman Bell

Covenant Communications, Inc.

Covenant

Published by Covenant Communications, Inc.
American Fork, Utah

Copyright © 1998 by Michele Ashman Bell
All rights reserved

Printed in the United States of America
First Printing: March 1998

05 04 03 02 01 00 99 98   10 9 8 7 6 5 4 3 2

ISBN 1-57734-243-7

Library of Congress Cataloging-in-Publication Data

Bell, Michele Ashman, 1959-
    An unexpected love / Michele Ashman Bell.
        p.   cm.
    ISBN 1-57734-243-7
    I. Title
PS3552.E5217U5 1998
813'.54--dc21   98-13773
                                           CIP

This book is dedicated to
Gary—
my husband, sweetheart, and best friend.

Acknowledgments

To my children,
Weston, Kendyl, and Andrea.
Thanks for sharing the computer with me.

And to my sisters—
Alicia, Nicole, Erika—
and my niece, Lindsay.
Thanks for liking everything I write.

Special thanks to
the wonderful women of Wasatch Mountain Fiction Writers;
the members of First Writes, Second Writes, and
LDSFW critique groups;
to Karla Jay, Shelley Thompson, Lynelle Spencer,
Caren Tucker, Lisa Payne
Lynnae, Mardi, Amy, Sue, and Craig;
my supportive friends and fellow instructors at Life Centre;
the Young Women of Willow Canyon 3rd Ward;
Anita Stansfield, for helpful suggestions and guidance;

and above all,

to my friend and editor, Valerie Holladay,
for constant encouragement, advice,
and "tweaking" that made the difference.
Thank you isn't enough.

Chapter 1

ALEX McCARTY HAD CONQUERED HER EATING DISORDER YEARS ago and was now in complete control of her health and her life. However, her friend and manager Sandy Dalebout didn't think so.

As Alex traveled from the Bay Area, through northern Nevada to Utah, up into eastern Idaho, she had plenty of time to think about the conversation she'd had with Sandy the day before.

"It's for your own good, Alex. You'll see," Sandy told her as she helped load suitcases into the trunk of the car. "The timing is perfect. Your sister needs help right now and you need some time off. Go. Relax. Eat. Have a nice visit. And don't come back until you've gained at least ten pounds."

Alex didn't plan on gaining any weight. She didn't need to. And she resented Sandy for questioning her judgment. She was a national health and fitness consultant, for goodness' sake. Her whole career was based on knowing the difference between being healthy and being too thin.

So, instead of enjoying springtime in California, she was plowing through skyscraping mountains in a raging blizzard, headed toward her sister, Jamie, and brother-in-law, Steve's, house in Island Park, Idaho, near Yellowstone National Park.

The narrow road, barely visible through the blur of snow outside, was slick and difficult to follow. Alex gasped, terrified, as the back wheels of her car shifted, fishtailed, then grabbed hold. As her car proceeded at a slow crawl, Alex's breathing returned to normal but her heart banged wildly in her chest.

Tightly she gripped the Mazda's steering wheel and searched through dense, whirling snow for pole reflectors. Had she driven past the town? Was she anywhere near civilization?

Keeping her eyes on the nearly invisible road ahead, Alex felt along the console until she located her cell phone. However, when she turned it on, the NO SERVICE indicator flashed. Either the heavy shroud of storm clouds or the towering mountains prevented contact with the world. She would have given anything to hear something other than the static on the radio and the scrape of wipers on the windshield. It was like being sucked into a swirling, white vacuum.

Darn you, Sandy. This is all your fault.

Sandy was concerned because Alex had lost "a little" weight, but Alex wasn't surprised she'd dropped a few pounds. Her career demanded constant traveling, extensive lectures, and long hours demonstrating new ideas in the ever-changing world of aerobic exercise. But Sandy wouldn't listen to reason. Sandy felt like Alex hadn't "been herself" lately; it seemed like she was lacking energy, always picking up whatever cold or flu bug was going around the gym, and just plain looking too thin.

And then, after the last fitness convention Alex had passed out in her hotel room and Sandy had completely overreacted when she found out. In all honesty, Alex had to admit that it had even scared her a little. She was relieved when the doctor attributed her collapse to overwork and lack of rest, which made sense to her, but Sandy was convinced Alex was anorexic.

Slowing the car to barely six miles an hour, Alex continued to follow the curve in the road. Even at a snail's pace the tires slid. She held her breath. The tires caught and the car inched forward.

Last night in her hotel room in Salt Lake City, when she had watched the news, the weatherman had said nothing about a major snowstorm hitting eastern Idaho. Would she have changed her plans had she known it was going to snow? Probably not. She had to get to Jamie's. Her younger sister needed her. After two miscarriages Jamie was finally expecting again but now she was having complications with this pregnancy.

The thought stabbed Alex with guilt. She loved her sister and wanted to help, support, and encourage her, but she'd kept her distance all these years because Steve and Jamie were such religious fanatics. The last time Alex, Jamie, and their mother had been together was at their grandfather's funeral in Lancaster, Pennsylvania, three years ago.

Alex and her mother sat through Steve and Jamie's explanation of life after death, then their "testimonies" about the importance of the eternal family unit. After that, Alex and her mother had spent the rest of the day avoiding the young couple.

Unlike her mother, Alex managed to separate her sister from her religion and tried to maintain some kind of relationship with her. She liked spending time with Jamie but she always had a plan ahead of time to dodge and divert their attempts at brainwashing her. She didn't want anything to do with this crazy cult they belonged to. Especially since this was the same religion responsible for killing their father nineteen years ago. To make matters worse, Jamie had left home after high school and gone to college—to BYU of all places— and joined the Mormon Church.

Things had never been the same since. Alex wondered if the tension between her mother and Jamie would ever cease. She was tired of getting caught in the middle.

Glancing down at the dashboard, Alex noticed there was a quarter of a tank of gas left. How long would that keep her alive if she was forced to stop and wait out the storm? There was nothing in the car to keep her warm once the fuel was gone. Wool blankets and mittens weren't exactly standard trunk storage items back home in Palo Alto.

The outline of a road sign appeared on her right. Snow clung to its surface, covering desperately needed information.

"Where in the world am I?" Alex strained to make out any words on the sign, but keeping the car on the road demanded her complete attention.

"Why didn't I call Jamie and Steve this morning?" She banged on the steering wheel with the heel of her right hand. At least then they would know to look for her if she didn't show up.

"And why do I keep talking to myself?"

Because I'm scared!

Alex fumbled with the heat switch, moved it to defrost, and bumped up the fan. The digital clock flashed 11:51 a.m.

Even with her headlights on she could barely see to the front end of the car. With a click of the lever she turned on the high beam. The snowflakes doubled in number and size. Quickly she clicked the lights back to low.

"You're going to be fine," she told herself. "Just keep going." There had to be a service station or house somewhere along here soon.

She leaned forward, stretching the tension out of her back.

"Come on, Texaco."

Her stomach churned, partly from nerves, partly because it was empty. She hadn't eaten since the bagel and diet drink she'd had the day before. To keep her appetite at bay, she kept plenty of gum close by, chewing it until the flavor left, then popping another piece in her mouth. Wrappers from three packs of cinnamon Trident littered the passenger's seat. But the gum didn't fool her stomach. Her system knew all that chewing was supposed to produce some kind of sustenance. But Alex had learned to discipline herself and refused to give into her appetite. Besides, she hated feeling full. It made her feel as if she'd lost control of herself.

The movement of the wipers broke the hypnotic slant of snow dancing toward her, scattering her thoughts. A flicker of light in the rearview mirror caught her eye.

Could it be? She glanced again at the reflection. Yes! There it was. Headlights. Two dim but beautiful disks of yellow moving closer.

Her mind raced. Somehow she had to flag down the driver and find out where she was.

She looked back at the lights in the mirror, and relief eased her knotted stomach. But when she looked forward again, she saw that she'd missed a turn and was headed straight off the road.

She spun the steering wheel to correct her course, but the rear end of the car whipped sideways, pulling it into a perfect spin. Once, twice. But it was too late.

"NO!" she screamed. She stomped on the brake and locked her arms against the steering wheel. Still spinning, the car careened off the side of the road and nose-dived into a canal, landing at the bottom. On impact Alex's head slammed into the side window and everything went black.

Chapter 2

"HI, THERE. HOW'RE YOU FEELING?"

Alex's forehead scrunched up at the sound of the man's voice, and a whomp of pain pulsed on the left side of her forehead.

"Ohhh." She lifted her fingers to the ache, but a warm hand gently clasped hers and set it on her stomach.

"I've just changed the bandage. I think you'll be okay, but you might have a scar. You could have used some stitches. Can you open your eyes?"

Alex rolled away from the voice. Why did he keep talking? She wanted to sleep, to make the pain go away.

"Hey." He jiggled her shoulder. "Wake up."

Using all her strength, she lifted an arm and let it fall heavily toward the voice. "Don't." Her lips barely moved. "Sleep."

"Sorry, no more beauty sleep for you." He shook her again.

She tried to make a fist but was too weak. How could she make him go away? And who was he anyway?

WHO WAS HE?

She bolted upright, and a searing pain shot through her head. Wincing, she demanded, "Who are you? Where am I?"

"It's okay," his voice soothed. "You're in my home. You had an accident."

"An accident!" She fingered the gauze and tape above her eyebrow. "How did you . . . what am I . . . ?" She tried to study the stranger in front of her through blurred vision. His mangy hair, dark eyes, and week's worth of stubble did little to comfort her. "Why did you bring me here?"

"I was driving behind you. Your car went into a skid and slid off the road just before the turnoff to my house. You hit your head pretty hard on the side window. I brought you here because it's thirty miles to the clinic and the storm's still pretty bad."

Skidding? Sliding? Of course, she'd been driving through the snow on her way to Jamie's. He was the pair of headlights behind her.

She eased herself back onto the couch. "I need to call my sister."

"The phone lines are down and the power's out. It's been snowing for sixteen hours straight."

"Doesn't this place have snowplows?"

"Sure," he said, "You got caught in the worst of it before they closed the road."

They closed the road!

"The plows can't seem to keep up. But I'm sure the power and phones will be working soon."

He appeared to be a decent person beneath all that hair, Alex tried to think positively.

"I'm glad I was behind you," he said. "We wouldn't have found you for weeks if I hadn't seen your car go off the road. It's buried. You can't even see it from the highway." He turned and lifted a cup of water off the end table. "I've got some Tylenol if you'd like." He held the tablets out for her to see.

She eyed them suspiciously, trying to remember what Tylenol looked like. "It doesn't really hurt that much." She wasn't about to take medicine from a stranger.

"I'll put them here if you need them." He placed the cup of water and pills on the table next to a stack of magazines. Mormon magazines. She recognized them because her sister sent articles from the periodical sometimes. They went straight to the garbage. Unread.

Was this guy a Mormon?

Alex clutched the blanket to her chest, averting her gaze when he looked at her.

"You had me a little worried. I thought you'd never wake up." He ran his hand up his forehead, his fingers catching in a tangle of curls. Now that her vision had cleared she realized he wasn't as old as she'd thought he was. Late twenties, early thirties, maybe.

"What time is it?"

"Almost four."

She glanced out the window. "It's so dark outside."

"We lose the sun early up here, and those clouds are pretty thick." He tilted his head to the side and leaned toward her, his eyes full of concern.

"I need to call my sister. She'll be worried."

"I'll check the phone again. Maybe they've got it fixed." He jumped to his feet and in five strides left the room.

Alex felt like she'd slipped through a crack in the earth into some strange twilight zone.

Propping herself up on the pillows, she studied the room. The cabin was rustic but still charming. Two Aztec-patterned couches flanked a large stone fireplace, flickering with low flames. Except for the forest-green leather recliner with a crocheted afghan slung over the arm, the house was in perfect order. Bookshelves were neat and orderly; the polished furniture glistened in the firelight. Not a cobweb or dust bunny in sight. Even the wood stacked near the fireplace was piled neatly. Either this man had a wife or a a a maid, or he lived with his mother.

"No luck." Alex heard his voice before he walked into the room. "Phones are still down. But I'm sure it won't be long. The last radio report said the roads are still closed but the clouds are starting to break up."

He carried a tray in with him and sat it on a cross-cut log coffee table. "You must be starving. How about some cheese and crackers? I can't really cook anything until the power comes on."

She started to protest but her stomach reacted with a hungry growl loud enough for him to hear.

"I take it that means yes?" He smiled. Even with his Tasmanian devil hairdo and grizzly beard, she couldn't deny the kindness in his voice and eyes.

"Well, maybe a cracker or two."

Alex leaned forward and reached for several of the saltines.

"Do you live here alone?" she asked.

He settled back into his chair, shifting a little to move the afghan. "Yup. Just me." Rubbing the whiskers on his chin, he said, "Tell me, what's a California girl like you doing in a snowy place like this?"

"How do you know I'm from California?"

"I recognized your license plates."

"Oh." She nibbled a corner of her cracker. The flames in the fire-place crackled and hissed. Its warmth took the edge off her fears.

"Believe me, just before I slid off the road, I asked myself the same thing. I didn't expect snow like this in March." She took another bite.

"We get weather like this in June."

"I'm on my way to visit my sister. She lives in Island Park."

"Who's your sister?"

"Her name is Jamie Dixon."

"Jamie! You're Jamie's sister?"

"Yes." She nearly dropped her cracker. "You know her?"

"Jamie Dixon, Steve's wife?"

"YES!" Alex sat up, cringing at the pain. "You know them?"

"Sure I know them. I'm Rich, Rich Greenwood. Steve's partner. I forgot he said you were coming for a visit. You must be Alex."

"That's right." She stared in disbelief. This was Rich? Jamie had talked about Rich for years. Somehow Alex never pictured him looking like a fur trapper.

"I don't believe this." He shook his head. "I guess I should have made the connection, though. I mean, how many women from California would be alone on the road in a raging blizzard?"

"Not many, I suppose." He made her sound foolish driving in such weather. But the snow had started so unexpectedly, without any warning.

Relaxing a little, now that she knew he wasn't going to whip out his chain saw, Alex couldn't believe the coincidence. She supposed she should be grateful for the stroke of luck that saved her life.

He studied her for a moment. "You look like Jamie except her hair's a lot shorter than yours and her stomach's out to here." He stretched his arm out in front of him then brought it closer to his middle. "Well, maybe only to here."

"She's finally showing?" Jamie was over five months along.

"She sure is proud of that tummy of hers. They've been waiting a long time for this baby."

Jamie had talked about having a baby from the moment she got married. Even as a child the only thing she'd ever wanted was to get married and raise a family.

He settled back into his chair. "Where in California do you live?"

"Palo Alto, near Stanford University."

He nodded. "How long do you plan on staying?"

Now, that was a good question. Until the next fitness convention, until Jamie and Steve bore their testimonies one too many times, until Sandy decided Alex had suffered long enough and let her come home. "A week or so. I don't have to get back right away."

"Jamie will love having you around. She's got her hands full with the baby coming, the rental business, and her calling in the branch."

So, he *was* a Mormon. Too bad. She was just starting to like him.

He unbuttoned his cuffs and rolled up his sleeves. "The church roof collapsed after the last big snow storm so the whole branch has been in a bit of a shock. Jamie and Steve have done a lot to keep things going until the damage is repaired."

He walked over to the fireplace and picked up the poker.

"I don't know how she does it all," he continued. "The doctor told her she needs to slow down, take it easy, but she's always on the go. I've never seen anyone like her. She's always sewing or painting some craft thing for a friend or a neighbor." He jabbed at the logs then tossed in another.

Jamie had already had complications with this pregnancy, spotting in her second month. This darn church of hers was going to make her lose a third child.

"I'm not a Mormon." Alex's words hung in the air.

"Oh." He paused then replaced the poker. "I didn't know. Anyway, Steve and Jamie are great. Almost like family to me. Steve and I go way back. We were mission companions in Bolivia." He went back to his chair and sat down. The fire caught the fresh log and the room brightened with its glow.

He looked like Daniel Boone having a bad hair day. She always pictured Mormons wearing dark suits and white shirts and shaking everyone's hand. That's what they'd done at her sister's wedding reception. Had this man been at the wedding?

Which was another sore spot, now that he'd brought up the subject of religion. What kind of church didn't allow family members to attend weddings inside that temple of theirs?

"Were you at their wedding?"

"No, I was still on my mission in South America. Steve wrote to tell me he couldn't wait until I got home before they married. He didn't want Jamie to have time to change her mind."

That meant Rich, like her brother-in-law, was probably close to her age, twenty-seven.

"Steve and Jamie are sure a great couple. She used to invite me to Sunday dinner when we were all at BYU. And she was forever setting me up with friends of hers."

That sounded like Jamie, who seemed convinced she needed to make everyone else in the world as happy as she was.

"You say you're from Palo Alto?"

Alex nodded. The cracker in her mouth tasted like a lump of paste. She tried to dredge up some saliva to wash it down.

"Jamie always said she was from New York."

Alex relaxed back into the couch. "That's where we grew up. My mother still lives there. Jamie hooked up with a few kids in Manhattan and followed them to BYU. That's where she got baptized."

"Your mom's not a member either?"

"No." If she didn't change the subject quickly, he'd probably pull out his Mormon Bible and start preaching.

"So," she said, "how's business?" Rich and Steve owned an outdoor rental equipment store for all kinds of summer and winter recreational activities.

"Great. You know Steve, always coming up with some new advertising gimmick or plan to expand the business. In fact, right now we have more than we can handle. Hiking and river trips in the summer and snowmobile and cross-country skiing tours in the winter—we're booked a year in advance. That's where I was coming from when I saw your accident."

"You'd been snowmobiling?"

"I'd just brought a group back from five days in Yellowstone. We barely missed the storm. I must look pretty scary. I haven't had a chance to shower and shave."

Because he'd been stuck taking care of her.

"I'm really sorry about the intrusion. I feel much better now. Maybe you could just drive me to Jamie's."

"Sorry, it's still a blizzard out there. We'd never be able to stay on the road. When it stops we'll give it a try."

So now what did they do? Sit here and stare at each other? She was reluctant to keep talking for fear something would trigger any more talk about religion.

"If you're feeling okay, I'll go jump in the shower and clean up."

"I'm fine, really," she fibbed. Her head still throbbed.

"Holler if you need anything."

She nodded.

He took one of the two lanterns off the mantel and was gone.

Alex got up and examined his collection of CDs. A lot of country/western, some classical, and of course, the Mormon Tabernacle Choir. He had several shelves of videos, too, including a complete collection of Disney animated movies, some recent hits, and several rows of John Wayne movies.

A half dozen pictures on the wall below the stairway caught her eye. She noticed one of a young woman with a generous smile, heavily made-up eyes, and a long blonde perm that was gathered on the crown of her head like a fountain.

Was she a sister? There was no resemblance. A girlfriend? The Barbie doll didn't seem the type for a tree-lover like Mr. Greenwood.

Alex shrugged then paced back to the fireplace, wondering how much longer she'd be stuck there. She admired a lovely watercolor above the mantel, a landscape of a beautiful green valley with a creek winding through, surrounded by tall pines tickling puffy pink clouds. Is that what Island Park looked like when it wasn't covered in snow?

Howling wind rattled the paned glass, reminding her of the raging storm that threatened to keep her captive. Alex shook her head in disgust. Who would have thought she would be here with a stranger, snowbound in a cabin in the mountains? How much longer could the storm go on?

Chapter 3

ALEX LEAFED THROUGH A *SPORTS ILLUSTRATED*, PAUSING BRIEFLY to scan an article called, "Should Kids Look Up to Athletes?"

She lifted her gaze from the magazine when Rich entered the room. Her breath caught in her throat. Gone were the beard and scruffy hair. Instead, he was clean shaven, his dark, wavy hair finger combed into place. He could have been advertising men's cologne, men's jeans, or for that matter, toilet bowl cleaner, and she would have rushed to the nearest store and bought it. He was handsome. Outdoorsy and rugged. Especially in a light blue denim shirt, neatly pressed jeans, and leather moccasin slippers.

Without the beard she could see his wide mouth, smooth skin, and strong chin. But still, even more striking were those molasses-colored eyes, peaceful and kind.

She recalled that when Jamie had talked about Rich during many of their phone conversations, she had briefly mentioned his good looks. Which were definitely worth mentioning, Alex added to herself. She wondered why he wasn't married to some nice Mormon girl.

He rested his feet on the coffee table. "You didn't eat much. Aren't you hungry?"

"I'm okay. I don't want you to fuss."

"Are you kidding? I'm thrilled to have some company. The only single females around these parts are the four-legged kind."

Even if she tried, she knew it'd be hard not to like him.

"So, what do you say? Should we grab something to eat?"

"Okay." She returned his smile.

They each carried a lantern into the kitchen.

"Does the power go out like this often?"

"Once or twice a year." He stopped in the middle of the floor. The flames bathed the cupboards in a golden glow. "They'll have things turned back on soon."

Alex shivered against the icy chill seeping in through the window.

"I can't guarantee anything. I haven't been shopping for a week." He opened and shut every cupboard in the kitchen, illuminating the contents with the lantern. He opened the fridge.

"Doesn't look very promising. This is more serious than I thought."

Alex peeked around him to look inside the refrigerator. Except for a ketchup bottle, a half-full milk jug, an egg carton with one egg, and condiments lining the shelves in the door, the fridge was practically empty.

Rich rummaged deeper. "I think we've been saved." He pulled out a package of hot dogs. "We can do these over the fire."

Alex shut her eyes, took a breath, then said, "Do you have anything else?"

"Not a big fan of hot dogs, eh?"

Alex shook her head. "Sorry. I make it a habit to watch my fat intake. Please, go ahead though. I'm not that hungry anyway."

"I could warm up some chili."

"I wouldn't care for anything. Really." She ran her hands through the sides of her hair and rested them on the back of her neck.

His smile faded. "Are you sure there's nothing I can get you?"

Alex suddenly felt embarrassed. Here she was, a total stranger, and he was waiting on her hand and foot, even when she was being as picky as a princess. But after years of teaching and preaching fitness and nutrition, she had trained herself to be careful about the kind of foods she ate. Of course, she tended to go overboard at times and barely ate enough to keep a bird alive, but that was partly due to the anorexia she'd suffered as a teen. It was inbred in her like DNA. She knew she wasn't anorexic now, but she couldn't change the tendency to fall into old habits any more than she could change the color of her eyes.

"I'll eat when I get to Jamie's."

"That may not be for hours." He thought for a moment. "Hey, how about a P-B-&-J?"

"What's that?" she asked.

He pulled a jar of Skippy peanut butter from the cupboard. "We'll have to use hot dog buns, though."

She swallowed, trying to ignore the emptiness in her middle.

"It's okay, really. I wish you wouldn't worry about me."

"Nonsense. I'm making you a sandwich." He grabbed a butter knife from a drawer. "After what you've been through, you need some nourishment. Besides, you're skinny enough. Why do you have to worry about fat, anyway?"

"I'm not skinny." To her that was an insult. "I'm *lean.*"

"You're lean all right, but you're also hungry and weak. Have a seat," he pointed to a chair. "I'll whip this up in a second."

"Easy on the peanut butter, please."

"Gotcha," he said.

She salivated as she watched him spread strawberry preserves and a light smear of peanut butter onto the bread.

"I can tell you've done this before." She accepted the plate.

"P-B-&-J's are a bachelor's staple. That and La Choy."

She laughed out loud. "I'm sure it's delicious."

"Here." He handed her a napkin. "Eat."

She nibbled on a corner of the hot dog bun. He pulled a can of apple juice from the cupboard, opened it, and poured them each a glass.

She licked her lips. "Mmmmm. This is good."

He sat down at the small square table across from her in the other chair. The flame of the lantern waltzed between them. "I'm glad you like it. Maybe it will put some color back into your cheeks." He leaned forward.

As much as she didn't want to, she kept eating, marveling at how good the sandwich tasted. Even though she knew she was consuming at least fifteen grams of fat, she was too hungry to feel guilty about it now.

"So, what is it you do when you're not sliding off snowy roads and not eating fat?"

"I'm a national fitness and nutrition consultant." After a few more bites, she set the half-eaten sandwich down on her plate.

"What does that mean?" He gazed at her intently.

"It means I travel to conventions and gyms across the country and lecture on nutrition and exercise. Basically, I teach other fitness instructors about new industry techniques and breakthroughs."

"Sounds impressive."

"It can be fun at times, but I travel a lot and the pace is hectic. I also just finished a workout series for ESPN."

"You mean you'll be like that guy on the beach in Hawaii?"

She licked jelly off her thumb. "Kind of, but better I hope. I want to reach those people at home who are too uncomfortable going to a gym, or have small children and can't get away. The workout has to be motivating but fun so they'll stick with it and achieve their goals. What good is all that work if they don't get results?"

Rich nodded and dug his hand into his shirt pocket, producing a tiny jar of Carmex. "It's nice to have a profession that benefits others. I bet you're good at what you do." He twirled off the lid, coated his finger, and rubbed his lips in a vigorous back-and-forth motion.

She smiled at the method he used to apply the balm, almost like he was brushing his teeth.

"How'd you get into this line of work?" he asked as he returned the container to his pocket.

Alex wasn't about to tell him that as a child she'd endured years of torment and teasing because she'd been overweight. "I majored in Exercise Physiology with a minor in nutrition. To support myself while going through school, I taught aerobics. I also got a job as a personal trainer at a gym. I started lecturing about nutrition to instructors and trainers in local clubs around the Bay Area and wrote a few articles on exercise and nutrition for national publications."

By the look of concentration on his face he seemed to want to know more. She shifted in her chair and continued, "My lecture circle kept growing and branching until I was going all over the country doing workshops and conventions. A year ago I was asked to do this video and the TV series. We finished shooting last August."

"So when do we see you on television?"

"Sometime in May. Do you get cable up here?"

"Not me, but Steve and Jamie just got a satellite hookup. They missed the weekly Church broadcasts and conference from Salt Lake City. The church building has a satellite but it was damaged in the collapse."

Just then the lights flickered on, went dark, then flickered on again.

Alex squinted at their brightness and sat up tall, gaining a new appreciation for Thomas Edison. Lanterns were only romantic when you didn't have to use them.

Rich glanced out the window. "Hey, I think the snow's stopped. We'd better take off while we can, just in case it starts up again."

"Do you think it's safe?"

"Sure, you're in good hands. But maybe we should change that bandage first before your sister sees you."

As he cleared the dishes into the sink, Alex pushed onto her feet and watched him swish them clean with soap and water then stack them neatly into the drainer.

The first-aid supplies were still in the living room where he'd bandaged her earlier. With the coziness of the fireplace pulsing around them, they sat facing each other on the couch while he doctored her wound.

"Can you hold these?" He placed the gauze, scissors, and tape into her outstretched hands.

"This might hurt," he said. Carefully he lifted the corners of the tape and peeled off the dressing.

Mixed with the smell of his lip balm was the faint odor of peanut butter. Secretly she stole glances at him as he busied himself with his task. The brush of his fingers on her forehead tingled her skin.

Each moment she spent with Rich replaced the shock and fear of her first impression of him. He was nothing like the wild mountain man she'd thought him to be. He was gentle, caring, and warm. And he was heartwrenchingly handsome. Too bad he belonged to such a screwy religion.

Chapter 4

FEELING LIKE SHE WAS WEARING A SLEEPING BAG WITH BOOTS, Alex hung onto Rich's waist as the snowmobile, or "sled" as he called it, roared through the frozen stillness, the single headlight beaming ahead, splitting the darkness.

Within the circle of light, Alex made out the forms of towering lodgepole pines, their branches groaning under heavy snow. Log cottages, straight off a Christmas card, were tucked away between groves of trees and lofty snowbanks. Somewhere beneath one of those mounds was her car.

Thinking of her Mazda reminded her of the accident, and thinking of the accident made her think of Rich, the person she had her arms tightly wrapped around. Once again she wondered why his girlfriend or some other smart Mormon girl hadn't grabbed him by now.

She nestled her head between his shoulders and sucked in several breaths. The icy air froze in her nostrils and lungs.

They plowed their way through the sparkling wonderland until Alex noticed Rich was trying to tell her something. He pointed straight ahead to what she figured was Jamie and Steve's house.

They were nearly up the lane when the snowmobile choked and slowed, then chugged to a stop.

The noise of the dying engine sparked through the air, then got lost in the trees. The silence had almost settled when they heard a voice. "Rich, is that you?"

Alex looked up and saw Steve in the front doorway.

"Hey, Dixon, I brought you a surprise," Rich yelled.

"You need some help?"

"Nah, I think I can manage."

The boots on Alex's feet were twice her size and with each step she nearly left one behind. Instead of walking, she had to slide her legs. Snow quickly filled in the gaps between her snowpants and the buckets on her feet.

Together they tromped up the front porch steps. "You'll never guess who I found," Rich said.

"What the devil? Alex, is that you? Jamie!" He yelled so loud Alex feared an avalanche.

"We've been sick with worry." Her brother-in-law hugged her tightly. "I'm so happy to see you." He hugged her again.

"What is it?" a voice called, then Jamie appeared by his side. "Alex, you're here!"

"Sorry I worried you," Alex said.

"Come in." Jamie pulled her inside. "We thought you'd been kidnapped by aliens." She threw her arms around Alex, nearly knocking her sideways. "Are you okay?"

"Fine. I'm fine."

Jamie released her sister and stood back. "I can't believe you're really here."

"I should've called before I left the hotel this morning. I had no idea it was going to snow."

Jamie drew Alex away from the front door into a large room with a stone fireplace. "Come in where it's warm, and let's get you out of these clothes. Then you can tell us everything." Alex stood woodenly while her sister peeled off gloves, scarf, and down-filled jumpsuit. Last to come off was the stocking cap. When it did, Jamie gasped.

"You're hurt! What happened?"

"It's nothing, just a small bump. I had a little accident."

"An accident!" Jamie said. "Are you sure you're okay?"

Steve told his wife to calm down and helped clear stacks of fabric squares from the green and maroon plaid couch next to Rich. Alex sat across from them on the matching loveseat.

She explained what had happened, making sure to play down the seriousness of her accident and injury, explaining how Rich rescued her and they waited out the storm at his cabin.

"You've been with Rich this whole time?" Steve asked.

"Yeah, pretty much," Alex said.

"We tried to contact you, but the phone lines were down and the storm was too thick to travel in," Rich clarified the arrangement.

"We heard over the short-wave that they've called out the Search and Rescue for three cross-country skiers lost over in Yellowstone. There's been dozens of accidents and people stranded in their cars." Steve rose from the couch, walked over and fanned the fire, then added another log. Sparks swirled and faded into the rising smoke.

"Alex slept most of the afternoon," Rich said. "I didn't even know who she was. Her I.D. was back in her car and she was unconscious the whole time. Like I said, she wanted to reach you but the phones were out. Driving would have been bad news even on a sled."

"You were smart to wait for the snow to clear," Jamie said, resting her clasped hands on her stomach.

Steve returned to his seat. "Pretty uncanny, you two meeting up like this."

"We thought so, too," Rich said.

"The Lord was watching over you, Alex," Jamie said softly.

Then he watched me slide off the road. Jamie always sized up a situation in relationship to "the Lord." But Alex noticed that he only seemed to get credit for the good things that happened.

"Of course," Steve grinned devilishly, "I'm sure Rich wasn't too opposed to helping out a girl as pretty as Alex, were you, Rich?"

Alex could have sworn she saw Rich's face wash red. He shifted in his seat.

"I'm sure I drove him nuts," Alex said. She and Rich exchanged looks. "But enough about all of this. What a fantastic place you have here! Where did you get all these great decorations?"

Stuffed bunnies, bears, painted birdhouses, and other wooden items snuggled into every nook and cranny of the home. Dried flower wreaths and arrangements covered most of the walls.

"Jamie decorated it," Steve said. "She makes all of these things, and she's decorated most of the homes in our branch and neighborhood."

"You really did, Jamie?" Alex was impressed.

"I haven't decorated all the houses in our branch," Jamie said.

"Ever since we got her that scroll saw last year, she's gone crazy with wood. I'm a little worried about all those pine trees outside."

"Oh, stop it, Steve." Jamie shoo'd him with her hand. "He's exaggerating. I'm not that crazy."

Alex wondered where Jamie had learned to make all the cute decorations. "Your house could be a boutique."

"Hey," Steve said, "great idea. We could make a fortune if we could just get her to sell some of this stuff. But that's the problem; she either keeps it for herself or gives it away. Every craft store around hounds her to bring in her things."

"But, honey," Jamie said, "I wouldn't enjoy it if I *had* to make it. Besides, I'm not a businesswoman. I want to stay home with my husband and our children."

"How are you and the baby doing?" Alex asked.

Jamie's face brightened. "I'm past the morning sickness, and she's growing just like she's supposed to."

"She? The baby's a girl?"

Jamie nodded proudly. "We had the ultrasound last week."

"That's wonderful. Have you thought of a name yet?"

"We like the name Katelyn. It was Rich's suggestion."

Alex nodded in agreement. "It's a lovely name."

She didn't mean to stare at Rich, but the flicker of light from the fireplace danced shadows on his face. Alex had known good-looking men before. Her old boyfriend, Jordan, at first had been the most gorgeous man she'd ever seen, but his jealousy and possessiveness turned him into an ugly monster.

Did Rich have anything hidden behind his handsome face? She intended never to find out.

He glanced her way. She turned her eyes to her brother-in-law.

Steve slid an arm around his wife's shoulders. "She can name the baby whatever she wants just as long as she slows down and takes it easy, like the doctor said."

Alex sat up with a start. "What's wrong? Is everything okay?"

"Everything's fine." Jamie rested her hand on her husband's knee. "My baby's healthy and strong and I'm surrounded by the three most important people in my life. I'm so blessed." Jamie smiled at each of them.

Alex swallowed the knot in her throat. She couldn't deny it, Jamie looked happier than she'd ever known her to be. Jamie had always been the eternal optimist, always looking at the bright side, always cheering others. So sweet sometimes it was nauseating. But then, Jamie had always had an easy life. She had never struggled with her appearance or her weight. Jamie had always been surrounded by friends, adored by adults. It would be easy to be cheerful without any challenges, Alex thought.

"Is anybody hungry or thirsty? I could whip up some hot chocolate to go with these incredible pumpkin cookies I made this afternoon," Jamie said.

Rich raised one eyebrow as he smiled at Alex. Alex returned his smile with an innocent expression.

"What?" Jamie noticed the exchange of looks. "Did I say something?"

"No," Rich shrugged. He searched his shirt pocket then patted the pockets of his jeans. "Not really. I just hope you have better luck finding something for her to eat than I did."

"All out of rice cakes, Rich?" Steve caught an elbow in the ribs from his wife.

Alex was grateful Steve didn't crack some kind of joke about how pudgy she was when she was younger. Instead he leaned over to the end table and pulled open the drawer.

"Is this what you're looking for?" He tossed Rich a tube of Carmex.

Rich briskly applied the salve and handed it back.

"We keep this here just for Rich," Steve said, displaying the tube. "He's got some kind of addiction. I find tubes and containers of this stuff everywhere."

Alex fought the urge to laugh.

"The dry, cold air is hard on skin," Jamie defended Rich. "And he's outside so much he has to keep his lips protected."

"Thanks, Jamie," Rich said. He checked his watch. "You folks probably need to get to bed. I think I'll go see if they need help plowing the roads."

"At least take a few cookies to eat while you plow," Jamie insisted. "And you'll be here tomorrow for dinner, won't you?"

"Are you kidding? Me miss a free meal?"

"With all the stuff you do to help us, we owe you much more than a home-cooked meal every now and then," Jamie said as she accompanied him to the front door. Steve and Alex followed behind.

While the conversation shifted to Rich's recent snowmobile outing, Alex visually toured Jamie's home. The furniture was a traditional style, in green, navy, and deep maroon plaid; Alex thought it was an excellent choice. It made the front room very cozy. On either side of the stone fireplace and oak mantel were bookshelves lined with leather-bound encyclopedias and church books. Two pictures were propped on the mantel—one of a temple and the other of three men in dark suits and white shirts. Over the fireplace was a large painting; a fall landscape of mountain peaks and colorful tree-filled valleys.

On the other side of the entry was a formal dining room. A polished oak table with a pedestal base was surrounded by six oak chairs. A braided rug in the same green, navy, and maroon covered the hardwood floor. A simple but elegant chandelier crowned the room.

Through the dining room was the kitchen, and down a hallway she could see what looked like a family room with a television.

"Alex?" A voice broke her thoughts. "Alex?"

"Sorry, I didn't hear you." Alex focused back on the three faces looking at her.

"We were just wondering how long you could stay," Jamie said.

"Oh, maybe a week. This is a slow time of year for me. I don't really have to hurry home."

"Then why don't you stay on for Easter?" Steve said.

"Gee, I don't know. That's still two weeks away."

"It may take that long to dig out your car." Rich zipped his snowsuit up to his chin and pulled the stocking cap onto his head and over his ears. He wrapped a long scarf several times around his neck.

"I'll have to see. That's a long time to have company."

"You're not company," Jamie said, "You're family." Jamie left the room for a moment and returned with a plastic bag full of cookies. "You're staying and that's final. It will take that long to catch up on everything. I want to hear about your video and the ESPN workout. Besides, I need you to help me do the baby's room. I couldn't wallpaper a dollhouse let alone a whole bedroom." She handed Rich the cookies.

"Okay." Alex held up her hand in the face of Jamie's persistence. "I'll check my schedule."

"We'd better let Rich get going so he can get those roads done and get some sleep tonight," Jamie said.

"Yeah, I wouldn't want him sleeping through any of those basketball games tomorrow." Steve clapped his hands then rubbed them briskly together. "Got that satellite just in time, wouldn't you say, Bud?"

"Should be great." Rich pulled on his gloves and held up the bag of goodies. "Thanks, Jamie." He kissed her on the cheek. "See you tomorrow. Nice meeting you, Alex."

"Thanks for all you've done, Rich," Alex said.

He smiled broadly. "My pleasure." Then he opened the door and with an Arctic whoosh was gone.

The man had been in her life, her conscious life, for less than twelve hours, and she couldn't help peeking out the window for one last look as he started up the snowmobile and rocketed into the night.

Chapter 5

A PILLAR OF LIGHT LANDED SQUARELY ON ALEX'S FACE, FRAMING her with morning sun. She pulled the pillow over her head, but it was too late. She was awake and something heavenly-smelling filled her room.

After a quick trip to the bathroom, she was off to seek the source of the spicy, appley smell that was driving her tastebuds wild.

On her way she explored the rest of the upstairs. She found Steve and Jamie's room, with its French doors and private deck. Dominating the room was a lofty four-poster bed that looked like it required a spring board to get into. Off to the side was a spacious bathroom with double sinks, whirlpool bathtub, and a huge walk-in closet.

Next to them was a small room, filled with a ladder, paint cans, and rolls of wallpaper. Katelyn's room.

Envy nicked Alex's heart. Up to this moment, her career had always been enough, but now she wondered, would she ever be like her sister? Or would she follow her mother's footsteps: strong-willed and married to her career, alone at forty-nine?

Her thoughts drifted to her own sparsely furnished apartment with its bare walls, hodge podge of furniture, and shriveled-up Boston fern. Her life was like her apartment, full of clutter, busy, but it was empty without someone to share it with.

She wandered across the hall and found the office where Jamie's sewing machine was angled into one corner. Towering in the adjacent corner was Steve's computer. Stacks of computer magazines and long banners of form-feed printer paper decorated Steve' desk.

A sewing project lay heaped on a table with squares of calico print strewn around. Nearby was a carousel containing a rainbow of paint bottles, and next to that stood a half-painted wooden Easter bunny holding a string of brightly colored eggs.

Obviously all the artistic talent in the family had gone to Jamie. And judging by the size of the clutter, her sister was planning some heavy-duty paint sessions. Alex wondered if she ought to get a lesson or two while she was there.

As she descended the stairs she noticed some more tole-painted items and decorations she hadn't seen the night before. She slipped through the dining room and entered the kitchen.

Jamie, wrapped in a bright red apron with a teddy bear on it, was busy at the counter.

"You're awake." Jamie left her mixing spoon in the bowl and hugged her sister.

"What smells so good?"

"I'm trying that applesauce oatmeal muffin recipe you gave me. They'll be done in a sec."

"Why didn't you wake me?"

"You're on vacation. I want you to relax."

"I took a tour of the upstairs. It's going to take weeks just to see all the crafts you've made."

Jamie gave an embarrassed smile. "You don't think it's too much, do you?"

"Oh, no," Alex shook her head. "Your house has so much charm and personality. Things seem to have worked out great for you guys here."

"The business started out a little shaky; now those two can't keep up. It's time for them to hire some help. Rich is gone every week with tours, and Steve is constantly trying to make the business bigger and better. He's determined to make his first million before he's thirty. Ask him about his newest ideas—disposable credit cards and gourmet fortune cookies."

Jamie pushed her bangs off her forehead with the back of her hand. "I can't keep up with him." She replaced the lids on the plastic tubs of flour and sugar.

Alex jumped to her feet. "You should be resting, not cooking breakfast. Let me do this. You need to take care of yourself."

"I'm fine," Jamie assured her.

"And I want you to stay that way."

Nevertheless, Jamie let Alex put the containers in the cupboard for her. "I was starting to wonder if I'd ever get pregnant again. And then, when the bleeding started this time . . ." Jamie rested back on the counter ledge and took a deep breath.

The phone rang.

Jamie cleared her throat and lifted the receiver. "Hello?" Cradling the phone with her shoulder, she picked up a roasting pan before Alex rushed over and took it from her. Jamie mouthed, "Thanks," and pointed to the oven.

"I'm so sorry to hear that, President Miles. How long will she be in the hospital?"

Jamie sat in a chair at the desk and wrote something on a pad of paper. "Please don't apologize. We're more than happy to have them come here. Hopefully the weather will let up long enough to get the roof repaired on the church."

Alex took an orange from a fruit basket and held it up so Jamie could see it. "Can I have this?" she whispered.

Jamie nodded. She listened a moment longer then wrote something else on the paper.

Alex had most of the orange peeled when Jamie hung up. "Something wrong?" she asked.

"That was our branch president. He and his wife are retired. Sister Miles had a stroke and had to go to Idaho Falls."

"That's too bad." Alex sectioned the orange and took a bite. The tang made her wince.

"What did he need?"

"We've been having church at some of the members' homes until the chapel's repaired."

"His house was one of them, right, and let me guess," she pointed at her sister with a section of the orange, "He wants you to have church here?" The tartness of the fruit matched the tone in Alex's voice. "I swear, Jamie, don't these people understand your condition? You don't want to lose this baby, too, do you?"

Jamie ripped the note from the pad of paper. "Of course I don't."

"Then maybe someone else should take a turn. Why can't you meet in a conference room at a hotel or lodge?"

"You don't understand. It's not that big a deal. It's just a simple meeting with twenty people or so. And it's only for a few weeks until the church is repaired."

"That's it?" Alex scooped the remains of her uneaten orange and peel into her hand and dumped them into the trash.

"Pretty much." Jamie looked down at her tummy.

"Doesn't sound very definite. There must be more. What else? Do you have to feed these people, too?"

"No, of course not." The oven timer buzzed loudly.

"Sit," Alex said. "I'll get it."

She shoved her hand into a mitt, pulled open the oven door, and retrieved the fragrant muffins overflowing in their cups. "So," she said as she set the tin on the stove top, "what else?"

"I'm responsible for the Primary in our branch. I'll need to prepare something for the children."

"The children?" Alex tossed the oven mitt onto the counter. "Let me get this straight. Not only do you have to have the meeting here, but you have to tend the other people's kids, too?"

"It's not like that." Jamie traced the outline of the bear on her apron. Alex realized that her sister hadn't looked at her once during the whole conversation.

Finally, Jamie looked up and said, "They are my responsibility and I care about them. The children need to learn the gospel just as much, no, more, than the adults. Not only am I supposed to do it, I want to do it." She thumped the desk with the heel of her hand for emphasis.

"I'm sorry," Alex spoke softly. "You're right, I don't understand." *I'll never understand.* "I just don't want anything to happen to you. Or the baby."

"I know that." Jamie rose to her feet and smoothed her apron. "And I promised we wouldn't drive you nuts with all our church stuff while you were here. I'm sorry."

Alex waved her sister's words away. "Don't apologize. I'm the one who should say 'sorry,' not you."

"We'll keep the meeting short and try not to bother you."

"Will you stop already? I'm serious. It's okay. I'll read a book or write some letters while you're having your meeting. I told Mom I'd drop her a line, anyway."

"You've talked to Mom?"

Alex talked to her mother every week.

"Just for a minute. I told her I was coming to visit you."

"Did she ask about me?"

Alex didn't know what to say. No, her mother hadn't really even asked about Jamie. Alex's heart ached because she knew Jamie missed having her mother in her life. But when Jamie was eighteen and had joined the Mormon church, against their mother's wishes, nothing had ever been the same between them. Now, after six more years, Alex thought it was time for her mother to forgive Jamie.

"She thought it was great we were going to spend some time together."

"Do you realize I haven't even seen Mom in three years?" Jamie removed her apron and lay it aside, then picked up a glass tumbler but stopped before opening the dishwasher. "I mean, don't mothers usually visit their children occasionally?" Her voice rose steadily as she clutched the glass in her hand. "Or at least contact them once in a while, even if it's only to find out if they're still alive? Don't they feel *some* kind of obligation when their daughter loses a child?!" Without warning she slammed the glass down on the counter, shattering it into a hundred pieces.

"Jamie!" Alex flew across the kitchen. "Are you okay? Did you cut yourself?"

Tears spilled onto Jamie's cheeks. Her voice was shaky as she replied, "I'm fine, honest."

"Here." Alex gently led her sister away from the shattered fragments. "Let me clean this up. You have a seat."

"Alex, I'm sorry. I don't know why I did that." Jamie found a box of tissues and blew her nose. "These stupid hormones!"

"Jamie, it's okay. It was an accident." Although her sister had always tried to hide it, Alex knew that Jamie was deeply hurt because of their mother's distance. But it disturbed Alex that Jamie's pain had manifested itself in such an angry outburst.

"I just don't understand why Mom can't seem to forgive me." Jamie's voice still tremored with emotion. "Why is she so mad at me for doing something that has made me a better person? Especially something that has brought me so much happiness." She wiped her eyes, then laughed sardonically. "Well, except for one little thing. My own mother won't speak to me."

Alex dumped the dustpan of broken glass into the garbage. "The only thing I know for sure is that Mom does love you. I think she's just disappointed. Maybe she just needs time."

"But she doesn't even seem to care that she's going to have a granddaughter."

Alex kept her breathing even, hoping to stay calm. She knew why her mom acted the way she did. But she didn't know why her mother couldn't get past it. Even though Alex didn't like Jamie being a Mormon, she still wanted to stay close to her and made the effort to keep up their relationship.

"Jamie, please don't worry about this. Be patient with Mom. She'll come around. I know she will."

"You really think so?" Jamie sniffled.

Alex nodded.

"I hope it's soon. It's getting easier to not care, some days. I'm so glad I have you, Alex."

"Me, too," Alex answered, wishing there was some way to change the feelings between her sister and mother. She held out her arms to Jamie, thinking it strange that she was the one trying to comfort her sister, when her sister seemed to be able to comfort everyone else.

"Now," Alex said, ready to move on to safer ground, "Let me do something to help you get ready."

"There's not much left to do." Jamie looked around. "We can make the potatoes when it's closer to lunch, the rolls are rising and the roast is in the oven. I guess we could set the table."

On top of a mauve-colored tablecloth, they set out Jamie's best china and crystal, linen napkins, and glistening silverware. In the middle of the table, Alex placed a beautiful centerpiece made from dried flowers, eucalyptus, and candles.

"How have you learned to do this kind of stuff?" Alex asked. "Cooking, entertaining, decorating . . ." When they were young their mother had rarely cooked. They were the only family she knew who went to a restaurant for Thanksgiving dinner.

"It's all Steve's mom's influence. She makes Martha Stewart look like a slob."

Steve banged through the back door and saw them laughing.

"What's so funny?" He stacked his boots, gloves, and hat on the floor inside the door and hung his coat on a hook. "Smells great in here."

"Thanks, honey. What brings you home this time of day?" Jamie walked over and hugged him.

Steve let his wife kiss him on the cheek then he cracked open the oven door. After assessing the contents and filling his lungs with the mouthwatering smells inside, he said, "You're making Rich's favorite."

"He loves pot roast," Jamie explained to Alex. "I just add onions and carrots."

"Things are slow at the office and there's a game on I want to watch so I thought I'd come home. Are you going to tell me what you two were laughing about?"

"I was just telling Alex about your mother."

"Oh," he said, like he wasn't sure if the information was good or bad. "I guess she is pretty incredible."

"Incredible?" Jamie blurted. "The woman vacuums the bricks on her house every spring."

"You're kidding?" Alex said. She bit her top lip to keep from laughing.

"Not *every* spring," Steve said. He picked up the message Jamie had written earlier. "Besides, I thought you liked my mother."

"I *love* your mother. She's more like a mother to me than my own mom. I didn't mean to give you that impression."

Jamie stroked her husband's cheek, then kissed it.

"What's this?" Steve absentmindedly rested one arm around Jamie's waist and read the note.

She glanced at Alex before answering, "Sister Miles had a stroke and they're in Idaho Falls right now. President Miles wondered about us having church here."

"Sure, that'd be fine."

The rumble of a truck engine directed their attention outside. "Rich is here," Steve said.

"Rich?" Alex glanced at the clock. It was barely ten in the morning.

"He came to watch North Carolina play."

"Let me out of here." Alex pushed past Steve. Rich had only seen her looking her worst. For once she'd like to be cleaned up and at least have her teeth brushed when she saw him.

"What about your muffin?" Jamie said.

"Give it to Rich. I'm hitting the shower." She was out of the kitchen, through the dining room, and barely had one foot on the stairs when a knock came at the front door. Like a clod, she missed the next step, tripped, and fell.

Rich walked inside just in time to watch Alex bump down the stairs and land at his feet.

Chapter 6

"WHOA, THAT'S SOME GREETING." RICH STOOPED DOWN AND helped Alex to her feet. "Are you okay?"

Alex wanted to melt along with the snow on his boots. "Yes, I'm fine." She rubbed her rear end.

"What happened?" Steve rushed to the entry with Jamie close behind.

"I missed a step," Alex said.

"I've never had a woman fall at my feet before." Rich held her steady a moment longer before letting go. "I don't think I like it though. Are you sure you're okay?"

"I'm fine. I don't know what's wrong with me lately. I'm like an accident waiting to happen."

"Maybe this will make you feel better." Rich held out a suitcase for her.

"My clothes, my makeup. You found my car!" She wanted to hug him.

"It's still stuck but we can get it out later when the tow truck's not so busy pulling everyone else out of ditches. I thought you'd appreciate some of your things."

"Thanks, Rich." She noticed all eyes were on her. "Well, the show's over." Alex spread her arms wide and curtsied. "Isn't the ball game about ready to start?"

Steve checked his watch. "It's tip-off time." He rushed to the living room and switched on the television. "Are you coming in, Jamie?"

"In a minute," she said, "I need to check the meat." She left for the kitchen as the roar of a frenzied crowd rattled the windows.

"Thanks again for getting my clothes," Alex said.

"Glad to do it. By the way, how's your forehead feeling?"

"I think the swelling's gone down, but I haven't really looked at it yet this morning."

"Mind if I take a peek?"

"No, of course not." She set down her suitcase.

He came closer and attempted to lift the corner of the dressing.

"Ow, that tape really sticks."

"Sorry." He tilted his head and peered closer. She smelled the musky sweetness of his lip balm. "I'll be more careful."

Alex winced as he dug at the tape again. It felt like he was taking skin grafts from her head. "I'm no doctor but the wound has closed and seems to be healing nicely. I think I'd leave that butterfly on another day or so."

"Oh, no!" Steve yelled as he fell back onto the couch. "That guy traveled at least ten steps. Right in front of the ref."

Rich laughed, "You'd think Steve was in the game."

"I sure hope you two are rooting for the same team. I'll see you in a bit. Thanks again for getting my things." She grabbed her suitcase and scurried up to the bathroom to take a quick shower so she could get back downstairs to help Jamie with dinner.

As she showered, she thought about the last time she'd had dinner with her mother. It had been in New York. Alex had been a guest instructor at the American Fitness Council's Winter Conference in the city, and then had stayed on to spend the weekend.

A small dinner party in her mother's Manhattan apartment had been Judith's usual social presentation—a catered affair with people Alex had never met nor wanted to meet again.

What a difference between her sister and her mother. While Jamie was worried about everyone else, her mother worried about trying to look twenty years younger with her bleached hair, tight-fitting clothes, and chunks of diamonds and gold hanging from ears, neck, and wrists.

Alex loved her mother but hated the life she led. There had to be more. There had to be . . .

When Alex joined the others in the cozy family room off the back of the kitchen, Jamie and the two men were gathered around the television. Bowls of M&Ms, peanuts, and pretzels orbited the coffee table as the enthusiasts nibbled without moving their eyes from the screen. Even Jamie whooped and hollered with every three-point shot and misguided call.

"Who's ahead?" Alex asked as she took a seat in a wingback chair. Rich was the only one who removed himself from the excitement long enough to answer.

"We're down by one."

"Hmpf." Steve grunted at the score.

Alex eyed the snacks on the table. She never had treats hanging around her house, mainly because she didn't trust herself. It was easier not to have anything, rather than try to stop after a few bites. Sometimes she couldn't stop, then she'd feel guilty for days. She hated not having control over herself; she hated not having willpower. She *never* wanted to feel the rejection that came from being overweight again.

Feeling like a child reaching into a cookie jar, Alex slid her hand across the table and took two colored candies from the dish. While the three spectators collapsed over a three-point shot, Alex slid the red M&M into her mouth, then the green. They were every bit as good as she remembered. In fact, so good, that through the rest of the second quarter she nearly emptied the dish.

As the halftime show started, Jamie turned down the sound while Steve and Rich analyzed the events of the first half. Just when Rich was ready to go out for a pillow pass from Steve, the phone rang. Within minutes Rich and Steve were out the door to meet a client down at the store.

Jamie and Alex watched them through the window as the two men hurried to Rich's truck. Steve grabbed a handful of snow, skillfully formed it into a ball, and launched it at Rich. Snow flew madly in the minute following, then suddenly stopped and they were off.

The house seemed quiet and empty without them.

When the men returned a few hours later, Alex helped her sister dish up the food. She felt a little resentful of the men who had immediately sat down in front of the ball game while she and Jamie slaved away in the kitchen. No sooner had she had that thought than Rich stepped into the kitchen.

"Can I help?"

"Sure, carry the juice pitcher and that dish of vegetables." She was grateful she hadn't voiced her feelings. In fact, Rich not only finished helping them transport the meal to the dinner table, he helped the ladies into their chairs while Steve triumphantly took his place at the head, ready for the honor of cutting the meat.

Alex looked at each member seated around the feast. Jamie was all smiles, her face flushed with excitement and the warmth from scurrying about the kitchen. She hadn't changed much in the last few years. The two sisters looked alike with identical noses and similar builds, but Jamie had their mother's high forehead, arched eyebrows, and round, brown eyes, and she wore her hair short, with full bangs. Alex's hair was blunt cut, shoulder length, no bangs, an easy hairstyle to pull back for workouts. Alex favored her father with powdery blue, almond-shaped eyes, and a small mouth. She'd always wished she had Jamie's full lips and generous smile, especially since, in her opinion, she was the one with the loudmouthed job.

"This looks delicious, honey," Steve said. "Hey, Rich, remember when we tried to make a pot roast on our mission?" Steve looked handsome in a navy-and white-striped rugby shirt. His winter-tanned face and brown curly hair made him look younger than his twenty-seven years.

"After spending a fortune for the meat, we nearly burned the whole apartment complex down," Rich laughed out loud at the mission memory. Alex liked the deep creases that curved from cheek to jaw on either side of his smile, and the easy way he chuckled and added details to Steve's story. To Alex a mission seemed all business, doing fanatical bible bashing and trying to drill religion into poor unsuspecting victims before dunking them in water to claim them as their own.

"The best thing I remember was coming home and finding sugar cookies from your mom once a month," Steve said.

"Even though they were in a million pieces."

"Did we ever figure out what shapes they were supposed to be?"

"I don't think we stopped eating them long enough to put one together."

Alex laughed hearing them retell their experiences. She realized that they had not only been devoted missionaries but also normal nineteen-year-old boys who liked to joke and have fun.

"We made the perfect companionship," Steve said. "I cooked and Rich ironed."

Rich's eyebrows arched and he said, "I think the correct explanation would be, you experimented in the kitchen." Rich turned to Alex. "He created all sorts of culinary Frankensteins. And then expected *me* to eat them!"

Everyone laughed.

"We were the best-fed missionaries in the mission," Steve said. "And absolutely wrinkle-free."

"You really liked to iron?" Alex asked with disbelief.

"Yeah, I still do," he said. "I find it relaxing. And I love putting on a crisp, freshly ironed shirt."

"I think it's a wonderful quality," Jamie said. "Especially since he volunteers to iron all of Steve's Sunday shirts."

"Fair exchange for all the button sewing and hemming you do for me," Rich said.

Alex was surprised to learn he couldn't sew his own clothes. He could do everything else.

Steve took a deep breath and said, "Before we pray, I'd like to take a moment and express a few feelings. Don't worry, Alex. I won't bear my testimony." Rich and Jamie laughed, and Alex looked down at her plate, feeling a warmth spread upward onto her face.

"I want to tell all of you how thankful I am we could be here together today. Especially for my wife and child. They are the most important people in my life.

"And my best friend and partner, Rich. We go back a long way. I can't seem to remember a good time, or a bad time, that you weren't there to share it with me.

"Then there's Alex, who practically risked her life to be here. I couldn't ask for a better sister-in-law . . ." Jamie was sniffing into her napkin ". . . nor a better sister and best friend for my wife. Not a day goes by that Jamie doesn't say how much she misses you and wishes you two lived closer. It means the world to both of us that you could come spend time with us. That's it. I'll go ahead and say the prayer now," Steve said.

Everyone bowed their heads. Alex noticed that Steve not only asked for a blessing for their families, but for the branch members as well. Even though she wasn't used to having a blessing on the food, she thought Steve's prayer was kind of sweet. She was glad her sister had someone like him for a husband.

When the prayer ended, Alex realized that her heart was beating wildly, her palms were clammy, and her bones were as weak as Jell-O. *Probably just a sugar high from all those M&Ms,* she told herself.

"Pass me your plates and I'll serve the roast." Steve scooted back his chair and stood, with serving fork in hand. "How about you, Alex? Are you going to break your code of ethics and eat real food?"

She swallowed quickly, grateful for the calm restored to her body, and said with a weak laugh, "I guess you didn't see me putting away the M&M's, huh?"

"You, eating chocolate?" Jamie asked in mock horror. "And I missed it?"

"Sorry. I'll let you know when I start on a bucket of ice cream." She looked back at Steve. "Thank you, I'll have a little."

"Me, too." Rich thrust his plate toward Steve.

After Steve placed a generous portion of meat on Rich's plate, Alex watched as Rich built a man-sized mashed-potato mountain. Squishing the center with a spoon, he added a large dollop of butter. When he showered it with salt, then flooded the entire plate with gravy, she had to bite her tongue to keep from saying anything. Taking a deep breath and then a long drink of water, she reminded herself that she had no right to impose her feelings on someone else. But it almost killed her to watch him and Steve drown their vegetables in cheese sauce and cover their rolls with a thick layer of butter. If they kept eating like this, they'd all be in for bypass surgery before their fifties.

"Honey, this looks incredible," Steve said.

The phone rang in the kitchen. Steve held up his hand. "I'll get it."

Alex took a small bite of the steamed broccoli without any sauce.

Steve returned to the room, a look of concern on his face. "Sister Beckstead just called. Her little girl is burning up with a fever. She wondered if we could give her a blessing."

Rich dropped his fork, jumped up from his chair, and grabbed his coat from the coat rack. "We can take my truck. I'm parked behind you."

"Little Sara . . . I wonder what's wrong." Jamie looked at her husband worriedly.

"We'll go see what we can do, honey. Don't worry. I'm sure she'll be fine."

Alex couldn't believe her ears. Of course, a sick child was something to worry about, but did they have to rush off right in the middle of dinner? And, if a blessing was so important, why couldn't the woman's husband do it?

It sounded to Alex like they needed a doctor, not a blessing.

She shook her head as more questions filled her mind about this strange religion her sister was tangled in.

Chapter 7

THE MEN RETURNED NEARLY AN HOUR LATER.

"How's little Sara?" Jamie asked.

"Doing better than her mother. Sister Beckstead worries herself sick." Steve removed his heavy coat and collapsed into a chair. "Sara's fever broke shortly after the blessing. She was sleeping when we left."

"I wish Sara's father could be more help," Rich added. "As soon as we arrived, he hightailed it to the other room."

"I'll call her later and see how they're doing," Jamie said.

Alex marveled at everyone's casual attitude about the dinner that had been ruined. No one even seemed to care.

While the men ate reheated food, Jamie and Alex started cleaning the kitchen. They didn't talk, just loaded the dishwasher and stacked pots and pans into the sink to soak.

"Jamie," Alex finally broke the silence, "you've been on your feet all day. Let me finish up in here. You go rest."

Jamie opened her mouth, then blew out a deep breath that lifted her bangs. "Let's both sit down and do them later. We've got everything soaking anyway."

"You talked me into it." Alex tried to be cheerful. She didn't want to ruin the rest of the day by acting childish about what had happened at dinner.

Entering the living room from the kitchen, Jamie walked over to the stereo. "Let's enjoy a few minutes of peace. In fact . . ." She clicked some buttons and soon the low tones of Pachelbel's Canon floated around the room.

"Ahhh, that's nice." Alex rested her head back and let the melody relax her. After a minute she lifted one eyelid and noticed Jamie softly snoring, her arms and legs sprawled, head cocked to one side.

Alex watched her sister's stomach carefully, waiting for a bump, a jiggle, anything. She leaned closer, almost as if she were studying a crystal ball.

She waited and watched, but nothing happened. Jamie stretched and rolled onto her hip and shoulder. When her sister got comfortable, Alex rested her hand softly on Jamie's abdomen. As soft as butterfly wings, she felt the tiny fluttering of movement under her fingertips. She held her breath and froze while again the little thumpety feeling tickled her fingers.

She was tempted to say something, to tell the baby she was there and loved her already. Instead, she blinked away a film of tears and felt the shifting of the little person cocooned within her sister.

After another moment, the baby grew still. Alex drew a flowered throw over her sister and walked to the front window.

The sun angled toward the horizon, casting shadows over untouched snow. Rich's black and chrome truck stood in the driveway, wearing a heavy coat of mud and salt. Two small rainbows of clear glass shone on the windshield. Beyond it a row of evergreens ran along the drive to the main road in front, and a gathering of pines and various shapes and sizes of boulders clustered in the other corner of the front yard. Even though it was cold, Alex felt the urge to get a breath of this wonderful mountain air.

She tiptoed to the dining room where Steve and Rich sat back, relaxed in their chairs. Steve rubbed his stomach with one hand and worked a toothpick between his teeth with his other.

"I thought you might be napping," he said, letting the toothpick bob between his lips.

"Jamie's asleep. I think I'll go for a short walk and have a look around."

"Want some company?" Rich sat up in his chair and set his wadded napkin on his plate.

"Sure." She liked the idea of having Rich along. His company was easy, comfortable, almost as if she'd always known him.

Alex layered herself with extra socks and a sweatshirt, then put on snow boots, gloves, and parka from Jamie. Rich was dressed and waiting when she pulled a knit cap onto her head.

"Are you ready?" Rich asked as he turned the knob on the door.

Alex nodded. "We won't be long, Steve. Don't let Jamie clean up the kitchen. I'll do it when I get back."

"And I'll help," Rich said. Alex grinned as Rich coated his lips with a shiny smear of Carmex, then offered some to Alex. Curious about his addiction, she dipped her finger and rubbed her mouth. Nothing special there, she thought. Just slippery lips.

Rich held open the door and Alex stepped through.

"Oooh, it's colder than it looks." She wrapped her arms across her chest.

"Compared to January, this is warm."

They stepped off the porch and crunched through the snow around the side of the house.

Taking her elbow, Rich helped her across a slick patch on the driveway, and they made their way across the backyard into the trees beyond. Pines mixed with quaking aspen, cloaking them in shadows. Alex's earlobes felt like they'd been dipped in ice.

Here the gentle slope took a steep incline. Rich offered his hand and together they climbed a few more yards to the summit. Alex found that the cold and altitude made it hard to catch her breath.

"What keeps you here?" she asked Rich, shivering.

"In Island Park?" He lifted his brow and looked at her.

She nodded.

"This," he swung his arm wide, "This is why I stay."

Words weren't necessary. The expansive landscape took Alex's breath. Startling blue sky swallowed the towering mountain peaks and rolling hills. Thickly forested hillsides broke the white blanket of snow. This was tranquility, perfect beauty, a masterpiece.

"I've seen this before."

Rich's expression grew puzzled.

"This is the same scene I saw above your mantel in that painting, except there's no snow. In fact, Jamie and Steve have some similar landscapes in their home." She looked into his eyes, which sparkled brightly against the reflecting snow. "They're beautiful. Did someone from around here paint them?"

"I did."

"You?"

He smiled at the obvious shock in her reaction.

"Rich, really? You're the artist? Why they're, they're . . ." she searched but couldn't find the adequate word, ". . . incredible."

"Obviously I don't seem the artistic type?"

"I didn't mean that." She was glad he was smiling. "I've just never met a real artist."

"I'm glad you like my work." They started walking again, slowly, across sun-kissed sparkles of snow. The low hum of a plane engine droned in the distance. Smoke from a fireplace drifted on the breeze.

"So," he said after a few moments, "did that answer your question?"

She thought a minute. "Yes, actually. Now it makes perfect sense. Where else could someone live who loves nature as much as you?"

"Even though I grew up in Boise, I really feel like my place is in the heart of these mountains. People here, for the most part, are good and hardworking. We don't worry about crime or gangs. It gets crazy in the summer with all the tourists, but that just gives us a little excitement. I can't think of a better place to live or raise a family."

"No place can be that perfect."

"Sure, we have our problems, but nothing like big cities."

"Can I ask you a personal question?" They walked slowly. Alex had forgotten about the cold, even though her nose was starting to run. From the ridge behind Jamie's house, they had a clear view that seemed to go on forever.

"Sure, I guess so."

"Don't you worry about being able to find a wife up here? There can't be too many available women around."

"You've got that right," he chuckled. "Actually the only single woman I know works down in West Yellowstone. She owns the taxidermy shop there. She's several inches taller than I am and has biceps bigger than my thighs."

Alex smiled at the mental picture. "So what's the problem?" she asked, her face glossed with innocence.

"Very funny. I'd like to marry someone who will let me carry *her* over the threshold."

"That's it?"

"What's it?"

"It's Amazon Annie or no one?" She raised an eyebrow and tilted her head.

"Actually, I have a girl back in Boise. But long-distance relationships are tough. I haven't seen her since Thanksgiving, although I'm going home for Easter."

So, the Barbie in the picture had to be his girlfriend. Alex was appalled that she felt a vine of envy wind itself around her heart. Certainly she wasn't interested in Rich. They lived in different worlds. His had snow, hers had palm trees. His had wild animals, hers did too, but they were the two-legged kind. His had cabins and snowmobiles, hers had mansions and Ferraris. He had a girlfriend, she had a Chia pet. He was LDS and she wasn't.

"It's almost dark; we'd better head back."

Traipsing through knee-high snow proved to be more of a workout than one of her step aerobic classes. Alex was panting when they got to the fence surrounding Jamie's house. The backside of the fence sagged to one side.

"Uh-oh, looks like the storm broke one of the posts," Rich said. He scanned their surroundings, picked up a stout four-foot pole, and studied the damage once again. "We need to brace this until the post can be replaced, or the whole side will come down."

Setting the pole down, he positioned himself against the broken section and attempted to push it upright. It gave an inch.

"Need some help?" Alex asked.

"Yeah, maybe you ought to go get Steve."

"Get Steve?! Hey, I don't work out just for the fun of it. I can help you as much as he could. Besides I'd love a chance to smash that crack you made about me being skinny."

He held up his hand to ward off her verbal blow. "Sorry, I didn't realize that was a bad word." Rich held his gaze on her until she wondered if something was wrong with her face. Had her nose been running and become frozen like an icicle?

He smiled then said, "All right then, let's push this thing back up."

She joined him against the fence and together they moved it into place. Rich held it steady while she braced the pole against the post.

"That should keep it until tomorrow." He gave her a big smile. "And I apologize. You are a lot stronger than you look."

Glad someone thinks so. Her manager's unnecessary concern about her weight loss still rankled.

As Rich led the way back to the house, Alex watched him curiously. He was unlike anyone she'd ever known. There was much more to him than just a handsome face; he was gentle, genuine, and thoughtful. He reminded her of her father.

She liked Rich. As much as she didn't want to and didn't need another man in her life, she liked him. Out of all men in the world she could be interested in, she had to pick a religious Idaho spud with a girlfriend!

Chapter 8

JAMIE WAS AWAKE WHEN THEY RETURNED FROM THEIR WALK. RICH explained about the fence while Alex took off the layers of outerwear. Although she'd worn nearly a closetful, she'd still been shivering.

The conversation turned from the fence to the subject of church on Sunday.

All their talk about "Brother So-and-so" and "Sister What's-her-name?" made them sound like a bunch of Quakers. Alex rolled her eyes.

"Sure will be nice when we get our building back," Jamie said.

Alex heartily agreed.

"If this sunshine keeps up, the roof will be finished earlier than planned." They continued talking about church business as they made their way to the living room, so Alex remained in the kitchen to tackle the mess there. Which wasn't much more than just washing the pile of pots in the sink and putting away the food.

Dinner had been more than three hours ago and Alex was hungry. After her binge on M&Ms, she hadn't eaten much of the meal. Nibbling on a piece of dinner roll, she dug through some drawers to find an apron. Having no luck, she took a broad dishcloth, tied it around her waist and rolled up her sleeves.

With suds up to her elbows, Alex scrubbed and scoured gravy pans, vegetables pots, cookie sheets, and glass serving dishes. She popped the last olive off a dish into her mouth and dunked the chrome tray into the water.

"Hey, you were supposed to wait for me."

Rich's voice startled her and she swallowed the olive whole. With a cough, she said, "You were busy." She coughed again, harder.

"Do you need a drink?"

She nodded.

Rich poured a glass of water from a pitcher on the counter. "Here you go."

The water cleared the food away.

"Thanks." She swallowed hard.

He looked at the counter filled with dripping, drying cookware. "Where's a towel?"

She opened a drawer and tossed him a fresh dishcloth.

He worked on the large pot while she dried the crystal.

"So . . ." Rich finished the pot and picked up a round platter.

"So, what?" she asked, peering at the stemware to check for spots.

"So, tell me why an intelligent, pretty girl like you isn't married."

She nearly dropped the goblet.

"I sure wish you'd get to the point, Rich," she said dryly.

He laughed. "Fair is fair. I'm only returning your question."

"Okay, well, things are different in California. There's not a big rush to get married or even consider marriage until your thirties. So I have a long time before I'll even start looking. Besides, I was only wondering about you, because," she inspected the crystal one more time, "you know, you're a Mormon and you're supposed to get married young. Right?"

Rich didn't say anything for a moment. He polished the tray one last time then slung the towel over his shoulder and leaned against the counter, his arms folded across his chest.

"Our church encourages us to not put off marriage and a family, if that's what you mean. But they don't expect us to marry the first single person we meet either. We are allowed to fall in love."

Gone was his usual fun, teasing tone. She hadn't meant to strike a nerve but she knew she had.

"I kind of figured out that much by myself. I mean, just look at Jamie and Steve."

"I'd say they're happy by anybody's standards, LDS or not," he said.

"Me, too. They sure are lucky."

"It's not all luck," Rich said. He was drying the serving utensils now.

"Do you mean because they're Mormons? LDS," she corrected herself, "and were married in the temple?"

"It's no guarantee for a successful marriage. But I feel it helps your chances."

Alex tossed her dishcloth onto the counter and leaned back against the edge of the sink. "Being LDS didn't help my father much."

"What do you mean?" He'd stopped drying. Alex wasn't looking at Rich, but she could feel his gaze upon her.

"He joined the Church when he was thirty-five and one year later, almost to the day, he died in a car accident."

"I don't understand the connection," he said.

"First of all, my mother asked him not to join the Church, but he did anyway. And when I turned eight he wanted me to get baptized. She wouldn't let me and all they did was fight about it."

Rich's expression softened, pulling her feelings deeper from her heart. "And then, one day, one beautiful clear spring day, he was coming home from church and got hit in an intersection by a driver who ran a red light," Alex whispered because she didn't trust the knot in her throat. Even after nineteen years, the hurt was just as painful, maybe even more.

"You don't think he got killed just because he joined the Church, do you?"

"He would have been home with us instead of at church, and he would still be alive today."

"I'm sorry. That must have been very hard for your family."

"The first few years after his death were awful. This was before my mother went back to college and got her degree in journalism. Now she works for *Today's Woman* magazine, but for a long time she worked at crummy waitressing jobs, leaving Jamie and me alone the whole night sometimes. I could never sleep when she was gone. I'd just lay there, holding Jamie, wondering where my daddy was and why he had to go. Was there really a heaven? Was he up there, watching his two little girls all alone, watching his wife cry constantly, wondering how she was going to keep a roof over her children's heads?

"I don't know, Rich." Alex shook her head slowly. "All the Church has brought our family is misery."

"What did you think when Jamie joined the Church?"

"I couldn't believe it, especially after what happened to Dad. And it nearly killed my mother. Things haven't been the same between them since. In fact, they rarely talk anymore. It's hard on all of us. I'd give anything to have us all be close again, like we used to be."

"It doesn't seem to be a problem between you and Jamie."

"As long as we don't talk religion, we're fine." Alex rubbed her forehead, wondering how they'd gotten into this discussion anyway. "She's my sister and I love her. As long as she's happy, that's all that matters."

"But wouldn't you like to be happy like her?"

Here it comes. "Of course I want to be happy like her. I *am* happy," she corrected herself. "But I don't believe her happiness comes from your church. She was lucky to find a good husband and she has a wonderful life here in Island Park. It's as simple as that."

"I think if you were to ask her, she'd tell you differently."

Alex shrugged. She'd heard the whole "spiel" before—the Joseph Smith story, the Mormon Bible, the "priesthood" stuff. She didn't need to hear it again.

"Probably." Alex poked at the remaining suds in the sink. "But she just found something that works for her. That doesn't mean it's right for everyone."

"But if it were right for you, and she believed with all her heart that it was, and she knew without a doubt that it would bring you more joy than you could ever imagine, would you blame her, or me, for wanting to tell you about it?" Rich persisted.

She looked at her shoes, hoping the sudden, inexplicable tears pooling in her eyes wouldn't fall. "No."

Rich stepped closer to her and she felt his hand on her arm. "I'm sorry, Alex. I didn't mean to upset you."

She cleared her throat and said, "You haven't," a little too brightly. But she still couldn't look at him.

Gently he took her chin and tilted her face to his. "Sometimes we don't understand why things happen. Life doesn't always make sense. What happens isn't always fair."

She certainly agreed with that. And thank goodness her tears were drying.

"Your father found the gospel, and he wanted to give you, Jamie, and your mother the same joy he had. Jamie did the same thing. It's like the way you feel about taking care of your body. You know how important healthy food and exercise are, and you want others to know it, too. In fact, you probably can't understand when they don't accept what you say, because to you it makes perfect sense—it's completely true."

She nodded. That was exactly how she felt. And she hoped to convince him *he* needed to change how he ate.

"That's how we feel about the gospel. It makes perfect sense, especially in this very imperfect world. I can't imagine going through this life without it. I'd feel lost and I know others would, too. The gospel can change people's lives completely. Why wouldn't we want to share it with others? Especially those we love."

She couldn't imagine him feeling lost or unsure. He seemed to possess a great confidence and total conviction. She also couldn't imagine him lying to her either. She believed that he believed what he was saying was true. She just didn't happen to buy it.

He dipped his chin and raised his eyes, looking straight at her.

"Okay," Alex finally spoke. "I understand the Mormon motivation to tell others. And you're right. I feel as strongly about nutrition and good eating habits as you do about your religion. In fact," she squared her shoulders, "watching you earlier at dinner nearly drove me insane. You must've eaten one hundred and fifty grams of fat, not to mention the calories and cholesterol overload."

Rich stepped back and looked at her questioningly. "A hundred and fifty. Is that bad?"

"It's almost three times your daily allowance. Your meal was a 'heart attack on a plate.'"

"I've eaten like this all my life. My whole family has."

"That's why I feel it's important to help educate others about it. If you keep eating like this, it will kill you one day."

"One of my grandfathers had a heart attack and died in his early sixties. The other ate bacon and eggs for breakfast every morning and lived until he was eighty-three."

"Imagine how long he would have lived if he'd eaten healthier."

A moment of silence passed. Alex twisted the dishcloth in her hands, then said, "I don't want to seem narrow-minded about religion. I believe in God and the golden rule."

His eyes were fixed on her.

"You seem to have your life in perfect order, just the way you want it. But that doesn't mean others' lives are messy. And even if they are messy, maybe that's the way they like it. You can't force someone to join your church just like I can't force someone to give up butter, red meat, and cheese."

"Cheese is bad, too?"

She smiled. "Maybe an occasional slice now and then is okay."

"Thank goodness," he said, "I wasn't ready to give up cheeseburgers quite yet."

She pulled the makeshift apron off and tossed it onto the counter. "Let's go see what Steve and Jamie are doing."

The lights were low in the living room, and music from the stereo drifted and glided along with Steve and Jamie, who swayed to the rhythm, in each other's arms.

Rich and Alex froze in the doorway and watched as the couple, lost in their own world, stole a moment of romance.

A pounding started in Alex's chest, her heartbeat increasing, drumming fast and hard. Her knees felt like melting butter, weakening her slight frame. Alex stepped back, sat in a chair, and took several deep breaths.

I probably just need a bite to eat. Maybe some juice would help or one of those oranges in the kitchen. But before she collected herself enough to ask Rich to get it for her, the trembling subsided and her heart calmed.

"You okay?" Rich said.

"Me? Yeah, sure I'm fine," Alex said breathlessly, wondering about her sudden lightheadedness. Usually when her blood sugar was low, it took twenty minutes or so for the cold sweats, jitters, and weak-kneed feeling to go away. This had come and gone so suddenly.

"Hey you two, come in here," Steve called from the other room. "Let's get a game of cards or something going."

"I should get home," Rich said. "I've got a group coming over from Jackson to pick up the sleds in the morning."

"Did you get that engine running?" Steve turned on a table lamp, filling the room with light.

"It just needed new plugs."

Alex's mind drifted, the conversation with Rich still running through her head. Could a religion really make that much difference in a person's life? Most of the people she knew who claimed no specific religion were basically decent people.

No. Jamie's church was too demanding. Alex couldn't belong to a religion that consumed her life the way Jamie's did. She didn't have time for it, nor did she want it.

Chapter 9

THE NEXT DAY JAMIE AND ALEX BOUGHT OUT THE SHOPS IN WEST Yellowstone.

"I'm so relieved we found a gift for Mom's birthday." Jamie led the way down the store-lined street. "She's going to love that southwest jacket and turquoise earrings."

"The minute I saw it, I knew it was perfect for her," Alex said.

"It will probably be the first gift from me she'll actually like. She never said anything about the purse I sent her for Christmas."

"I'm sure she loved it. You know how busy Mom is."

"All I know is that she's obviously too busy for me."

"Jamie, I don't think that's what it is at all."

They stopped on the sidewalk in front of a souvenir shop, next to a tall, carved wooden Indian. Tourists hurried in and out of shops to escape the icy breeze knifing between the buildings, and cars sloshed down the street where the snow was melting and turning to slush.

"I wish you were right, Alex, I really do. But I think Mom has just written me off. She doesn't care what happens to me."

"I know that's not true. She loves you very much."

"A phone call at Christmas and fifty dollars in a card for my birthday doesn't do much to convince me, Alex."

There was pain in Jamie's voice. Alex sensed it and could see it in her eyes, but there was a stronger emotion that Alex was concerned about. It wasn't like Jamie to lose her temper or get mad. It was a side of her sister she rarely saw. But she could tell Jamie was mad, and the more anger that filled her sister—pushing the hurt away—the less likely Jamie and her mother would ever work out this problem.

"You know what?" Jamie said. "I don't really want to talk about this anymore. We were having so much fun. Let's forget about it, okay? I'm starved. You want to grab a bite to eat?"

Alex's frustration grew. These strong feelings between her mom and sister were building a massive wall between them.

"Yeah, sure," she said, following Jamie to the deli next door.

They found a table next to a cozy fireplace and placed their order. Jamie had a club sandwich with avocado on sourdough, and Alex ordered turkey on whole wheat with mustard and vinegar.

They talked about light subjects—the weather, Alex's work, the decorations inside the deli—until Jamie said, "You haven't eaten very much."

"I'm not really hungry. I'll pack it up to take home and eat later."

"You look awfully thin, Alex. I know you don't like to talk about this, but are you okay?"

Alex knew the best defense was to not overreact when this question was asked. If she stayed calm, they stayed calm.

"Jamie, good heavens, I'm fine. Stop worrying." For added impact she took a bite of the pickle on her plate. "I lost a few pounds while we were shooting the workout series, but I plan on putting the weight back on."

Thank goodness Jamie didn't know about her collapse.

"Okay, I won't pester you. I mean, you know a lot more about health and nutrition than I do. But ever since, you know . . ." she stirred the ice in her lemonade with her straw ". . . the time you got so sick in high school, I worry. Anyway," she brightened, "it's great having you here."

Relieved that her sister let the subject drop, Alex said, "I'm glad I came. Island Park is a lot different than I expected." She took another small bite of the pickle.

"What do you mean?"

"I thought your home would be, I don't know, kind of like *The Waltons,* or something. Rustic. Instead it's elegant, spacious, and beautifully decorated. I can see why you and Steve are so happy."

"I'll never forget when Steve came up with the idea to open an outdoor equipment rental shop. I told him I'd give it one year. And I swore I'd never even unpack the boxes because I was convinced we'd be heading back to Provo in twelve months."

"What happened?" Alex pushed the rest of her uneaten sandwich away and wiped her mouth with a napkin.

"After only one month, I was in love with this place—the people, the scenery, the slower-paced lifestyle. And business really took off. Better than we ever could have imagined. The winters are long, even for people who like snow, but I love it here. We have a wonderful branch and great neighbors. But I'd give anything to have a close friend. Like Steve has Rich. It would be perfect if you lived close by. You're my best friend, Alex."

The sincerity in her sister's voice touched Alex deeply.

"I wish we lived closer, too." Alex felt like a clod that she'd stayed away so long. But at least she'd kept in touch with Jamie. Why wasn't her mother even contacting her sister? Alex knew her mother carried a lot of resentment toward the Church, but she couldn't imagine that her mother had abandoned Jamie altogether. Especially with all the problems Jamie was having with her pregnancies.

"I'm glad you're happy here," Alex continued. "You and Steve seem to fit in well with the community. And it's neat that Steve and Rich can be in business together."

"I don't know what we'd do without Rich. He's as much my friend as he is Steve's. He helps me hang curtains and ice cookies and plant flower bulbs."

"He seems like a really great guy." Alex took a sip from her drink and pushed it aside. "But he's so immaculate. I've never known a guy who keeps everything so tidy. He's so perfect it's scary."

"Scary?" Jamie laughed. "I guess you have to be married to appreciate those traits. I'd love to not have to pick up clothes off the floor, scrub the shower before I use it, put the toilet seat down . . ."

"Okay, okay. I get the picture. But don't you think he's a little extreme? I mean, the man loves to iron. That's a little strange, if you ask me."

"The way Steve tells it, Rich wasn't a fanatical 'neat freak' on his mission. He became that way after he got home." Jamie leaned her elbows on the table. "I'm glad you've had a chance to meet him. Of course, I didn't expect you two to meet like you did," she laughed. "I still can't get over what a coincidence that was."

"I hate to even think what would have happened if he hadn't been directly behind me."

"He told me that he'd planned on spending the day at the lodge in Yellowstone with the group of people from the tour, but he felt like he needed to go home instead, even in that terrible storm."

"Really?" Alex felt sudden goose bumps and wondered if someone had opened a door and let in the chilling breeze from outside.

"I know how you feel about this, but I have to say it. I think something prompted him to leave when he did. Seriously, Alex, you might never have been found, especially if you were knocked out cold like that for so long."

Alex shuddered. "I don't even want to think about it."

The bell jingled on the front door of the deli. Alex looked up and saw a six-foot-tall woman walk inside. She wore a knitted stocking cap, logging boots, and a sleeveless down vest over a plaid flannel shirt.

"Hey, Mac, you got my lunch ready?"

"Sure thing, Rose. Did you want slaw or potato salad?"

"Gimme some slaw."

"Okay, comin' right up." The man behind the counter walked through a swinging door into the kitchen. Rose leaned onto the counter and tapped her fingers to an upbeat tune on the radio, whistling slightly off key.

"Who's that?" Alex mouthed to her sister.

"Rose Timmins," Jamie whispered. "She owns the taxidermy shop."

Alex stifled a laugh. So this was the only single available female in the area. No wonder Rich wasn't interested. She looked more like Paul Bunyan's type.

"You ready to go?" Alex placed several dollar bills on the table and pulled on her jacket.

"I need to stop at the grocery store and get some things for dinner."

"Good," Alex said. "I think I'll pick up some of that Carmex Rich is always scrubbing his lips with. Mine have been so dry since I got here."

They giggled about Rich's unique way of applying lip balm as they walked out of the sandwich shop. Rose nodded their direction when they passed by.

"Did we get everything? The sack with Mom's jacket? I don't want to lose it."

"I've got everything right here," Alex showed her the package. Everything except the sandwich she'd promised to take home and eat.

"I'm so excited to give her this jacket. For once she's going to like what I give her for her birthday." Jamie pulled her collar up against the chilly breeze tingling the air.

When they were teenagers, Jamie and Alex used to drag their mother everywhere with them. She had been more like their sister than their mother. But too many things had changed and Alex didn't like it. She especially disliked the cold distance between the two people she cared for most in the world. Although she didn't want to, she knew it was up to her to intervene, to get her mother and sister back together again.

The first step was getting their mom to pay a visit to Island Park. Her birthday fell on Easter Sunday that year. They would give her a birthday party she'd never forget.

The phone call had been tricky to time just right, but on Saturday morning, while Jamie showered and Steve worked in his office, Alex took a chance and called.

"Hello!" Judith always answered the phone extra cheerfully.

"Hi, Mom, it's me."

"Alex, darling, hello. I didn't expect to hear from you this weekend. I thought you were going to Idaho."

"I am in Idaho."

"At Jamie's?"

"Yes. I'm having a wonderful time." She shifted the phone to her other ear and strained to hear if Jamie's shower water was still running.

"That's nice, dear," Judith said.

"How are you, Mom?"

"Marvelous. I went to Connecticut last weekend with friends. We had a lovely time."

"I'm glad." Alex straightened her shoulders and said, "Mom, I want to ask you something."

"Sure, dear, what is it?"

"I was wondering how hard it would be for you to get away for a few days around Easter."

"My friends and I were talking about going to Vail skiing. But not until after the holiday. Why?"

"So you're coming out west?" What a lucky break.

"Alex, what exactly are you fishing for?"

"Mom . . ." She shut her eyes and thought, *Please say yes.* "I wondered if you'd consider coming to Island Park for Easter and your birthday. Even for just a few days."

"Island Park? Did you move to a new condo?"

"No, Mom, Island Park is in Idaho, where Jamie lives." She rubbed her forehead.

"I thought she lived in Yellowstone."

"Not exactly. Island Park is a small town thirty miles or so from Yellowstone. Haven't you got her address?"

"Of course I do. It's just that I never write. I prefer to call."

Alex wanted to tell her she needed to call more often, but knew that would only upset her.

"What do you think, Mom? Any chance you could make it?"

"To Yellowstone?"

"Yes, Mother." She didn't try to explain the difference between the national park and the town again.

"I don't know. I'm under a magazine deadline right now. I was planning to work that weekend."

"Isn't there any way you can come?"

"I don't know, Alex. Besides, it's not just my work schedule."

Alex knew what was coming.

"You know I don't feel comfortable with Jamie and Steve. All that religious talk . . ."

"It hasn't been like that this time." Alex searched for the right thing to say. Somehow, something had to convince her. "Mom, Jamie would never ask but she could really use some support right now."

"How is she, anyway?"

Maybe that was the ticket, Jamie's baby. Even though Alex knew her mother was having fits about being a grandma, one thing she knew for sure—Judith McCarty had always *loved* babies.

"She had some problems during the first trimester but seems to be doing better. By the way, it's a girl."

"A girl!" Her mother's voice rose two octaves higher. "A grand-daughter?" She was quiet for a moment.

"Mom?"

Her mother's voice was bemused. "I wonder if she'll look like Jamie. She had such dark, curly hair when she was a baby."

The water stopped running. Alex's heart thumped wildly in her chest. "Mom, listen. I need to run, but would you come? Please? We haven't been together in a long time."

"I guess I could try. But I can't really promise anything. Besides, do planes even fly to Yellowstone?"

"I'm not sure." Alex lowered her voice. "You might have to fly into Idaho Falls. But I'd come and get you."

"I'll have my travel agent check into it, but don't plan on anything until I let you know for sure. This new project isn't falling into place like I'd planned."

"What new project?"

"Favorite childhood Christmas stories of former first ladies."

"Oh, that's right. How did your interview with the president's wife turn out?"

"Delightful. She was absolutely charming."

"We'd love to hear about all the things you're working on and spend some time together. Please try, Mom."

"Give me a week to work on it."

"Thanks, Mom. I love you."

"Love you, too, sweetie."

She would come. Alex just knew it.

* * *

"Cannonball!" Steve took a flying leap into the pool and landed with a ka-whoosh. They were the only four people in the whole place.

Going swimming at the Island Park Resort's indoor pool had been Steve's idea. Asking Rich to come along had been Jamie's. Alex breathed a grateful sigh that she hadn't packed a swimsuit; she had declined Jamie's offer to borrow one of hers, opting instead for something more concealing—a tank t-shirt and baggy shorts.

"Hey, you big moose, try and leave some water in the pool, would ya?" Rich pushed himself out of the water and stood on the side. Jamie and Alex were at the shallow end bobbing on small rafts, enjoying the bathtub temperature of the water.

"That's the whole idea behind a cannonball, the bigger the splash the better." Steve grabbed his towel and dried his face and neck.

"Those two act like they're twelve years old sometimes." Jamie swirled the water with her hands and spun her raft around to face her sister.

"When was the last time Steve's legs saw the sun?" Alex asked.

"He can't even sit by a window without getting sunburned."

"I sure hope the baby gets your olive skin." Alex dangled her hand in the water.

"I do, too, but you should see Steve's mom's skin. It's beautiful. She's almost sixty and hasn't got a wrinkle."

"Hey," Alex said, "how come it's quiet all of a sudden?" She barely had time to lift her head off the inflated pillow when the side of her raft lifted up and over.

She came up sputtering. Wiping her eyes, Alex shook her head and looked Rich square in the face. "You're dead, Greenwood."

She lunged forward, landing on his back, and pushed him under the surface before making a quick getaway to the other side of the pool. Rich surfaced like a periscope, located her, and began his pursuit.

Alex barely had time to scream when Rich grabbed her from below and pulled her under. After a few long moments they exploded out of the water together, gasping. Taking only a second to catch her breath, Alex tackled him from the side and knocked him over.

"I surrender," he said when they cleared the surface. Alex's legs were circled around his torso, and she had one arm locked around his neck. Their faces were inches apart.

"I don't trust you," she said softly.

"I promise," he said, smiling. "I won't dunk you again."

Alex released her hold on him, but they remained close, maintaining eye contact as they held onto the side of the pool. Her breath caught and held in her throat. She didn't like what his cinnamon eyes and wide smile did to her heart.

"Want to sit in the hot tub before we go?"

"Sure," she said. Did he even realize the effect he had on her?

He pushed himself onto the ledge first, then turned and offered his hand, pulling her up beside him. "You may be tiny, but you're stronger than a buffalo."

She sat up and smiled. "Thank you. I think."

He helped her to her feet, and she grabbed her beach towel off a lounge chair. With one smooth motion, she wrapped it around her as they walked over to the hot tub where Steve was relaxing, his head back, his eyes closed.

"Where's Jamie?" Alex asked.

Steve spoke without opening his eyes. "In showering. Oh, I meant to tell you, Alex. The mechanic at the station said your car will be done first thing Monday morning. There wasn't any damage to the frame. He only needed to replace the headlight."

"That's a relief. I wasn't excited about repairing a two-month-old car." She was silent for a moment and then said, "Steve, I've done something I think I ought to tell you about." She sat on the edge of the tub, letting her feet dangle in the hot, bubbling water.

He opened his eyes and looked at her with interest. For a moment his gaze slipped over to Rich then back to Alex.

"I know it's not my place to extend invitations to your home, and I'm not sure how you feel about this, but," she took a deep breath, and said quickly, "I invited Mom to come out here for her birthday. It's on Easter Sunday."

"That's great! Is she coming?" Steve pushed himself up onto the ledge of the spa.

Relieved at his reaction she said, "I don't know yet. She has a project she's working on but she'll let me know as soon as she can."

"Jamie isn't one to complain and she'd never say anything, but she really struggles with her relationship with Judith. I mean, the only time your mom called after the last miscarriage was when Jamie was sleeping. She said she would try to call back, but she never did. Jamie didn't leave the house for a couple of days, she was so afraid she would miss her phone call. I knew your mom wasn't going to call back, but I kept hoping just this once she would. If Jamie didn't have you, I don't know what she'd do."

Alex sensed a harsh edge to her brother-in-law's voice, but the truth was he had every right to be upset. She swirled one foot in the bubbling water. "I just wish those two could work things out. I'm afraid if I don't get involved they never will."

"Inviting your mother out to visit is a great idea. I've thought a million times about calling her myself." He patted her on the knee.

"When you talk to her tell her it's better to fly into Idaho Falls. We can pick her up there," Steve said.

"And if Steve can't get away, I'd be glad to help out," Rich said. "If I'm still here."

"When are you leaving for Boise?" Steve asked.

"I'm not sure. We're getting that big shipment of camping gear right before Easter. I hate to leave you with all that stocking to do."

"Don't worry about that. I can handle it," Steve said.

Alex had no right to care if he went to Boise. She didn't want to care. But she did.

"Excuse me." A young girl with a pony tail rushed toward them. She wore a Hard Rock Cafe t-shirt and baggy jeans that threatened to fall off any second. "You know that other lady who was swimming with you earlier?"

"She's my wife." Steve sat up.

"She just passed out in the dressing room."

Chapter 10

A Jeep Cherokee pulled up in the driveway. Alex let the curtain drop and ran to the front door, flinging it open.

"Dr. Rawlins?"

"Yes, I'm Dr. Rawlins." He pulled off a leather glove and extended his hand.

"I'm Jamie's sister, Alex. Please, come in." She reached out and shook his hand. "She's in her room lying down."

The doctor followed Alex up the stairs. They stopped outside the bedroom.

"It's probably nothing to worry about." The doctor gave Alex a reassuring smile and stepped inside.

"Good afternoon, Jamie. Hello, Steve."

Steve jumped to his feet and approached the doctor with an outstretched hand.

"Boy, are we glad to see you. Thanks for coming."

Dr. Rawlins looked down at Jamie. The calm on his face helped ease Alex's fears.

"I hear you've been causing some excitement down at the pool."

Jamie raised herself up on one elbow but the doctor patted her on the shoulder, gently coaxing her back down. He sat in a chair Steve had placed behind him.

"I feel so stupid. I don't know what happened."

"Well now, you don't have to feel stupid about anything. Pregnant women are always pulling stunts like this. Last week one of my patients was waiting in line at a fast food restaurant and her water broke."

"Oh." Jamie covered one side of her face with her hand. "I would hate that."

"Let's see if we can figure out what happened." He located her pulse and studied his wristwatch. Alex felt every second tick by.

"Did you eat before you went swimming?"

"An hour before."

"Did you overdo it at the pool? Any fancy dives or relays?"

Jamie shook her head.

He untangled a cuff and pump from his bag and fastened it around Jamie's rolled-up sleeve. Again there was silence as the doctor took her blood pressure.

"A little high." Dr. Rawlins removed a pen from his shirt pocket and made some notes in a notebook. "I really don't think it's anything to worry about. Probably just a drop in blood sugar. That place is like a sauna, which makes it difficult for your body temperature to stay regulated."

It made sense to Alex. The pool room had been steamy and warm, and Jamie hadn't been able to finish her salad before they got ready to swim.

"Why don't you stay in bed the rest of the day and drink plenty of liquids. Take it easy. I'd like to see you at the clinic in West Yellowstone on Monday. We'll do some blood work and check your iron level."

"Okay, Dr. Rawlins. I'm sorry you had to run clear out here."

"It was on my way home. Besides, I do this for all my favorite patients." He snapped his bag shut and patted her hand.

The doctor's thick gray hair gave him an older appearance, but judging by his smooth skin Alex guessed him to be in his early fifties. He dressed in Dockers and a plaid, button-down shirt. What was an Ivy League doctor like him doing in this neck of the woods?

"I'll walk you out," Steve said.

The doctor turned to Jamie. "Any further complications or worries, you call me, day or night. Understand?"

Jamie nodded, "I will."

He patted her hand one last time and walked over to Alex. "It was nice meeting you. Will we see you tomorrow at church?"

"Uh," Alex stumbled over her words for a second. "I-uh . . . I don't know."

"I hope so. We could use another pretty face in this branch."

Alex smiled. A breath of warmth colored her cheeks.

Dr. Rawlins walked to the door where Steve waited. Before leaving he turned and pointed at Jamie. "Get some rest. These two look like they can handle things around here."

Jamie crossed her heart and held up her hand. "I promise."

"Steve," Alex remembered, "Rich wanted you to call him at the office after the doctor left."

"Will do," Steve said.

Jamie and Alex listened as Steve and the doctor talked about the NCAA tournament on their way down the hall and to the front door.

"What a guy," Alex said when they were gone. She walked around the bed and sat on the edge next to her sister. "He treats you like a daughter."

Jamie rubbed her stomach slowly. "He's such a sweet man and he's a great doctor."

"What's he doing in Island Park?" Alex asked.

"He used to vacation here for years. He has a beautiful home on Bill's Island."

"Bill's Island?"

"We'll take you to Henry's Lake sometime and show you the island."

"Who named all these places anyway? A couple of bass fishermen?"

Jamie laughed. "I don't know the history behind them. They don't sound like the names of great explorers though, do they?"

"More like a couple of tourists, if you ask me. They probably have a Winnebago Canyon around here or a Coleman Cove."

"Okay, okay. Stop it already. It's not that bad," Jamie defended her home territory. "Besides, you don't find an obstetrician like Dr. Rawlins in a city like San Francisco. He came down from Idaho Falls a few years ago after his wife passed away. He decided he needed a change, so he quit his practice in I.F.–that's Idaho Falls– and moved here permanently. And am I glad to have him."

"I wasn't sure what kind of doctor you'd have here in the boonies."

"The 'boonies'?!" Jamie exclaimed indignantly.

"This isn't exactly Times Square."

Jamie reached over, pulled a pillow from the other side of the bed, and smacked her sister with it.

"Hey, don't take it personal. But I admit, I wouldn't be surprised to see Barney Fife pull up in a patrol car."

"Enough with the 'hick town' jokes. I love it here. Now help me sit up."

"Okay, I'm sorry. I just can't believe a New York girl like you doesn't miss ballet and opera and Bloomingdale's." Alex helped her sister sit up, then slid the pillow beneath her neck and shoulders. "How's that?"

"Better." Jamie shifted to a more comfortable position. "I miss it sometimes, but I really do love the slow, easy lifestyle we have here. The worst part is not having a close friend. I haven't really got someone to call and gab with, or go to lunch with. I can't bear the thought of you leaving. It's been so nice to have another female around, a friend."

"If you haven't noticed, I'm not exactly in a hurry to get home. I haven't even missed California or all that traveling."

"And what about guys? You haven't mentioned that you're dating anyone."

"Tripping around makes it difficult to have a relationship," Alex said dryly.

"What happened to Justin, I mean Jason . . ."

"You mean Jordan?"

"Yes, Jordan. I thought things would work out with you two."

"How can I describe Jordan?" She stared out the window while she thought. "He's the type of guy who parks in handicap spaces."

"I *hate* that," Jamie said.

"And," Alex sighed, "he was getting too serious about our relationship."

"Too serious? What do you mean?"

"He was getting so demanding and I didn't like how jealous he was," Alex explained. "I had to account for practically every move I made."

"That's awful. I'm glad you got out of it."

"He freaked when I told him it was over. He's called me a few times since then, but I think our relationship is pretty much history now."

"Thank goodness." Jamie rested her hand on her chest. "Sometimes I wonder if I'd ever get married again if something happened to Steve. I've given so much to our relationship, I don't think I have it in me to start all over with someone else. I couldn't hack playing the cat-and-mouse game again."

"Only if you can be the cat once in a while."

They both laughed.

"You and Steve have a great relationship."

"Yeah," Jamie agreed. "I know I'm blessed to be married to such a great guy. So many of my friends are either divorced or miserable in their marriages."

Alex noticed that Jamie didn't say "lucky" but "blessed."

"*Every* one of my friends who was married has gotten divorced," Alex said.

"That doesn't scare you from marriage, does it?"

Alex picked at a thread on her jeans. "A little. I would like to have someone special in my life, but I haven't had a whole lot of luck lately. All the guys I meet are such jerks."

"You sure you're okay?"

"Yeah, I'm doing great," Alex said.

"But." Her sister added.

"But nothing. There is no 'but.'"

"It sounded like there was a 'but' coming."

Alex shifted on the bed. Outside the light had been snuffed out by heavy gray clouds.

"Nope. No 'but.'"

"Hey, this is me you're talking to. What's up?" Jamie rolled onto her side, resting her head on her elbow.

"Nothing's up. Really, I don't know why you think I'm not telling you something."

"Because, you always pick at your pant seams when something's up."

Alex quickly released the thread on her jeans. "I do not."

"Alex, I know you too well. You're a thread-picker when something's on your mind."

Alex opened her mouth to say "ha" but froze for just a second with her mouth gaping wide, then released a sigh.

"I guess I've just been thinking about my life and where it's going. I see you with your husband, this lovely home, and a baby on the way, and I wonder if I'll have the same someday."

"I didn't realize you were worrying about these things."

"I'm not *worried.*" Alex slid off the bed and walked toward the window. "I was just wondering, that's all."

"Maybe it's a little more than that."

"No," Alex said. "There isn't any more."

"Maybe you're looking for more than what you have."

Alex whirled around. "I don't need anything else. I've got a great life. I'm going to be a 'television exercise star.' What could be neater than that?" She looked at her sister, lying helplessly on the bed, cradling her stomach with one arm. "I don't need anything else," she repeated, although she nearly choked as she made her last statement again.

Jamie looked up at Alex with a worried expression. "Can I tell you something? Can I be open and honest?"

Oh no, here it comes. "Of course you can, you know that."

"I worry about where your life is headed."

"You shouldn't be, Jamie. I'm fine. This conversation has really gotten out of control. I mean, I didn't have any problems when I left California, but now it sounds like I'm in deep depression and suicidal."

"You know I don't mean that." Jamie twirled the wedding band on her finger. "I just wonder what you're looking for in life."

Alex opened her mouth to respond and stopped herself. Then she whispered, "I didn't know I was looking for anything until I came here."

Chapter 11

THE NEXT MORNING WAS CHURCH. ALEX HELPED STEVE ARRANGE chairs in the living room for the members. When he went to shower, she checked on Jamie.

"How are you feeling this morning?"

"I don't like everyone fussing over me like this."

"No one's fussing. But until Dr. Rawlins checks you again today, you're just going to have to stay put."

"I need to get something together for the Primary kids."

"Nothing doin'." Alex crossed her arms. "Steve or someone else can help you with this. Especially with that scare you gave us all yesterday."

Jamie's reply came slowly after a moment of thought. "You're right. I'll see if Steve will take the kids. There may be only one or two anyway."

Alex pulled the curtains and exposed the stormy day. Snow had been falling most of the morning and now the wind whined through the trees. "Maybe you'll get lucky and not have anyone show up. It's pretty yucky out there."

"They'll come. Up here a little snow doesn't stop anyone. What are you going to do while we're having church?"

Alex shivered and moved away from the window. "I'm outlining a new lecture on exercise and fat metabolism based on a study done at Stanford. Do you think I'd be in the way if I sat at the bar in the kitchen?"

"Heavens no. But I could have Steve hurry and clean his desk if you'd be more comfortable there."

"I'll be fine in the kitchen."

The doorbell rang. "I'll get it. You," she pointed at Jamie, "stay put." She scurried down the hall, descended the stairs, and swung open the door. There was Rich, smiling, with his arms full of bright red and yellow tulips.

"Wow. Those are beautiful. Come in."

He wiped his feet on the mat inside the door. "I thought these would look nice for church."

"How thoughtful." She closed the door behind him. "Here, let me take some of those."

He handed her two of the four potted plants. Out of the corner of her eye she noticed how handsome he looked in his navy blue suit, starched white shirt, and maroon striped tie. She nearly tripped over an extension cord as they entered the living room together.

"How about one on either side of the mantel?" He looked around the room. "And maybe one over there by the window. What do you think?"

She nodded. "And this one could go on the piano." She walked the flower over and set it in the center of the spinet that had been their mother's.

They turned as footsteps thumped down the staircase. Steve bounded into the room. "Hey, Rich, you're early."

"Look at the beautiful flowers he brought." Alex motioned to the plants placed about the room. "A little breath of spring."

"Those are nice, thanks." Steve was also wearing dress clothes, tan pants, and a navy blazer. Alex felt out of place in her trademark leggings, turtleneck, and oversized Nike sweatshirt.

Rich held up a plastic bag with tiny cups inside. "I brought these. Should I go ahead and prepare the sacrament?"

"Sure, go ahead and get started. I'll be in to help in just a minute. I need to go salt the front porch."

While the men went about the business of preparing for the meeting, Alex hurried up to her room and snagged the materials she needed for her outline. She wanted to get situated before the members arrived.

On her way down downstairs Alex stopped at Jamie's room. Jamie was wiping at her eyes when Alex cracked open the door. "Jamie, what's wrong?"

"Nothing." She turned away so Alex couldn't see her face.

"But you're crying." Alex threw her books into a chair and rushed to the bed. Wrapping an arm around her sister's shoulders, she said, "Please, tell me what's the matter."

"I don't know."

"Are you sick?"

"No. I don't think so." Silent tears continued to fill her eyes. "My stomach's tight. I feel pressure inside. I'm so scared."

Alex hugged her sister close. "I'm sure everything is going to be fine. You'll see. Dr. Rawlins is coming and he'll tell you there's nothing to worry about."

"But I can't shake this feeling. It's almost like someone or something's trying to tell me to prepare myself."

Alex blinked hard and held onto her sister. What could she say to help her feel better?

"Could you—" Jamie blew her nose and wiped at her eyes again. "Could you get Steve?"

Alex didn't like the shakiness in Jamie's voice. Her sister, the one with the easy life, carefree and disgustingly happy, was devastated and distraught. It scared her, seeing Jamie like this.

She jumped from the bed. "He's just downstairs. I'll be back in a sec." She hollered as she charged down the hallway.

Steve met her at the stair landing. "Alex, what's wrong? What is it?"

"It's Jamie. She needs you." She hadn't noticed Rich behind him until she turned to point in Jamie's direction. They watched Steve take the stairs in twos.

"Rich!" Steve's voice traveled back to them a moment later.

Like a cannon, Rich hauled up the stairs with Alex right behind.

They skidded to a halt when they reached the bedroom. Steve and Jamie's hands were entwined and resting on her swollen abdomen.

"Could you help me give her a blessing?" he asked, looking up at Rich. The doorbell rang. Alex stepped back and out of the room, pulling the door behind her. Again she scrambled down the stairs and yanked open the front door. To her relief, it was Dr. Rawlins.

"I'm so glad you're here," she said. "Something's wrong with Jamie. They're upstairs with her now."

Dr. Rawlins went directly to Jamie's room, but stood waiting outside the door. Alex paused with him, watching through the narrow crack.

Jamie lay still on the bed, the two men stood at her side, with their heads bowed and their hands resting on her head. Steve spoke slowly and softly. Alex couldn't make out his words.

When Steve finished speaking, Jamie opened her eyes and smiled up at them. Steve leaned over and kissed her forehead and whispered something. When he stepped back, Rich leaned over and kissed her on the cheek, took her hand, and patted it reassuringly.

"Thank you," Jamie said softly.

Steve turned and noticed the two standing at the door. "Dr. Rawlins, come in, please. I'm so glad you're here."

Rich retreated and stood by Alex as the doctor sat next to Jamie and spoke to her in low, soothing tones. They stopped talking while the doctor took her temperature and blood pressure.

After he finished he turned to Steve and said, "I don't see anything wrong, but I'd like to take Jamie to the West Yellowstone clinic so we can check the baby's heartbeat and do a more thorough examination."

"Now? Should we go now?" Steve clasped and unclasped his hands.

"I'd rather not wait."

Steve looked at Rich and Alex.

"Don't worry about things here," Rich said. "I can take care of the meeting."

"And I'll help him," Alex said.

Jamie's eyes filled with tears. "Thanks, sis. I'm sorry to leave you with all of this."

"We'll be fine. You just take care of yourself."

Steve scooped her up, blanket and all, and started for the door.

"Steve, I can walk. This is ridiculous." She argued with him all the way down the hall and outside. The front door slammed shut, sending waves of silence through the house.

Alex held her breath and let the stillness press down on her. Then she glanced up at Rich. One look at his understanding expression and she dissolved into the security and safety of his outstretched arms.

Chapter 12

A KNOCK AT THE FRONT DOOR SEPARATED THEM.

"Are you going to be okay?" His questioning eyes were filled with concern.

Alex blinked back the tears that threatened to spill over. "I have a feeling it's going to be a long morning."

The knock sounded again.

"I'd better get that," he said. "You could probably use a few minutes alone. I'll let you know if I need anything."

Although she knew full well that she wouldn't be able to concentrate on her outline, Alex sought cover in the kitchen. She heard Rich greeting and welcoming the handful of members who trickled through the front door.

While looking for a pencil, she turned and saw Rich setting an armload of coats on the dining room table. She managed a smile and their gazes remained locked until a bearded man, as burly as a grizzly bear, approached Rich.

Alex dodged out of sight and forced herself to take a seat at a bar stool. The stack of papers held no interest for her. But she had nothing else to do but shuffle through computer printouts containing charts and graphs and other research she'd gathered. She stopped when she heard Rich's voice.

"Good morning, brothers and sisters. I'm happy to see you all made it here safely. I'd like to excuse President Miles and his wife and Brother Rawlins this morning, as well as Brother and Sister Dixon. The Dixons graciously opened their home for our Sabbath meeting, but were called away unexpectedly. We'll open the meeting by singing,

'Welcome, Welcome, Sabbath Morning,' hymn number 280."

There was silence. Alex looked up from the papers and wondered why they weren't singing.

"Sister Morris, you play the piano, don't you?"

"Um, not very well," a woman said.

"I'm sure having you play would be better than no accompaniment at all."

Alex shut her eyes and shook her head. She knew Jamie usually played the piano for their church meeting.

Poor Rich.

"Sister Anderson, could you lead the singing?"

Alex heard some shuffling and a cough. Then the music started.

Streaks of cold shivers rippled Alex's spine with each sour note. The congregation sounded like they were doing their best to keep up with the choppy rhythm, but it was a losing battle. Alex covered her forehead with her hand and thought again, *Poor Rich!*

She could almost hear the sigh of relief as the final discordant note hung heavily in the air.

Even though she focused herself on her article, her concentration dissolved when she heard Rich's voice again. He covered some church business then introduced the next song.

Alex rolled her eyes. She didn't think she could stomach another song.

". . . one verse of 'I Stand All Amazed,' hymn number 193."

The title of the song described the moment perfectly. Alex was amazed that this song could be worse than the first one they sang.

They'd be better off singing a capella.

This time the singing and the piano never did get together.

Alex shook her head and went back to her research.

A moment later Rich startled her by coming into the kitchen.

"I forgot to fill the sacrament cups," he whispered.

He rushed to the sink and stuck the silver tray under the faucet. When he turned on the knob, the water hit the tray full force and sprayed everywhere.

Alex jumped up from her stool and grabbed a dishcloth.

"Here, let me do that."

While he mopped off his dripping front, Alex filled the little cups. Then Rich exchanged the tray Alex held for the damp dishcloth.

"I wish there was something I could do to help," she whispered.

"Me too. You don't know how to play the piano, do you?"

He was joking and desperate.

"Actually I can." She knew she'd regret volunteering, but when it came to Rich, she realized, she didn't think clearly.

"You're kidding?"

She shook her head.

"I'll pay you, I'll do anything . . ."

"Exactly what would I have to do?" She took a step back, hoping she hadn't made a mistake.

"Just the closing song."

"One song? And that's it, right?"

He nodded.

She paused before answering. The pleading expression on his face, the needy look in his eyes, was more than she could handle. "All right. But only because my ears can't take it anymore."

"Thank you *so* much." He grabbed both of her hands, squeezed them tightly, then hurried back to the living room.

Crazy Mormons.

Not only was her concentration shot, she had to go into that meeting with those people and play while they sang a hymn. Was Rich really worth it?

Yes!

After another prayer and more silence, she heard Rich's voice again. Resting her chin on her knuckles, she listened to his voice, smooth, yet powerful.

". . . I know that there are times when the Lord tries to talk to us, to prompt us, and we don't make ourselves available to partake of his Spirit. Maybe we're too busy, or too stubborn, or there is something amiss in our lives that is preventing us from hearing that still, small voice. But brothers and sisters, I want to testify to you that I know the Lord is there. He wants to help and bless us, but we have to ask, especially at those times when we feel most unworthy to ask for the Lord's help. *That* is the time when we should be constantly on our knees, pleading for his forgiveness and the strength to live our lives the way we should."

Alex dwelled on every word he said. Never before had she thought about Jesus in that way. That not only could she approach Jesus, talk to him, and confide in him, but that he *wanted* to bless her, *wanted* to "talk" to her. Was he really a living being? A caring, understanding person? Someone who was concerned about her?

In that moment of pondering, when she was just about to doubt it, her understanding seemed to expand enough to grasp the whole wonderful concept. Her heartbeat quickened and her palms grew cold and moist.

She drew in several uneasy, shaky breaths.

Food, she thought, *I need food.* Grabbing a banana she went back to her chair.

The meeting continued but she blocked it out. She heard voices but didn't listen.

Finally, she became absorbed in her project and lost track of time, until, as if she'd been equipped with "Rich Radar," she heard his voice.

"I think we'll go ahead and close our sacrament meeting at this time. The closing song is 'Where Can I Turn for Peace?' hymn number 129. I've asked Sister Morris if she would lead the music this time, and Alex McCarty, Sister Dixon's sister, who is here for a visit, has offered to play for us."

Wondering what she'd gotten herself into, Alex jumped to her feet and met Rich in the hallway connecting the kitchen to the living room.

"I owe you one," he said softly as they joined the congregation.

Alex glanced at the audience and smiled briefly, then took her place at the piano. A woman pointed at a page and Alex nodded. Fumbling with the first few notes, she played the introduction. Then, on the upsweep, she launched into the song, hoping she had the phrasing and counts correct. Sight-reading had never been her strength, but it was a simple tune with a predictable rhythm. She watched 'Sister Morris' wag her arm from side to side, and did her best to keep up with her.

Even for the small group the song was spirited and lively. Alex tingled with exhilaration as six years of piano lessons kicked in.

A rush of silence followed the last chord.

The chorister found her seat and an older gentleman came forward, stood in front of the congregation, and folded his arms. Alex stayed on the piano bench while he offered a short, simple prayer. He asked a blessing upon those in need, the sick and the afflicted, the poor and the homeless.

His next statement caused Alex to lift her head and stare at the man. "And Father, please bless those in our midst who may be seeking the truth and may not know where to look. Soften their hearts, and open their minds to Thy spirit. Let them feel of Thy love and the truthfulness of Thy gospel."

Alex remained with her head down after the "Amen" was said. Why did it seem that people were telling her to look for something she wasn't interested in finding?

A few members introduced themselves to her and the next thing she knew she found herself back in the kitchen with "Little Sara," who was the only child at church and didn't want to sit with her mother through a grown-up Sunday School.

"You look like Sister Dixon," the golden-haired child said, looking up from the picture she was coloring.

"You think so?"

"You're pretty like she is, and nice, too."

"Thank you, Sara. I think you're pretty, too."

The little girl straightened her shoulders. "You do?"

"You look just like a porcelain doll I used to have when I was younger. Do you know what a porcelain doll is?"

"My mommy has some dolls that are made of glass. Sometimes she lets me hold them."

"You have to be careful with them because they're very delicate, don't you?"

Sara nodded. "Delicate," she said slowly. She smiled.

"One year, when I was a little older than you, Santa brought me a beautiful porcelain ballerina doll for Christmas. She was dressed in a fluffy, light pink tu-tu."

"Will you draw me a ballerina?"

"Me?" The child didn't know that Alex was the only person on earth who could botch up a paint-by-numbers picture.

"With a tu-tu like your doll," Sara added.

Alex took one look at the sweet face in front of her and picked up a pencil. She made some lines on the paper. Sara tilted her head to one side as Alex drew a fluffy skirt and pointed slippers on the dancer. One leg was skinnier than the other but Sara got the idea.

"I saw a ballerina on TV. A man was lifting her high in the air."

"That's the kind of doll Santa brought me. She had honey blonde hair and big blue eyes like yours."

"She did?"

Alex nodded.

"Do you still have her?"

Alex hadn't thought about that doll for years. Most likely it was in storage with a lot of her things at her mother's. "I think so."

"Could I be a ballerina someday?"

Now that was a tough one. Where in Island Park did a child take ballet lessons? "Maybe when you get a little older. You'll have to ask your mother, okay?"

"Okay." Sara studied the picture. "Sister McCarty?"

The name made her sound like a nun. "Yes, Sara."

"Can I keep this picture?"

Alex ran her hand down the girl's soft hair and said, "Of course."

The low tones of voices from the meeting filtered into the kitchen. Alex looked around for something else they could do. She saw a few books Steve had left on the counter and began sorting through them. One was full of church pictures.

"Have you seen this picture before" Alex asked the little girl.

"That's Adam and Eve in the Garden of Even."

Alex thought for a second then said, "The Garden of *Eden*?"

Sara nodded.

They flipped through picture after picture. Sara was able to identify many of the New Testament pictures.

"That one is Joseph and Mary going to Bethalem." Alex hid her smile at the child's pronunciation of the town's name.

"That one is baby Jesus. And this one is when they had to leave because the mean king wanted to kill baby Jesus."

Sara turned to another picture.

"Mommy told me this is where Jesus threw bad men and their money out of the temple. And this one is when he gets baptized. I'm going to get baptized when I turn eight."

"How old are you now?"

"Five and a half," she said proudly.

Sara went to turn the page but Alex said, "Wait, I'd like to look for just a minute." The picture had John the Baptist and the Savior standing in a pool of water. John the Baptist's hand was raised to heaven. Alex studied the picture. She hadn't seen her father or her sister get baptized. Was this how they'd done it?

Alex jumped when a voice said, "Hi girls, how's it going?"

"Look what Sister McCarty drew for me." Sara ran over to Rich.

He took the picture from Sara. Alex wanted to snatch it and hide it.

"Wow, that sure is a pretty picture."

Alex studied her cuticles.

"Sister McCarty even has a doll that looks like me."

"*Sister* McCarty does?"

Alex glanced up to see Rich struggling with a smile that threatened to burst into laughter as he handed her picture back.

"You know what, Sara? Our meeting is over. Your mommy is waiting for you."

"I can show her my picture." Sara headed for the living room, holding her picture safely to her chest. Then she turned, ran back to Alex, and threw her arms around Alex's neck. "Thanks for the picture. I'm glad you were my teacher."

For a moment Alex was so surprised by Sara's display of affection that her arms wouldn't move. Then quickly she embraced the child and said, "I'll see you soon, okay?"

"Okay. Bye." Sara waved as she ran from the kitchen to join her mother in the living room. Rich sighed, loosened the knot in his tie, and undid the top button on his shirt.

"You two sure hit it off," he said.

"She's an angel."

"That she is." Rich looked down at the picture in the binder. "Were you two looking at these?"

"Yes. Is that how you guys get baptized in your church?"

"Yup, just like that. But we use a font at the church. It looks like a big hot tub without the bubbles. We believe in baptism by immersion. The way Christ did it."

Alex had never known that was how Jamie had been baptized. She'd always pictured Jamie getting sprinkled on the head with water.

Alex licked her dry lips, wishing for some of Rich's Carmex. "Do you think it's too soon to call the doctor and see how Jamie's doing?"

He looked down at his watch. "It's been almost two hours. Let's call right now."

He opened a cupboard above the desk and found the phone book. After thumbing through a few pages, he ran his finger down a column of names.

"Here it is."

He punched in the number and held the phone to his ear. Alex chewed the edge of her thumbnail.

"I'd like to speak with Dr. Rawlins, please." He lifted his eyebrows at Alex and waited.

"Hello, Dr. Rawlins? This is Rich Greenwood. We've been wondering how Jamie's doing." He looked at Alex as he listened.

"Good, good. That's what we wanted to hear." He gave her a thumbs-up and kept listening. Her heart calmed as she released a deep breath.

"Okay, great, we'll watch for them, then." He turned to the desk.

Alex didn't realize she'd been clenching her fists so tightly. She shook her hands to relax the tension in them, noticing fingernail marks on her palms.

"Thanks again, doctor. Bye." Rich hung the phone on the receiver and looked at Alex. "The doctor said they ran several tests, hooked her up to a monitor, and everything looks normal. The baby's heartbeat is strong and regular. The doc's puzzled but not worried."

Alex's shoulders slumped with relief. "When are they coming home?"

"He wants her to stay on the monitor a while longer. Then they'll be on their way."

"Good." For a moment they stood looking at each other until the doorbell rang.

"I'll get it," he said.

Alex watched him walk out of the kitchen, then placed a hand on her chest and rested back against the refrigerator door. Jamie was okay. She shut her eyes and said a soft "thank you." Alex was incredibly grateful to have Rich around to help shoulder the concern for her sister. She realized how much she had relied on his faith and strength.

Her eyelids flew open. What was she doing? She couldn't rely on Rich, couldn't get involved with him. No matter how much she cared for him, there was one fact she couldn't ignore—he wouldn't marry outside that temple of his and she wouldn't marry inside of it. They could only be friends.

"That was Morty." Rich came back into the kitchen. "He forgot some things."

"I thought I'd make something to eat." Alex kept her eyes focused on the fridge. "Would you like to stay for lunch?"

"Sure, if you'll let me help."

She looked over her shoulder at him. He had his suit coat off and was rolling up his shirt sleeves. During the church meeting he had seemed so important and commanding. Now, with his tie gone, he was the everyday Rich. Both ways were equally impressive, equally unnerving.

"Why don't you put those noodles in to boil?"

"You're the boss."

They worked silently for several minutes. She rinsed vegetables. He waited for water to heat. Soon he dumped the box of pasta into the boiling water and poked at stray ends with his finger. "Ow, that's hot!" He shook his hand and joined her at the sink. "What next?"

"Use that brush and scrub the carrots for me."

"Why don't you just peel them?"

"The skins have most of the vitamins."

He picked up a carrot and examined it. "So, where'd did you learn to play the piano so well?"

"Six years of lessons. Jamie's much better than I am."

"You saved us today, you know."

They stood side by side, elbows bumping, hands brushing under running water.

You've got to have some flaws somewhere, she thought. *I just need to find out what they are.*

"I'm glad I could help," was all she said. Glancing up at Rich, she saw that his face had a faraway look about it.

"Holding church in members' homes like this reminds me of my mission."

"Did you like having Steve for a companion?"

"He was my favorite, but he sure had some strange eating habits."

"He still does," Alex grimaced. She had never known a person who abused their stomach like Steve did.

"His mom used to send him boxes of cake mix on his mission. He'd mix up the batter then sit down and eat the whole thing."

"Without baking it?"

"Yes," Rich laughed. "I'd wait for him to get sick, but he never did." Rich shook his head. "He used to make breakfast every morning. His specialty were 'gut bombs.'"

"Gut bombs? Sounds tempting." Alex cut the stems from the last of the mushrooms and tossed them into the drainer.

"They were these incredibly heavy pancakes smeared with peanut butter and covered with maple syrup. It made you feel like you'd eaten a load of bricks. Sometimes we could barely walk to our appointments, we felt so heavy. But we wouldn't get hungry again until dinner that night."

Alex couldn't help but laugh. What a pair those two must have been. "What would you have for dinner? Or do I really want to know?" she asked as she chopped the celery into angled pieces.

"'Slimers' were his favorite."

"Slimers?"

Rich rinsed his hands under the water and wiped them on a dish cloth. "They were pretty good, actually. He used flour tortillas, diced ham, cheese, and mushroom soup. They were kind of like enchiladas."

"I was afraid they had something to do with worms or slugs."

"No, no. Steve may be weird but he's not gross. We still get together every once in a while and have some of his famous mission food. We've even got Jamie hooked on slimers."

"I don't have anything special planned for lunch—just safe, identifiable vegetables over pasta."

"Sounds delicious."

Rich had the table set and the pasta drained when she announced, "The vegetables are done. Let's eat."

They dished up their plates in the kitchen and carried them to the table where Rich had arranged placemats, goblets with ice water, and two lit candles between them. He held her chair then walked around the table and sat directly across from her. Their gazes locked over the flickering candles. Alex returned Rich's smile. And she knew . . .

There was far more between them than just friendship.

Chapter 13

"I'M STUFFED. IF I DON'T GET MOVING I'M GOING TO FALL ASLEEP." Rich rested his head against the back of the chair and sighed. "You sure didn't eat much."

Alex looked down at her plate, still almost full of food. "I guess I'm just a little worried about Jamie." She didn't tell him that she didn't like feeling full, didn't like herself when she ate a big meal. She'd spent years training herself to ignore hunger pangs, to accept the hollow feeling. The emptiness in her stomach was her barometer. She equated hunger with thinness, and thinness with being good enough. But good enough for what, she didn't know.

"Yeah, me too. But Dr. Rawlins assured me she's fine."

They sat in silence for a moment.

"Hey." Rich sat up and slapped the table. "I've got an idea. I need to run out to the shop and check to see what time a group from Reno comes in the morning. Do you feel like getting out?"

She wondered if he'd read her mind. She wasn't used to being cooped up inside all day long and was grateful for an excuse to go outside, even if it was cold and snowy. "I'll just clean up the kitchen, then go change my clothes. Remind me to leave Jamie and Steve a note so they don't worry."

"Why don't I put things away while you go change?"

She scampered up the stairs and flew into her room. *He's going to break your heart, you idiot.* She knew it was true. There was absolutely no future for her and Rich, but she couldn't help herself. She enjoyed being with him. With other guys she always felt like she was being scrutinized, judged, sized up, like a contestant at a beauty contest. Not with Rich though.

She pulled on cream-colored leggings, a long-sleeved tee, and a bulky cable-knit sweater. Over thick wool socks she laced up leather ankle boots and brushed her hair into a loose pony tail. Just before leaving the room, she spritzed herself with perfume and wondered when the last time was she'd had butterflies.

Rich was finished in the kitchen when she bounded down the stairs. They slid into their coats and headed out the side door to Rich's truck.

"How come Sara's dad doesn't come to church?"

Rich opened the door for her. "He's not a member."

Alex climbed in the truck, and as Rich went around to his side of the truck, she wondered how the family functioned with one of the parents being a nonmember.

Rich climbed in behind the steering wheel and continued, "It's a sad situation. I'm surprised he allows Sara and her mom to attend meetings, he's so negative toward the Church."

I guess that answers my question.

"Having opposite views on religion can be a huge strain on a marriage." He started the engine and put the truck in reverse.

"Are your parents members?"

"Yeah." He swung the truck around and headed down the driveway. "I've got great-great-great-grandparents who came from England, then crossed the plains with handcarts."

"Really?" She didn't even know who her great-great-great-grandparents were, let alone where they came from or what they'd done.

The storm clouds had cleared, leaving the day sunny and bright. They drove past snow-burdened cabins peeking through high drifts and past trucks and vans pulling trailers of snowmobiles. Several cars had ski racks loaded with skis. Alex noticed a gas station, a market, several souvenir shops, and even a pottery shop.

Rich turned off the main highway and the truck bumped down a snow-packed road toward a cozy log structure.

"Is this your house?"

"You probably don't remember much about it, do you?"

"Not the outside. It was dark when we left."

"This is home. It's not much, but it's mine."

The lodge-pole cottage was perfectly symmetrical, with a window on either side of the front door and a wrap-around porch. There were even flower boxes under each window. It was wonderful, and probably even more charming in summer, surrounded by flowers.

"I love it. How long have you lived here?"

"Just a couple of years. Steve and I built it. We had help with the wiring and plumbing, but the rest he and I did."

Rich steered the truck around to the side of the house and slowed it to a halt. She nearly hopped out her side until she realized he was coming around to get her door. It had been a long time since a guy had opened a door for her.

"Thanks, Rich." They paused briefly, eyes connecting, her heart pounding.

The crunch of snow and the purr of an engine broke their trance.

"Hey, it's Jamie and Steve," Rich said. "What are they doing here?"

They ran to greet them, and Alex swung Jamie's door open. "What a surprise. How are you?" Jamie was still in her robe and slippers, and looked pale and tired.

"I'm fine. I just want to go home and soak in the tub. What are you guys doing? We saw you from the highway." Jamie reached for Alex's hand and scooted over to make space for her to sit. Alex perched on the edge of the car seat.

"Nothing, really. We made lunch—we left some of it for you. Rich was going to show me around town."

"I'm starved," Jamie said. "The doctor wouldn't let me eat a thing until we finished the tests."

"Did he have any more to say?" Alex asked.

"My iron's a little low, but that's all."

"How did church go?" Steve killed the engine.

Rich leaned over and looked inside. "We started off a little shaky, but thanks to Alex, things turned out great." Rich patted her on the shoulder, then left his hand there for a moment.

"Thanks to Alex?" The surprise on Jamie's face made Alex laugh.

"She bailed us out with the music," Rich explained.

"You did?"

"I *do* know how to play the piano," Alex said.

"After one song with Sister Morris playing, I thought we were going to send out shock waves and start an avalanche," Rich said.

"I didn't know Sister Morris could play the piano," Steve said.

"She can't!" Rich and Alex said together. Everybody laughed.

"Do you want to come in? I was just going to change clothes." Rich rubbed his hands together to warm them.

"You two go ahead," Steve said. "I'm getting this little mother home to take it easy. It's been one rough day already."

Alex looked at Jamie. "Do you want me to come back with you?"

Jamie shook her head. "All I need is some food and a bath. Why don't you join us later, though? We can play games or something."

"Good idea," Rich said.

Alex leaned over and hugged her sister. "Take it easy, Jamie. Okay?"

"I will. You two have fun."

Rich and Alex stood side by side as Jamie and Steve backed down the driveway and out of sight.

"You're worried, aren't you?" he said.

"I just don't understand why she keeps having problems. I don't know what she'll do if she loses this baby, too."

As Rich opened the back door of his house for her, Alex noticed it hadn't been locked. In fact, she realized Jamie and Steve never locked their doors either. That was unheard of where she came from.

She stepped into his house and Rich followed her. "It was rough seeing Jamie go through her other miscarriages," he said. "But she's tough and has a lot of faith. She'll be okay."

Would that be enough? Alex wondered. To have faith? Her father's faith didn't spare his life.

Everything looked familiar inside the cabin—the small table in the kitchen, the polished pine stairway, the lovely painting over the mantel. Dark embers smoldered in the fireplace. Rich opened the screen, threw in some tinder, and added another log. He blew on the kindling until the new wood ignited.

"I'm going upstairs to change clothes. I won't be long."

Sitting next to the warmth of the fire, Alex picked up a magazine and leafed through the pages. Not ten minutes later, Rich loped down the stairs.

"That was fast." Alex put down the issue of *The Great Outdoors* she was reading and stood up.

"Sorry I didn't have anything more interesting to read."

"Actually, the article about hiking the Grand Tetons was fascinating."

"You're welcome to borrow it. In fact, you can borrow anything you want." He gestured around the room.

"Well, I do have my eye on this painting." She motioned to the canvas above them.

"I'm glad you like it. Spring up here is unbeatable, I don't care where you've been or what you've seen."

"If it ever stops snowing around here, maybe I'll get to see for myself before I go home."

"Jamie's going to have a hard time when you leave. She really loves having you around."

"I hate to leave her, but after Easter I'll need to get back. I'm already feeling a little fidgety."

"Because of your job?"

"Kind of. But mostly because I haven't been able to work out. Back home I rarely miss a day, and I'm just not used to staying inside all the time. But I can't seem to squeeze in a workout between snowstorms."

"Sounds like you've got a case of cabin fever. You've just been cooped up inside too long." He rubbed his chin with his thumb. "I might be able to help you out. Let me think on it for a while." He stood and offered his hand. She wondered what he meant. What could he do about the snow? Accepting his hand, she let him pull her to her feet.

They left through the back door, and again he helped her into the truck. After he started the engine he slid a CD into the stereo. Soft instrumental music filled the cab. After a few moments Alex recognized the tune.

"Hey, this is the song I played at church."

He adjusted the volume louder.

"How beautiful. It sounds so different with an orchestra."

Alex thought the flowing music served to sharpen the beauty of the day. Beneath the sun's rays, the melting snow sparkled with blinding whiteness.

"Tell me about Island Park," she said.

Rich was glad to oblige. "It's primarily a tourist town made up of empty cabins, used off and on throughout the year, mostly in summer."

Down the highway they traveled with Rich pointing out different landmarks and spots of interest—a hotel and dinner club, a general store, the post office. After they crossed a bridge over Henry's Fork, a finger of the Snake River, Rich steered the truck down a snowy road to a building with a sign *Recreation Headquarters* across the front. Rich pulled up to the door and parked the truck. "This is it."

"Wow."

The front of the building was rustic with lodgepole pines and stonework, but the body was a storage warehouse with two huge garage-like doors on the side.

"Let me show you around," Rich said.

Even in the bright sunshine, their breath came in vapory puffs. Alex bounced from foot to foot trying to stay warm while Rich opened the door.

"You'd be warmer if you had a decent coat." Rich examined her canvas jacket as they walked inside.

"This coat is decent." She tried to look offended.

"You know what I mean, something designed to keep your body heat in." He swung the door wide. "You're so thin you don't have any body fat to insulate you. I have just the thing."

Alex didn't admit that she'd been cold ever since she'd crossed the Utah/Idaho border. As long as she wore several layers of clothes, the temperature was bearable.

They stepped directly into the showroom where every piece of outdoor equipment imaginable was found—camping equipment, survival supplies, any item an outdoorsman would need to enjoy the wilderness.

"Looks like you've got everything here but the kitchen sink," she said.

"We have one of those, too. They're collapsible and fit in a backpack."

Alex laughed. She wasn't surprised.

"You take this pretty seriously, don't you?" She picked up a canteen and examined it.

"Being outdoors isn't much fun if you're caught unprepared. We make sure our customers have safe, enjoyable experiences up here. Most of what we get are 'city slickers' who don't know a Swiss Army knife from a port-o-potty. So we have to provide everything they need. That way they're satisfied and we get repeat business. In fact ninety percent of our clients are repeat customers or referrals. We've even thought of opening another shop in Jackson Hole, but we're so busy here we don't have time to get plans together. In fact, we could use some help around this place, now that Jamie isn't able to work."

He showed her the back room, which housed their joint office, along with a bathroom and a lounge area that held a vending machine, a television, and a couch for clients. The rest of the back room was filled with canoes hanging from the rafters, rows of ATVs and snowmobiles, and heaps of sleeping bags, backpacks, and assorted boots and outerwear. All in chaotic disorder, in complete contrast to Rich's house. She was surprised Rich didn't have it color coded, sized, and stacked in neat rows.

"Gee, Rich, how do you find anything in here?"

Rich looked embarrassed. "We just never seem to have the time to clean up and organize it all." He walked over to the shelves and pulled down a red bundle. Untying the strap, he shook the contents. It was a bold red parka, with fur-trimmed hood. "Now this will keep you warm."

He held it for her. She slid out of her jacket and thrust her arms into the cushy sleeves of the coat. He twirled her around and zipped the front.

"It's like wearing a hairy sleeping bag." She looked up into his face. It was only inches away.

"But it'll keep you warm." His voice was soft.

"I bet it will." Her tone matched his.

"You look like an Eskimo." He smiled and leaned in closer.

"I feel like an idiot." She tilted her chin up toward him. Her palms were sweating and it wasn't from the warm coat.

Her heart pumped wildly as he drew even closer. More that a few times she had dreamed about him kissing her, but now that it was about to happen, she felt like she was going into cardiac arrest.

Alex closed her eyes.

Chapter 14

JUST BEFORE HIS LIPS TOUCHED HERS, THE PHONE RANG.

With an exasperated sigh, Rich said, "Excuse me, I'd better get that." He strode to the office.

Alex ripped down the zipper and tore the hood from her head before she suffocated. Or had it been the close brush with disaster that had her gasping for air? Because if Rich had kissed her, that's exactly what it would have been. Disaster.

Alex collapsed onto the couch in the lounge and massaged her forehead with her fingers. *I have to get away from him and stay away.*

But as true as that fact was, her heart just wouldn't shut him out. Rich was the kind of man she didn't think existed anymore. Warm, thoughtful, sincere. But he wouldn't have her if she wasn't a Mormon and she didn't want him if he was one.

Panic hit her with the force of a meteor. What in the world was she thinking? She'd only been there five days and look at her. She would have let him kiss her. She wanted him to kiss her.

"Sorry for the interruption. We've got a group from Chicago coming in this week and they wanted to confirm their dates." Rich's frame filled the doorway. Alex sat up with a start. She forced herself to look at him.

"That's okay." Her voice sounded strained. She fought to prevent her face from betraying the pain filling her chest.

"Is something wrong? Your cheeks are flushed."

"I'm not feeling well." It was true. She was heartsick. "Would you mind taking me home?"

"Not at all." He rushed to her side. "Can you make it to the truck?"

She nodded.

"Here let me wrap this around you so you don't freeze." He lifted the red coat.

"No. It's fine. Really. If I need a warmer coat I can just borrow one from Jamie."

"Oh." His voice cooled. "Okay."

Silently they left the building. He helped her into the truck then came around to the other side. Before starting the engine he reached over and felt her cheek, then her forehead. "I can't tell if you have a fever or not."

After giving her one last worried look, he turned the key. They drove in silence.

When they arrived at Jamie's, Alex jumped out and rushed up the front steps before Rich could come around and help her out.

"Hi . . ." Jamie's voice faded as Alex ran past her and up the stairs.

Alex rushed into her room just as a sob tore from her throat. *Stupid, stupid, stupid! Why did you let yourself fall for him?*

A knock sounded at her door. She wiped furiously at her tears and swallowed the emotion clogging her throat.

"Alex, it's me. Can I come in?" Jamie's voice was muffled through the door but her concern was evident even so.

"Sure." Alex grabbed a pillow and hugged it close. She didn't want to see anyone or talk to anyone. It was hard to admit stupidity, even to her sister.

"Rich said you weren't feeling well." Jamie walked around to the side of the bed. "You haven't been eating at all lately. Are you sick?"

"I *have* been eating and *no*, I'm not sick. I just have a headache." Alex sat on the bed so hard the headboard banged against the wall.

"Sorry. But you're so thin. I worry, you know, that you might be getting anorexic again."

"Jamie! It's just a headache."

Jamie flinched at Alex's lashing words. She turned to leave.

"Wait," Alex said.

Jamie stopped.

"I'm sorry. I didn't mean to yell at you."

Jamie turned slowly to face Alex.

"Did something happen while you were gone? Rich is really worried."

"No. Yes." Alex covered her face with her hands. "I don't know."

"Rich was worried he'd said or done something to upset you."

"I'm fine. Tell him I'm fine. And I'm sorry I yelled at you like that."

"It's okay." Jamie sat down on the bed next to her sister. "I don't want to stick my nose in where it doesn't belong, but I have to be honest, Alex. I think there's something you're not telling me."

Alex shut her eyes, willing her sister to go away. Not only did Jamie want to stick her nose in where it didn't belong, she'd keep sniffing until she uncovered the truth.

At last Alex opened her eyes and sighed. As Jamie waited patiently, Alex propped the pillow behind her back. She bit her bottom lip then looked at her sister and said, "I've done something really stupid, and I'm embarrassed to admit it."

Confusion creased Jamie's brow. "You know you can tell me anything."

"Yeah, but it's still hard."

The sisters sat in silence until Alex gathered her thoughts. "I've only been here a few days. And in that short time I've really managed to make a mess."

"No you haven't," Jamie jumped in. "You've been the perfect houseguest."

"I don't mean mess, mess. I mean MESS MESS."

By the look on Jamie's face, Alex was making a bigger "mess" out of the explanation.

"I'm not sure if it's love, but I've think I've fallen for Rich." Alex quickly shut her eyes and froze. She couldn't bear to look at her sister.

Instead, she felt Jamie's arms circle around her.

"So, tell me something I don't know." Jamie rubbed Alex's back. "I saw it happen and I honestly didn't know what to do or say. How do you stop the sun from rising?"

Alex wiped at her dampened eyes as Jamie released her hug.

"What do you mean you already know?"

"Maybe we haven't seen each other for three years, but I still know you pretty well. I could tell just by the way you looked at him. But one thing really gave it away."

"What?"

"I know how you feel about Mormons. But to actually play the piano for sacrament meeting? I mean, come on, give me some credit here."

"I just wanted to help."

"I know." Jamie said.

"That's it," Alex said resolutely. Somehow she had to wipe that smirk off her sister's face. "I was helping out."

"Help, schmelp. You wanted to be with Rich."

Is that why she'd done it? No one had forced her to volunteer to play the piano.

Yikes! It was true.

"So, now what are you going to do?" Jamie leaned against the bed post.

"Do? I'm not going to do anything but stay away and try to forget about him."

Jamie shot to her feet. She planted her fists on what was left of her waistline. "Are you crazy?" she said.

"No. Stupid, yes, but not crazy."

"How can you let a guy like Rich just slip through your fingers? He'd be a perfect husband and father. The man is incredible."

"Shhhh . . ." Alex waved her hands in front of her trying to push down the volume in Jamie's voice. "You think I don't already know that? But you're forgetting a few things like, one, he's a Mormon, I'm not. Two, he's got a girlfriend in Boise. And three, I live in California and he lives here. That's three strikes, I'm out."

"Whether you like it or not, there's something between you and Rich. I've never seen you as content as you have been these last few days. You're usually running at warp speed like you've only got one week to live."

Alex had to admit, she usually felt that way.

"But look at you. You haven't even called your office or home, have you?"

Alex shook her head.

"Isn't that unusual for you?"

Alex had to admit, her behavior recently had been odd at best.

"Don't you see?"

"See what? That I've fallen for a man I can't have, that I've lost my desire to work or go back home, and I've been sitting around like a beached whale? Oh, I see. I'm really something."

Jamie shook her head, sat down in front of her sister and grabbed Alex's hands. "You don't see it because it's happening to you and this is all strange and weird, but you are going through a change."

"I thought I'd have hot flashes and be in my forties when that happened," Alex grimaced.

Jamie giggled. "Alex, will you listen to me?"

Alex faced her, daring her sister to convince her of anything.

"I've picked up on this lately when we've talked on the phone. You've hinted a lot at the fact that your life is crazy, unpredictable, and hectic. And I've heard you say more than once, 'I know dozens of girls who would kill for my job, and on days like today I would gladly give it to them.'"

But Alex hadn't actually meant it, had she?

Jamie continued, "It's like you're looking for something more, and you just don't know exactly what it is. But to me, as the person standing back and watching, it's all so clear." Jamie reached up and smoothed a strand of hair off Alex's face. "Don't get me wrong; what you have is good. But, Alex, you have to feel like there's a purpose to all this running around you do. There has to be someone to share it with. I don't care what people say, money *can't* buy happiness."

Alex shut her eyes and let the words sink in. A purpose. Someone to share your life with. How many times on Red Eye flights, jetting from coast to coast, had she had those exact same thoughts? Maybe in different words, but basically the same meaning. "*Why am I doing this?*"

The fame, the glory, the excitement. Sure, those things were wonderful, but they didn't last. Once the conferences and commotion, the huge receptions, the pictures, and the autographs were over, she was still alone, in her hotel room, waiting to catch that next flight and go on to the next lonely hotel room.

Jamie squeezed Alex's hand and held tight. "Change is uncomfortable and hard, but I'm here to help you and I know the Lord is, too. And if I were you, that's exactly who I'd be talking to about this. He knows a lot more than I do. All you have to do is ask." Jamie rose from the bed and looked at her sister, her eyes large and filled with love.

"Alex, because you're my big sister, I've always leaned on you and so has Mom. But maybe it's time to let someone help you." Jamie hugged Alex, then left the room.

* * *

She must have fallen asleep. And she must have been dreaming, because she remembered running, or at least trying to run but not being able to move her legs. And crying out for help. She'd pleaded for someone to help her but no one was there. She was alone.

Alex woke up, rolled off the bed onto her feet, and walked over to the window. Streaks of evening stretched through the pines. Everything was quiet. Sparkling above the tallest tree was one single star dangling in the clear sky like a diamond on blue silk. *They say You're really up there and that You want to help me,* she began.

Tears blurred her view and she blinked them away. *Why am I so confused? Is what Jamie telling me true?*

She thought about her mother who seemed to be whirling around the same vicious cyclone, overly involved in her work and her friends, trying to fill the emptiness in her life. But her mother never complained. Had she found the contentment Jamie was talking about?

Do You know what I should do? Can You really help me?

What about her dad? Hadn't he committed his life to the Lord and his church? Had the Lord been there and heard his prayers?

Doubt filled her and she turned away. She didn't trust this person she couldn't see or feel. If faith was what she needed, then she was in big trouble because she didn't have any.

Chapter 15

THE NEXT MORNING ALEX AWOKE TO BANGING AND YELLING AT the front door. She pulled a robe over her T-shirt and ran into the hall and halfway down the stairs, then stopped short.

Steve backed through the door carrying a large, black metal object.

"Careful, don't scrape the newel post," Jamie said.

"You okay, Rich? You've got the heaviest part," Steve grunted and stepped back until one foot was on the bottom stair.

"Yeah. Let's get it through the door and set it down. I'm losing my grip."

"Just a few more inches," Steve said.

In through the door came a treadmill. Alex's mouth dropped open and stayed that way until Rich stepped through and looked up.

"Hi," he said with a groan.

"Set it down right there," Steve instructed.

Steve's side went down first, then he rushed around to help Rich ease his end to the floor.

"What is this?" Alex lifted her hands and scrunched up her shoulders.

"Gee, Alex," Steve said. "I thought of all people you'd recognize a treadmill when you saw one."

Weak with shock, Alex sank down onto a step.

Rich straightened and pressed his hands into his lower back. "This is called 'the Cure for Cabin Fever,'" he announced.

"You did this for me?" she asked softly, unable to take her eyes off his face.

"It was just gathering dust at my house."

"And Dr. Rawlins said he wants me to get some light exercise," Jamie said. "Isn't this great, Alex?"

Alex was still looking at Rich.

"Where should we put it, honey?" Jamie pulled her husband into the living room. Looking around, she said, "I'd like it somewhere near the TV so we can watch while we walk."

Rich sat down next to Alex on the step. "Looks like we woke you."

"I must look awful." She ran her hand down her rumpled hair.

"Don't forget, I've seen you looking worse."

"Yeah, I guess you have. Thanks for reminding me." Of course, she'd seen him looking like a serial killer. She shook her head. Boy, how wrong first impressions could be.

"This means so much to me," she said. "How can I thank you?"

"With all the meals you've fed me and your playing the piano at church, I'd say we're even."

Rich's arm rested casually on the step behind her, but having him so close sped her heartbeat up faster than the treadmill ever could.

"Are you doing better today?" he asked.

"Much better, thank you."

"I was worried." He looked down at his gloved hands. "I wondered if maybe I'd done something . . . if I was the problem . . . Did I—"

"Everything is fine, Rich. And what you've done today is the most thoughtful thing I think anyone has ever done for me."

She looked into his face. Then, without checking her brain first, she reached her arms around his neck and squeezed him tightly. He circled his arm about her waist and pulled her close. It was brief, but wonderful.

"Hmm, umm." Steve cleared his throat. "Are you ready to get moving again?"

Rich released her and jumped up. "Ready when you are."

How was she ever going to get him out of her system?

* * *

Revving up the treadmill, Alex established a brisk walking pace then picked up the remote and began flipping channels, beginning with the morning news, past the PBS children's shows, and through the shopping networks. She stopped briefly to catch the amount of an overpriced gold chain necklace before moving past various other movies, cartoons, and cooking shows until she reached the sports channels.

She looked at the clock. Eight a.m. straight up. Come June first this would be her slot on the morning line-up. Prime workout time on the sports networks. ESPN had high hopes for her series. She'd gone to five different tropical locations for the shoots with top instructors in the fitness industry—two men, both national aerobic champions, and two women, both international aerobic champions. In fact, Alex had been approached several times to participate in aerobic competitions, but she didn't have the time or the desire to put in the extensive training necessary.

Their music was hot, their format fun and motivating, and their backdrops of seascapes, waterfalls, palm trees, and sandy beaches couldn't be beat. So why wasn't she on top of the world?

Because Rich would be gone on a snowmobile tour for the week.

"How's the treadmill?"

She hadn't heard Steve come in. He perched on the arm of the couch and watched a commercial for a sports highlights show.

"I like the automatic incline. This is a sturdy machine."

"Rich was sure excited to bring it over for you this morning."

She nearly tripped. "He was?"

"Yeah. He figured you'd be happy to see it."

"Is he always like that?"

Steve raised an eyebrow, confused. "Like what?" he asked.

"You know, doing stuff for other people?"

"He'd give his house away if he knew someone needed it more than he did."

So her heart was doing flip-flops for nothing. He would have dragged that treadmill out for anyone. Besides, it was for Jamie, too.

She changed the subject and the TV channel. "Are these snowmobile trips he goes on very dangerous?"

"They can be, but Rich knows what he's doing. He takes all the right precautions and stays in contact."

Steve watched the falling snow out the window for a moment then said, "Have you heard anything from your mom?"

"Not yet."

"I sure hope she comes to visit. Jamie was talking about your mom again last night before we went to bed. Dr. Rawlins asked me not to say anything, but he's concerned about her ability to carry this baby full-term. The pattern from her first two pregnancies is repeating itself with this one, too. She could use all the support she can get. I'm afraid to think what might happen if she loses this baby, too. I don't know how much more she can take. Having you stay with us has given her such a boost."

Alex smiled her thanks, trying to hide the sick curdling in her stomach. She'd already decided it was time to go home, as quickly as she could. The only way to get over Rich was to get away from him. But how could she leave Jamie? Especially now, when her sister needed her so much?

If Mom were here then I could leave.

"I better shove off for work. Make Jamie take it easy, will ya? She thinks she's going to get on this treadmill *and* clean the house today."

"Don't worry, Steve. She's not lifting a finger or a toe." Alex wondered how it would feel to have someone be so concerned about her health and well-being. Being independent wasn't all it was cracked up to be. She wondered what it would be like to have someone want to take care of her. It was hard to be strong all the time.

Thirty-five minutes later Alex was still logging miles when Jamie came into the room with a glass of water. "You planning to catch up on all the exercise you've missed in one day?"

"Feels great to work out." Alex slowed the machine to a stop and wiped at her brow. "Helps clear my head."

"Thirsty?"

"Wow, am I. Thanks." She drank so fast water spilled down her chin onto her sweat drenched t-shirt.

"Here." Jamie tossed her a towel. "You really get into this, don't you?"

Alex wiped her neck and forehead then blotted the front of her shirt. "It's the only thing that keeps me sane some days. What have you been doing?"

"The wash. I need to change sheets and I have piles of towels to do."

"Why don't you let me do that? I'm a pretty good sorter, you know." Sweat dripped from strands of Alex's hair and her nose, and she dabbed at them with her towel.

"You don't need to do my wash," Jamie said. Her gaze wandered past Alex. Flakes as large as potato chips floated past the window. "Wow, look at that snow. I hope Rich delays the trip a day. I hate having him go out in this."

Alex thought about him out in the cold, blinding snow. Rich wouldn't go if it weren't safe. She did know that.

"I can't believe how much snow you're getting for this time of year."

"It's a little unusual, but it will start warming up pretty soon. They said on the news this is the second snowiest March in fifty years.

Alex rolled her eyes. *I'm so glad I could be here for it.*

While Jamie showered, Alex sprang into action. First, she stuck the wet clothes into the dryer, and added another batch to the washer. She hurried and loaded the dishwasher, wiped off the counters, and put the waffle iron away. Then she filled a bucket with hot water, added vinegar, and started washing floors.

First, she cleaned the oak floors throughout the kitchen, dining rooms, entry, and living room. When she'd finished, she located the vacuum and set it to whirring. While vacuuming she'd noticed the tulips needed water, so she gave them a dousing, and then polished the furniture.

Just as she was ready to tackle the bathrooms, Jamie appeared on the stairs and said, "Stop!"

With dust rag poised in mid-air, Alex froze and looked up at her sister.

"Just what do you think you're doing?"

"Cleaning," Alex said. "Guess I'm not doing such a good job if you have to ask."

"You don't have to do this." Jamie tiptoed across the drying floor onto the living room carpet.

"I need to do this," Alex insisted. The more she cleaned, the less she thought about Rich. Too bad the house wasn't bigger. *Maybe the neighbors could use some help,* she thought.

"I just feel weird having you clean my house."

"Don't, Jamie, please. I want to and it is helping me."

"What am I supposed to do in the meantime? Sit and watch?"

"Why don't you read a book or watch TV or just relax?"

Jamie ended up sorting through papers on Steve's desk and organizing her craft projects. Then, while Alex finished the bathrooms and folded laundry, Jamie made a shopping list of things she would need for the baby.

By late afternoon the house was "realtor" perfect. It smelled clean, looked clean, and felt wonderful. The two sisters sat on the couch, leaned back, and smiled at each other.

"You know, once the baby comes, you won't be able to leave these pretty glass figurines out, or those books, or have those plants down like that."

"I know," Jamie said. "Won't it be wonderful?"

Alex nodded. Jamie would live in a hut if she had to for this baby.

The phone rang. "Stay put, I'll get it." Alex pushed herself to her feet and snagged the cordless off the piano. "Hello?" she said breathlessly.

"Jamie? Alex?"

"This is Alex."

"Hi, it's Rich."

Rich! It was Rich. Would Jamie think something was up if she turned a cartwheel right there in the living room?

"Where are you? Is everything okay?"

"Yeah, fine. This storm delayed our trip a day. The Tarvers weren't able to make it from Idaho Falls. Steve wanted me to call Jamie and tell her he'd be late for dinner. We're working on some of the engines. It's a good thing we didn't go today. We would've had a breakdown on the trail for sure."

"How awful."

"Kind of sucks the fun out of a trip. But we'll have them ready for tomorrow."

"Why don't you come over for dinner tonight?" she said, then added, "If you want. I was going to make lasagne."

"I love Italian food."

"Great. What time should we expect you two then?" She twisted a strand of hair around her pinky finger.

"Sevenish. That is, if Steve will quit ruining all the tools. He's on his third screwdriver."

"Second," Alex heard Steve yell in the background.

"It's really his third," Rich said a little softer.

"I heard that," Steve yelled. "The first one wasn't my fault."

"See you later," Rich said. "Oh, one more thing, I checked with the station. They said your car's ready. Steve and I will stop by and bring it home."

Alex thanked him then hung up the phone. Rich was coming to dinner. And if her arms and hands would stop tingling, she'd start cooking.

Then she stopped. Just how deep of a hole did she plan on digging for herself to fall into, anyway?

Chapter 16

"THAT LASAGNE WAS INCREDIBLE." RICH RUBBED HIS STOMACH and stretched back in his chair.

"I don't get it," Jamie said, "You could barely scramble an egg when we lived at home. When did you learn to cook?"

"I got tired of eating out all the time so I started experimenting with ways to make dishes lower in fat. The problem is, it's no fun to cook just for yourself."

"Speaking of experimenting, you should have been around during the first year of our marriage," Steve said. "Jamie gave new meaning to the term 'charbroiled.' You remember Jamie's cooking, don't you, Rich?"

Rich held up his hands. "I refuse to answer anything on the grounds that I may never be invited back to eat again."

"It wasn't that bad." Jamie threw her napkin at Steve. "Was it?"

"No, honey. Really, I needed to lose those twenty pounds anyway."

"Steven!"

"I'm just teasing, honey." Steve walked around the table to her chair, leaned over, and nuzzled her neck. "You did very well considering we were poor struggling students and didn't have much money for food anyway. But I do have one question. What was in that meatloaf surprise you used to make?"

She popped him with her fist.

"Ow!" He rubbed his shoulder.

"So," Rich said, "did anyone try out the treadmill? Does it still work?"

"Are you kidding? When Alex is finished with that thing it's not going to have any tread left on it," Jamie said.

Rich looked pleased. "It's about time someone got some use out of it."

"I'll tell you what." Jamie pushed her plate away. "If walking on the treadmill does for me what it did for Alex, I'll have that shed out back built by summer."

Steve laughed at his wife. "What do you mean?"

"I mean, Alex walked on that thing for a while this morning then hit the ground running—washing, folding clothes, scrubbing floors and scouring bathrooms, dusting, vacuuming, changing sheets," Jamie took a big breath, "and then she made dinner."

Everyone looked at Alex then broke into applause. She bowed her head to each of them and said, "Thank you, thank you," like she'd just been given an Academy award.

"If you ever run out of things to clean here," Steve said, "come on down to the shop. I could find plenty of work for you there."

"Yeah, and my house is always open." Rich crossed his arms and rested them on his stomach.

"Okay, that's enough," Alex said. "You make me sound like some cleaning tornado. I just got a burst of energy, that's all. I'll probably sleep until noon tomorrow and watch TV the rest of the day. Besides, Rich, your house is perfectly clean. In fact, I'd like to know how you get the chrome on your faucets so shiny."

"Vinegar and Windex. It's great at removing hard water spots," he said.

Steve looked at him with wonder.

"Since you're such a cleaning whiz, Rich," Jamie added, "maybe you could come up to the baby's room and show me how to get a spot off the rug."

"Sure, I'll take a look."

"Can you stay and play cards for a little while?" Steve asked.

Rich checked his watch. "Maybe for an hour or so. We pull out pretty early in the morning."

"We'll clear the table while you two check out the baby's room, then we can get started." Steve lifted the stack of dishes in front of Jamie's place and started for the kitchen. Alex rounded up the glasses and looped her finger through the handle on the jug of juice. In the kitchen she and Steve loaded the dishwasher.

"Alex, thanks for all your help. I feel guilty having you do so much."

Alex grabbed his wrist and looked her brother-in-law straight in the eye. "You don't have to thank me or feel guilty. I love you guys. I appreciate you letting me stay for so long, and I'm happy to help. Okay?"

He looked at the floor, then slowly back to her, "Okay. But I don't know what we'd do without you."

"You'd manage."

"You mind if I ask you something?" Steve scratched at a spot on the counter with his thumbnail.

"Course not."

"Are you okay?"

Feeling her defenses rise, she calmly said, "I'm fine."

"You're not . . . I mean, we've noticed . . ." Steve ran his fingers through his hair. "Jamie and I . . . well . . . we've noticed you aren't eating very much. We're a little worried about you."

"I eat."

"But you look awfully thin."

"I lost some weight while I was shooting the workout series. I'll gain it back though."

She walked over to Steve and placed her hand on his shoulder. "I appreciate your concern, I really do, but I'm fine. Besides, I'm a nutrition expert. You think I'd do anything that would jeopardize my health?"

"No," he laughed, "of course not."

They went back to work, Alex wiping down the counters, Steve stretching plastic wrap over the leftovers and putting them in the fridge.

Alex was grateful he let the subject drop and made a point of eating the corner off a piece of garlic bread. But she was always afraid to eat something she knew she liked. Occasionally there were times when she couldn't stop herself and ate way too much. She hated herself when she did that.

"You and Rich seem to be having fun together," Steve said. "I haven't seen him out and about like this for a long time."

"What do you mean?"

"Usually by this time every year, he's got a bushy beard and straggly hair. With all his snowmobiling he says it keeps him warmer. And we hardly see him except for church. It's been great having him at the house so much lately."

"I appreciate him keeping me entertained."

"Believe me, he's enjoying it as much as you." Steve had a glint of mischief in his eye.

Alex would have played along with the little game except there was something larger than "just having fun" at stake.

"I hope his girlfriend doesn't get upset. You know, with him spending so much time with me."

"His girlfri— Oh, you mean Monica. He told you about her?"

"Yes." Alex noticed something odd in his voice.

"He hasn't said much about her since he called off their engagement."

Alex had to clamp her lips together to keep from shrieking, "What?" Instead she said, "I didn't know he'd been engaged."

"Actually," Steve kept his voice soft, "this is his third engagement."

"His THIRD!" This time she did shriek. She couldn't help it.

"Shhhhh." Steve looked toward the stairs and listened for any reaction from upstairs before going on. "He's been engaged to different girls each time. But don't say anything to him. He's very sensitive about it."

She'd been wondering what kind of flaw this guy had and she'd finally found one. A big one! She wondered how deep this commitment problem he had really went.

Steve went on, "Rich told everyone that Monica called it off because she wasn't sure about moving here to Island Park and she didn't want to leave her teaching position at the elementary school in Boise. She teaches second grade."

Alex still couldn't believe her ears. She caught herself just before she put the leftover salad in the oven instead of the fridge.

"But after they broke it off Monica called the office one day looking for Rich. He was out so we talked. She told me her side of what really happened."

Alex wrapped the lasagne dish with plastic wrap then realized the dish was empty.

"She said it was true that she wasn't sure about quitting her teaching position but it was Rich who broke their engagement. She was okay with moving to Island Park; in fact, she was kind of excited."

"Hmm." Alex tried to act like she wasn't stunned by every word he was saying.

"I'm not sure where their relationship stands now. He won't talk about it. The only thing he said was that they needed more time and that they were going to date other people. Problem is, you're the closest thing to a date he's had in over a year. Not much to choose from around here."

Alex tried to sound casual. "Why do you think he keeps breaking off engagements?"

"Honey," Jamie's voice called from upstairs. "Where'd you put the cards?"

"We'll have to talk later," he said. Then he yelled, "In the closet in my office."

"I can't see them," she hollered.

"I'd better go help her." He started walking but stopped. "You've been good for Rich, Alex. It's like he's been brought back to life."

Steve shrugged and walked out of the room, leaving Alex curious. So she'd brought Rich back to life, huh? To a life with someone else?

* * *

"POPEYE!" Alex shouted.

"No way, not again!" Steve threw his cards on the table then pounded it with his fist.

"That's three times in a row," Rich said, adding his cards to the pile. "I thought you said you'd never played this game before."

"I haven't."

"Okay, folks." Steve shuffled the cards and started dealing. "This is it, last game. So make it good, and remember, Alex has won every game. Maybe if we gang up on her we can shut her down."

Alex faked offense. "Thanks a lot. So, it's three against one?"

"Yeah. Now it's even," Steve smiled devilishly.

"Is everyone ready?" Rich held up his hand and looked around the table. "Go!" He smacked the table with his palm.

Cards flew, hands slapped and all four yelled, groaned, and cheered at one time or another. When the dust settled, Alex came out victorious. Again.

"What's your secret? No one can be that lucky." Steve tossed his cards in the center.

"I don't have a secret. It's luck. And maybe the fact that I can get my card on top before you."

"Face it, Dixon, you're just getting slow in your old age." Rich smiled and stretched his arms above his head. "And you're a poor loser, too."

"Yeah, well, I'm not proud of it," Steve said, "because it's all true. But I've never seen a beginner win every game like that."

"Next time I won't win one hand. You'll see," Alex said.

Steve snorted. "If there is a next time."

"I oughta get going." Rich pushed away from the table. "You know, the best part about losing to you, Alex, was that Steve went down with me."

"That's what friends are for." Steve slapped Rich on the back. "Do you need help getting off in the morning?"

"Nah, I did the prep work today. I'll holler when I get home Saturday." He pulled on his parka and gloves. "See you all."

Alex barely had time to lift her hand as he whirled out the door. Her mind spiraled with the confusion she felt, knowing he'd been engaged three times. She didn't know the statistics, but three seemed like a lot for anyone, LDS or not. What was going on in his life to keep him from commitment? What was he afraid of?

Chapter 17

ALEX WOKE BEFORE THE SUN ROSE THE NEXT MORNING. RICH HAD been on her mind all night long. She couldn't quit thinking about him even in her sleep!

Had he already left to meet the group of snowmobilers? Maybe the weather would be bad again today and he'd have to stay home.

And what if he does stay home?

Staying in touch with reality as far as Rich was concerned seemed to be a further stretch for her each day. Why would any intelligent woman want anything to do with him? He was a fanatically clean, engagement breaker with a serious Carmex addiction.

She couldn't keep him off her mind.

With a flutter of blankets, Alex scrambled for her fleece robe and wrapped it tightly around her shivering body. She peered through the window. Clear skies. Morning stars twinkled. Fogging the glass with a disappointed sigh, she dragged herself back to the bed and sat on the edge. He was leaving. Hitting the trail. Braving the elements.

She missed him already.

Alex looked out the window at the blush of dawn sweeping the sky. What was he was doing right that moment? She wondered if he thought about her even half as much as she thought about him.

The rush of water from the shower in the back bathroom broke into her thoughts. The clock read six-fifteen. Steve wasn't usually up so early. Maybe Rich wasn't gone yet and Steve was meeting him at the shop.

Alex decided to surprise her brother-in-law with a warm breakfast before he rushed out into the cold day.

Fifteen minutes later, he joined her in the kitchen. "Hey, what are you doing up so early? Boy, that sure smells terrific." He peeked around her shoulder at the scrambled eggs cooking in the pan.

"This will be done in a sec. You have time to eat, don't you?"

"I'll make time."

"I was awake when you got up so I thought I'd make breakfast."

"Thanks." He slid onto a bar stool. "I was just going to have cereal."

"Why are you up so early?"

"I'm going to help Rich, then I've got tons of paperwork to catch up on."

Alex scraped the contents of the pan onto a plate and pulled two English muffins out of the toaster and set them on his plate. "Here you go."

"Is this stuff low-fat too?"

"As low as I can get it."

"Delicious." His mouth was full. He chewed and swallowed. "If it has less fat, does that mean I can eat more?"

Alex gave her brother-in-law a wry smile then said, "Steve, can I ask you something?"

He eyed her suspiciously. "This is about Rich, isn't it?"

She lifted her hands helplessly. "I can't help wondering why he's called off three engagements and what the girls were like."

"The second girl, Trish, I didn't know, but Stephanie, the first, was in our BYU ward. Nice girl, not really his type though. Wasn't much for athletics and the outdoors. I'm glad he didn't marry her. I'm glad he didn't marry Trish either, or . . ."

"Monica?"

"I didn't say that."

"You were going to."

Steve cleared his throat. "Monica's a nice girl. But . . ." He rubbed his freshly shaven chin. "She's critical of Rich and very uptight. He's so easy-going, you know, a real mellow kind of guy. I wish I could tell you why he hasn't gone through with any of these marriages. I think it has something to do with his dad walking out on his mom the day after Rich got home from his mission."

"Really! Why did his dad leave?"

"That's what's so hard for Rich. His dad just didn't want to be married anymore."

"That's it?"

Steve nodded.

"There's got to be more to the story. And besides, what's that got to do with Rich?"

"He's worried he'll do the same when he gets his father's age."

"That's crazy." Alex tossed the potholder onto the counter. "Just because they're related doesn't mean he'll do the same thing." *I'm related to Jamie but that doesn't mean I'm going to join her church.*

"I agree."

"Do you think he'll ever get married?"

Steve shrugged. "You'd have to ask him that question. I don't know."

They didn't speak for a moment. Steve ate. Alex wondered. She was supposed to be turned off by the things she was learning about Rich. Mr. Perfect wasn't so perfect after all.

But it tore at her heart and made her yearn for him even more.

She decided she couldn't sit around all day fretting about him.

"You mentioned last night that you could use some help at your shop. I'd like to come down if you think I'd be of any use to you."

"You would?"

"Sure, as long as Jamie doesn't need me."

He took a long drink of orange juice. "Tell you what, I'll get things organized down there then give you a call. If you and Jamie aren't up to your necks in wallpaper, I'll put you to work for a few hours."

After he left Alex deposited the dirty dishes into the dishwasher, filled the detergent cup, and pushed the button. Was this what married life was like? Visiting in the quiet morning hours, discussing plans for the day? Looking forward to that mid-day phone call?

Once the kitchen was put in order, she headed straight for the treadmill, but was stopped in the entry when the phone rang.

She rushed back to the kitchen to grab it before it rang again. "Hello?"

"Hi, Alex. This is Rich." Like he had to identify himself. "Is Steve still there?"

"No, he left a few minutes ago." Her heart beat double time.

"Good. I need his help locating some of the gear. I can't find a blasted thing in this storeroom."

"He should be there any minute."

"Okay, thanks."

She waited, not wanting to say good-bye. He was quiet, too.

"Well," he finally said, "don't have too much fun while I'm gone."

"I'll try not to." Then she added, "Rich, be careful."

"Always," he said, his voice softer now.

She clenched the phone tightly and shut her eyes, trying to picture him.

"I'll see you Saturday. Bye, Alex."

"Bye."

The line hummed when he hung up. She listened to the annoying sound for a second then placed the receiver back on its hook. At least she'd talked to him before he left.

* * *

"I love these colors, don't you?" Jamie held up the pink and white striped wallpaper and pastel-colored teddy bear border.

"Katelyn's going to love her room. Especially when we fill it with toys."

"Katelyn." Jamie hugged the paper to her chest. "I can't imagine what it's going to be like, having a baby around."

"Hectic, fun, scary at first maybe, but wonderful," Alex said.

"I get so excited sometimes I can barely stand it."

"I hope I'm able to be here when the baby's born."

"Oh," Jamie's voice raised with alarm. "You have to. I need someone there with me. Steve will be out cold with the first contraction."

"What do you mean?"

"He can't even use ketchup, he gets so queasy around blood."

Alex laughed. "I never knew that."

"It's true. Alex, you will be here, won't you? I mean, I guess I could ask Rich, I know he'd do it, but it would be a little uncomfortable."

"You're serious, aren't you?"

"Yes. Steve's already sweating the baby's birth. Alex, I'll do anything to have you here."

"Then I'll be here. Who knows what I'll be doing by July anyway?"

Alex opened the step ladder and climbed up, wondering what the future would bring.

"What do you mean?" Jamie's forehead wrinkled.

"Here, hand me the paper so I can measure it," Alex said.

Jamie gave her a roll of the stripes.

"I don't mean anything, really. I just never know with my job. A lot of it depends on how many requests I get for appearances. So far, I'm only booked for two workshops, Dallas in May and Portland in June."

Alex let the roll drop to the floor. "I'll hold it up here. Can you mark it down by the baseboard?"

Jamie stooped down and drew a line along the edge. "This is going to look so cute." She sat on the floor and looked at her sister. "You're not worried about your job, are you?"

"No, of course not. How busy my schedule is depends on how much I'm willing to put into it, how much I promote myself. That's the problem. I feel like I'm losing my desire a little."

"It must be hard, trying to figure out what you want to do for a career. I mean, not just a job, but something that you'll do for years and years. I still don't know what I'd do if I ever had to go back to work and help support us."

"What about your degree in English?" Alex climbed down and cut the paper with scissors, then started brushing the back side with a wet paintbrush.

"I could teach, I guess. Do you want me to help you with that?"

"Just hold the other end while I wet the paste. It keeps rolling up."

They anchored the sheet of wall covering and Alex finished wetting it.

"My problem is, I like being a homemaker and a wife. I'm content to be here, cooking, cleaning, having babies. I feel strongly about being here for my family. Partly, I guess, because Mom was never there when we were growing up. I don't know what I would have done without you."

"Mom had no choice, though," Alex reminded her.

"I know. I just don't want her life, that's all."

Me, either.

"Well, here goes nothing." Alex lifted her end and climbed up the stepladder backwards. Jamie swung the bottom around, then slowly they moved the paper to the wall.

"Hand me that plastic doo-dad so I can smooth out the bubbles. Is it lined up down there?" Alex asked.

Jamie handed her the tool, then pushed on a big crease in the middle of the paper. "This stuff has sucked right into the wall. It won't," she pushed with her fingertips, "budge."

Then it ripped.

"SHOOT!"

"What happened?" Alex leaped off the ladder.

"It tore. I ruined it." Jamie held up the jagged piece. Her eyes filled with tears.

"I must've gotten it too wet. Hey, don't worry," Alex said, "you've got plenty of paper here."

"I'm sorry." Jamie wiped away the moisture in her eyes. "These hormones are a real pain sometimes."

During the next four hours, Jamie stopped to answer the phone, make them some lunch, and do some church business for next Sunday's meeting. Alex continued cutting and hanging until the wall was complete.

"Jamie, come and take a look."

Jamie ran in from the office and stopped short when she entered the nursery. "I love it, I love it!" She ran her hand along the smooth stripes and smiled like a lottery winner.

Alex eyed her work. At least the stripes ran up and down the wall like they were supposed to.

"Why don't we finish up tomorrow? I'll bet you're exhausted."

"I'm not stopping until those bears are dancing around the ceiling."

Jamie ran to answer the phone while Alex finished the border. When she returned she couldn't believe her eyes.

"Alex, I never could have done this without you. Katelyn's lucky to have you for an aunt."

"Aunt Alex." She thought about it for a moment. At least it sounded better than "Sister McCarty." "I like it. Makes me feel kinda old, though."

"I almost forgot. Steve just called and wondered if you wanted to help him out tomorrow morning."

"Sure," Alex said, "Unless you need me."

"I'll just be sewing curtains and a bed ruffle for the crib." Jamie gathered up the unused rolls of wallpaper. "One more thing, Steve said Rich radioed in a few minutes ago and said to tell you 'hi.'"

Alex stopped gathering tools. So, Rich was thinking about her. She guessed it was only fair, since he was all she could think about.

Chapter 18

THE NEXT DAY ALEX HELPED STEVE AT THE SHOP.

When they stepped inside the back room, Alex was speechless. It was an even bigger mess than the first time she'd seen it. A seven-point earthquake couldn't have caused such a disaster. Aside from the outdoor equipment—fishing poles, rafts, canoes, tents, cross-country skis, and snowmobiles—there were piles of coats, snowsuits, boots, hats, fishing waders, life jackets, and items Alex couldn't even identify.

"Have you ever thought of using a bulldozer? I'm surprised Mr. Clean allows such a mess."

"Hey, we're too busy to clean," Steve defended himself.

"What do you two do? Shut your eyes and throw things the general direction it belongs?"

"You're very funny, you know that?" He jabbed his finger at her. "You could be a stand-up."

"This is certainly no laughing matter."

Against his protests she pushed him out of the room and shut the door. "I'll call you when I need to bring in the heavy equipment."

Several hours later, after sorting, stacking, hanging, sizing, and organizing until she was out of breath and exhausted, she called for Steve.

"Whoa." He took a step back. "Alex, this looks great."

He examined shelves, bins, and boxes.

"I was wondering if you have any hangers," she said.

"What? Hangers?"

"Yeah, you know those things you hang clothes on."

"I know what they are. We don't have any though. I'm running to Rexburg tomorrow. Why don't you make out a list and I'll pick up what you need. This is great. Hey," he pointed to the backpacks hanging on the wall, "I like this."

Alex was pleased with the results, too.

"By the way," he said, "Rich checked in. They got to the cabin and had a good night last night."

She'd been hoping to talk with Rich when he called. "I'm glad they made it. Did everything go well?"

"No problems. We were worried about the one engine, but it ran okay."

"Good." It was awkward talking about Rich. She wanted to know every detail of what he was doing, but had to force a front of vague interest.

"I've done all I can do today," she finally said. "Guess I'll go on home."

She hated leaving. Being there made her feel close to Rich. Then she reminded herself that was exactly the reason why she needed to leave.

* * *

Jamie and Steve were snuggled on the couch watching TV so Alex headed upstairs to give them some privacy.

She wandered into the office where she'd left the research she'd been working on.

Sitting in Steve's chair, she picked up a recent issue of the *Ensign*. On the cover was a painting of Jesus on the cross. She studied the beauty of the colors and the artwork, then focused on the Savior's face. Something stirred inside of her, prompting her to open the magazine. Inside she found another picture, this one of Jesus outside the tomb.

She turned a few more pages and paused, stopping at an article entitled, "For They Shall Be Comforted."

Scanning the words and unfamiliar phrases, she read where a woman had just suffered the death of a child to leukemia and said that she couldn't imagine surviving the trauma of the death of a loved one without the comfort of knowing the Savior and his teachings.

Alex paused. How she would love to feel that kind of comfort, that kind of peace, about her father's death.

She realized that although she did not agree with the Mormons' beliefs, she had developed respect for them. She admired their solid understanding of what they believed, be it craziness or not, because it gave them perspective and hope and faith. And these were three things she knew she didn't have.

She picked up the magazine and reread the last paragraph. The scriptural references listed in the article meant nothing to her, but she was curious. What did they say that helped the woman survive the death of a child?

On Steve's desk was a copy of the Mormon scriptures with three names on the cover: The Book of Mormon, The Doctrine and Covenants, and The Pearl of Great Price.

She turned to the contents in the front and found the list of books contained in the Book of Mormon.

There it was, First Nephi. She ruffled through a few pages until she located the first chapter. She read the heading.

Flipping the page, she read the heading of the second chapter, about a man named Lehi taking his family into the wilderness. She skipped over to the third chapter, found the seventh verse and read:

> *And it came to pass that I, Nephi, said unto my father: I will go and do the things which the Lord hath commanded, for I know that the Lord giveth no commandments unto the children of men, save he shall prepare a way for them that they may accomplish the thing which he commandeth them.*

These people felt that the Lord was telling them to go places and do things. They believed he wouldn't ask them to do anything they couldn't do. What a thought!

It would be a fascinating concept, if it were true. It would also explain why these people obeyed without question. They figured that it was all part of the Lord's "plan."

She didn't believe it herself, but it helped her understand where Jamie and the rest of them were coming from.

What about that other scripture? The Doctrine and Covenants. What exactly did that name mean, Doctrine and Covenants?

She turned a chunk of pages and opened the book to section 21.

From section 21 she turned pages until she found section 122. Here the heading read, *The word of the Lord to Joseph Smith the Prophet, while he was a prisoner in the jail at Liberty, Missouri, March, 1839.*

She started with verse one and started reading until the end of verse four where it said, *"and thy God shall stand by thee forever and ever."*

Did this go for everybody or just prophets? She liked the idea. In fact, she'd thought more about God and Christ in the last week than she had in her entire life. Except for the negative reinforcement she'd had as a child regarding the Mormons, she'd never been instructed about religious things. In fact, she'd never even read the actual scriptural account of the Christmas story or Christ's resurrection in the Bible.

She continued reading until she finished verse seven. At the end of the last verse, she read again the words: *"God shall be with you forever and ever."*

She closed the book. What did it all mean? She didn't dare ask Jamie or Steve. If she showed even the slightest interest, they'd pounce on her for sure. Rich was a possibility. He'd been more than eager to talk to her about the gospel, but because of her strong feelings for him, she decided against it. Her actions might be misread, like she was interested in the Church because she was interested in him. And she wasn't about to join some kooky church for a man, no matter how incredible he was.

But she had to admit to herself, she wouldn't mind finding out a little more about some of these things, not so much about the Church, but about the Lord—who he was and what he had to do with her. And she would like to know a little about Joseph Smith and why he was in jail. That story about Nephi sounded interesting, too.

Then she stopped. She dropped the book as if it had burst into flames in her hands. What was she thinking?

She needed to go home. Tomorrow.

Just when she thought things could get no worse, they did. Not only was she attracted to a Mormon, she was actually getting interested in finding out about their God.

Alex covered her face with her hands and clenched her eyes shut. How could she have gotten herself confused in all of this? She'd been happy, content, fulfilled. Her life wasn't lacking.

Tears began to seep through her fingers. She didn't believe these Mormons, and even worse, she didn't believe herself anymore.

Chapter 19

"HI, MOM, THIS IS ALEX."

"Alex dear, what is it? You sound funny."

Alex looked down the hallway and listened for any movement upstairs. "Everyone's still asleep. I don't want to wake them."

"Are you still at Jamie's?"

"Yes, I've been trying to help her a little. She's had a few bad spells since I've been here."

"Bad spells?"

"Like fainting, contractions, stuff like that. Please don't say anything to her"—as if she had to worry about her mother talking to Jamie—"but the doctor's concerned about her carrying the baby full-term."

"He doesn't think she's going to miscarry again, does he?"

"No, I don't think so. But he's watching her closely. Have you found out about your plans?"

"Actually, it looks like I can get away on the twenty-eighth, that's a Saturday. I fly into Idaho Falls."

Alex closed her eyes gratefully. "That's great! Jamie is going to be so excited."

"To tell you the truth, I wasn't real crazy about the idea at first, but the more I thought about it, the more excited I got. We haven't been together for so many years and I think it is high time we were."

Alex was thrilled. With her mom coming she could easily go home.

"You're absolutely right. I'm so glad it worked out."

"My plane gets in at four thirty-five, your time. It's flight number 1436 on WestAire. If anything changes I'll let you know."

"This is really going to mean a lot to Jamie and Steve."

"Well, like I said, I think we need to spend some time together, and I've been thinking that it's time to give you girls something I've kept stored away for many years. Something very special."

Alex wrinkled her forehead. "Special? What do you mean 'special'?" She didn't want her mom to bring anything special. She didn't want her to bring anything that would complicate her leaving. She'd have to revise her plan to leave Island Park. She'd stay until Easter, but that was it, she decided firmly.

"I want it to be a surprise. You girls are going to be so excited. It's going to take some looking to find it though. I'd better get digging through those boxes in storage."

That reminded her. "Mom, while you're looking I wondered if you'd try and find that porcelain doll of mine. You know, the ballerina?"

"Ballerina doll? The one with blonde hair and the pink tu-tu?"

"That's the one."

"I'll see if I can find her."

"Thanks, Mom. And thanks for coming."

"I'm glad you invited me, honey. I hate to say it but I haven't really put out as much effort to visit the kids there in Yellowstone as I should. I know it's awful to admit this, but I just don't feel comfortable around Jamie and Steve. It seems like everything they talk about has to do with that church of theirs. In fact, I've been a little nervous about you spending so much time there. I wouldn't want them to convert you, too."

Alex grimaced. "I promise, you don't have to worry about that."

"Thank goodness I have one sensible daughter."

"Jamie's sensible, Mom. And she's very happy. I know her religion seems extreme, but I think it's helped her have the strength to deal with her miscarriages."

"That may be so. All I want is for her to be happy. I just don't like to be around them, that's all. I don't think I'd come and visit if you weren't going to be there."

Hearing that, Alex gulped. There was no way she could leave Island Park now.

"I'll see you soon, then. Bye, sweetie. Love you."

"Love you, too."

Alex hung up the phone slowly, her emotions churning. She was excited to spend time with her mother and sister, but she just didn't trust her feelings for Rich any longer.

This stupid church anyway. If he didn't have such a commitment to the religion, they could possibly have a future.

She knew his beliefs would never change and neither would hers.

Funny though. No one spoke directly to her about the Church, yet she felt like it was practically being shoved down her throat. She thought about the man's prayer at church and Jamie's constant claims about the joy and happiness in her life that came from her beliefs. Alex didn't doubt that Jamie and all the others were sincere in their feelings, but she was growing tired of dealing with the Church every time she turned around. Somehow she had to find a way to get away from there.

"Alex! Alex, come here, quick!"

"I'm coming, Jamie," she yelled as she ran from her bedroom.

"In here." Jamie's voice was weak, shaky.

Alex burst through the bathroom door. Jamie sat slumped over on the toilet.

"I'm bleeding." A sob gripped her. She wrapped her hands around her abdomen and rocked and cried. "I'm bleeding."

"It's okay, everything's okay." Alex forced her voice to stay steady as she knelt beside Jamie "I'll call Dr. Rawlins. He'll know what to do."

"Oh, Alex, my baby, my little Katie. I don't want to lose her. My baby." Jamie buried her head into her sister's shoulder and wept.

"Don't cry. I'm here, Jamie. I'm here."

"Little Katie. I want her so badly."

"I know you do, I know." Alex stroked her sister's hair and kissed the side of her head. She looked up to the ceiling and thought, *"Thy God shall stand by thee forever and ever."*

Where are You, God? She needs You. I need You. Help us. Alex clenched her eyes shut and held her sister close.

"Everything's going to be okay," she whispered.

* * *

"Except to go to the bathroom, she is not to get off that bed." Dr. Rawlins pulled on his coat and gloves then stopped at the front door.

"I'd like to say that she's going to be fine, but for some reason her body is determined to abort this baby. Any activity, any stress, and she could go into premature labor."

Steve's pale skin matched his white BYU sweatshirt.

"Doesn't she need to be in the hospital or something?"

"You two can do more for her here than they can there. She needs rest and she needs to stay calm. The best thing you can do for her is keep her spirits up. Read to her, talk to her, anything, but don't let her get upset about this."

Steve looked like he would pass out with the next breath. Alex slid her arm around his waist. "We can do that, doctor. We'll take good care of her."

"I know you will. She'll be much more comfortable here than in a hospital. Call me if she experiences any pain, contractions or more bleeding."

"Gotcha," Alex said.

"I'll check back tomorrow morning."

"Thanks, Brother Rawlins." Steve extended his hand and the two men clasped hands, not as doctor and patient's husband, but as friends. Dr. Rawlins wasn't just Jamie's physician; he was a caring part of their family.

"She's young, strong, and healthy. I'm still optimistic. Don't worry, son."

The fear and worry on Steve's face was matched by the consuming ache in Alex's heart. She hated feeling helpless, unable to change the situation, unable to make it better or take away her sister's pain.

With all her heart she wished the Lord were real, as Jamie and Steve said. He could do all these things and more. He could give them the courage, hope, and comfort they all needed.

But they felt none of these things. Because, Alex knew, He just wasn't there.

Chapter 20

ALEX DIDN'T GO BACK TO HELP STEVE THE REST OF THAT WEEK, even though he purchased the items she'd requested to finish up the back room. She spent most of the time keeping up the housework and the cooking, and writing down her recipes with Jamie's assistance.

They sat on Jamie's bed as they categorized recipes. Alex couldn't believe she was actually considering pulling together a cookbook. When she had checked in with her manager, Sandy had come up with the idea of putting together a low-fat cookbook to go along with the release of her video. She assured Alex that whatever recipes she could contribute would be great but her staff could flesh out the rest of the book with more. Most of all they wanted Alex's name on the front to sell the product. But Alex wasn't about to take credit for something she didn't do. If it was her cookbook, then the recipes were going to be hers.

"I thought I'd include the recipe for that English trifle I made the other day," Alex said.

Jamie licked her lips. "I've been craving it all week. You have to make it again."

Alex wrote the word "desserts" on a piece of paper and set a stack of cards on it.

Jamie fiddled with the buttons on her shirt. "Alex, you know how much I love having you here. In fact," her voice broke, "I don't know how we'd do it without you. But I'm sure we would manage. The branch would help out and Steve's mother has offered to come for a few days."

"What are you saying?"

"I just don't want you to stay if you need to get back to Palo Alto."

Alex put down her pencil and looked at her sister's worried expression. Her sister was giving her a chance to leave. To be free from Rich.

"Sandy would let me know if I was needed."

"Are you sure?"

"Sure I'm sure. Why do you ask?" They sat on the bed facing each other. Three-by-five cards were scattered between them.

"You seem distracted," Jamie said. "I know you must go crazy, cooped up in the house all day."

"Listen, Jamie." Alex crossed her feet and sat Indian style. "Being here with you, especially with your health like this, is what I want to be doing. This is a slow time at work so I can stay as long as I'm needed." She didn't tell Jamie that Sandy had basically "grounded" her from her job anyway, like a naughty child, until she got her weight up.

"I've been worried that I'm keeping you from something important."

"Jamie, *you* are important."

"That's what I was hoping you'd say." Jamie let out a sigh of relief. "So, you really are going to do a cookbook?"

"They want to release it the same time my workout video hits the stands."

"That doesn't leave you much time."

Alex gathered the papers into a pile. "I know. I need a lot more recipes than I have here."

"Could you make cheesecake a priority on your list?"

"They already have low-fat cheesecakes on the market."

"But they all taste nasty."

"I doubt I can improve them."

"Hey, they can put men on the moon," Jamie reasoned. "Surely you can make a better-tasting cheesecake."

"I'll see what I can do. What time is Steve going to be home for dinner?"

Jamie shifted to her right side and scooted up higher on her pillow. "Early. He said he'd stop by Rich's and borrow some videos so we'd have something to watch tonight. I'm in the mood for an old-fashioned romance."

"Me too," Alex said. *More than you'll ever know.* "I'll make some popcorn, and I want to try a strawberry milkshake idea I have."

"Oooo, yummy."

They heard the door close downstairs, then a heavily accented voice called, "Lucy, I'm home from the club. Ethel, are you here, too?"

Alex and Jamie looked at each other and burst out laughing.

"Ricky darling, we're up here," Jamie called.

Footsteps sounded on the stairs and in the hall, then Steve charged through the door and struck a pose. "Babaloo. Babaloo Aye-aaa," he yelled, dancing around like a Mexican hat dancer until he dove onto the bed and grabbed for his wife. She giggled and screamed. Alex laughed for a moment, watching their playful affection. She pushed Rich's face out of her mind, took her papers, and left the couple snuggling and laughing.

Rich comes home today.

The thought filled Alex's head as she took a quick shower then bundled up and braved the Arctic morning. Ten minutes later she pulled up outside Recreation Headquarters.

It took a second to open the shop door, but she wiggled the key the way Steve told her and the lock turned. She shivered when she stepped inside the building's warmth. For a brief second she caught a whiff of Rich's cologne, the musky, outdoorsy fragrance he wore. The familiar scent triggered his image in her memory and nicked at her heart.

"Get to work," she said. Staying busy was the only way to get Rich's smile out of her head. But even then the thought of him putting Carmex on his lips, or the way he cocked his head to the side when he listened to her, found a way to sneak into her thoughts.

Trying to clear her head, Alex worked fast, sizing, hanging, and arranging the snow clothes onto the rack. By noon she had all the equipment and gear organized. She even straightened the fishing poles, waders, and tackle boxes. Her stomach growled as the two bites of banana she had for breakfast burned out, but she kept going. With broom and dustpan in hand she swept and straightened the rest of the back room. At last she found herself in the office again where she straightened stacks and sorted mail. These men definitely needed a secretary.

Just as she thumbed through the last of the envelopes, a pale lavender one caught her eye. It was addressed to Rich and the sender was Monica Foster, from Boise, Idaho. The handwriting was small and swirly, not bold and straight like her own handwriting. What kind of woman was this who interested Rich?

"What I'd give to open this." She didn't like the pang of jealousy that twisted her heart.

He's taken.

Just a little peek.

He's taken.

Maybe it's not sealed shut all the way.

HE'S TAKEN.

She dropped the letter like it was full of scorpions and ran for the door.

With one last look, she squared her shoulders and turned out the light.

She closed the shop, climbed into her car, and started the engine, amazed that her Mazda would start in below-freezing weather.

Shifting the car into reverse, she glanced in the rearview mirror to back up and caught her reflection in the mirror. She looked at the trace of scab left from her injury. By now it was almost undetectable, except for the shine of the tiny scar along her hairline. Someday her torn heart would heal, too. She was sure she'd have scars left to remind her of Rich, but she would get over him. She had no choice.

She planned to stop at Rich's house to return the videos Steve had borrowed. As she drove she thought about that first day she'd driven into Island Park in the record-breaking snowstorm. Right in front of her was the Texaco and the houses she'd needed so desperately to find that day. Perhaps had she found them, instead of Rich finding her, she wouldn't be dealing with the thick fog of confused feelings that impaired her vision so badly.

With a few deep breaths she steadied her romping heart as she pulled off the main road onto Rich's driveway. She wasn't sure what time he'd be home, but she couldn't help looking around for his truck anyway. The idea was to avoid him, not plop herself onto his lap.

Whisking the videos off the passenger seat, she stepped out into the afternoon sun. Not surprised, she found his back door unlocked and went inside. The place was ice cold and dark. Her nerves jingled being in his house uninvited.

She knew right where the videos went and hurried to the bookshelf to put them back.

A rumbling outside the house caught her attention. She glanced out the front window and saw a diesel truck cruise by on the interstate.

She would die if Rich caught her inside his house. With a shove, she returned the videos to their spot on the shelf and tore for the back door. She swung the door open and screamed.

"Sorry, I didn't mean to scare you," Rich said.

"I . . . I . . ." Her breath came in spurts. "I-yie-*yie.*" She placed her hand on her heart and tried to calm its erratic pounding.

"I saw your car pull in and thought I'd stop on the way to drop off the trailer."

Rich's face was scruffy and his hair stuck out in spikes around his stocking cap. He was still in snow clothes and boots and had white rings around his eyes from his sunglasses. He looked wonderful!

"I was returning some videos for Steve."

"Oh, okay." He wasn't bothered in the least by the fact that she was inside his house.

"I should have just left them on the table."

"Whatever. You know you can help yourself anytime." He walked around her and removed his hat, gloves, and boots. "Sure is cold outside."

"How was your trip?"

"Great." He shoved his hand into his pocket and pulled out the Carmex. "Lots of fun, but I'm mad. I lost my camera somewhere along the way."

"I'm sorry."

"That's okay, it wasn't an expensive one, but it had some great pictures on it from our branch talent night. Some real funny ones of Steve and Jamie. By the way, how's Jamie doing? Steve told me about her scare the other morning." He offered the tube to her.

"He did?" She squeezed a dab onto her finger and glossed it over her lips.

"When I checked in yesterday."

Alex watched him shove the balm back into his pocket. He removed his coat and pulled his sweatshirt over his head.

"Jamie seems to be doing better. Dr. Rawlins isn't sure what to think. He says he's seen situations similar to this and some have turned out fine, others . . ." She didn't finish.

"How's she holding up?"

"After losing two babies already, she seems to expect the worst."

He ran his hand across his matted hair. "Wish I could do something."

"We all stand around feeling useless. There's nothing we can do but wait."

"I'd like to see her. Do you think she'd like a visitor?"

"She'd love some company. In fact, I'm making Chinese food tonight. You wouldn't want to come over for dinner, would you?" Now why did she go and do that? Just when she'd decided to get him out of her life and system, she was setting herself up for another fall. Dumb. She was definitely dumb.

He walked over to the refrigerator and opened the door. She looked in behind him.

"Why bother having a fridge if you never put anything in it?" she said lightly.

He turned his head and smiled at her. "I really do need to get some groceries. I never can find time though."

"Then it's decided. You're coming for dinner."

"I'll get cleaned up first and come over. Plus I need to stop at the shop and unload the trailer. Do you know if Steve's there?"

"He's with Jamie. Do you need his help?"

"Kind of, I can manage though."

"I'm not doing anything. I can help."

"Just give me five minutes to shower."

"I'll be here when you're ready."

* * *

Rich flipped on the back room light and stared in surprise. "Whoa, what happened in here?"

"Steve asked me to straighten up a little."

"A little? This place should have been condemned it was such a mess." He walked over to the shelves and peeked in several of the boxes. "This looks wonderful. I hope he paid you for all your work."

She planted one fist onto her waist. "He didn't have to pay me. I volunteered."

"I don't know what to say. Except that I'm impressed. " He looked the room over again. "*Very* impressed."

The next thing Alex knew, Rich had his arms wrapped around her. "Thanks for all your help," he said softly. He held her several more seconds.

"You're welcome." She patted his back lightly, then strained against his arms, trying to free herself. He loosened his hold but still held her elbows.

"You know, Alex." His voice was low and soft. "Jamie and Steve have talked about you as long as I've known them. But until I met you I never realized what a wonderful person you really are."

She ceased to struggle in his embrace but kept her distance as best as she could in his tight grasp.

"I'm not really that neat."

He chuckled. "You are. You're not only beautiful, but you're hard-working, kind, and generous."

"Gee, I do sound pretty good, don't I?" Now she was squirming. He pulled her closer, his face drew nearer.

Her mouth started to open as she waited for her mind to provide some words, but nothing came.

His kiss was as delicate as the brush of rose petals. And she had every intention of fighting the urge to return his kiss, but her intentions dissolved right along with her fears. In his arms she felt safe, protected, and loved.

She was in big trouble.

Nothing could come of this; there was no future for them. The more involved they became the harder it would be when reality hit.

And it hit like a semi.

"Alex, what's wrong?"

She ran for the office and shut the door. Leaning against the wall for support she buried her head in her hands as the tears flowed. *I'm a regular leaky faucet.* What was she doing? Not only was she playing with fire, she was holding a can of gasoline in each hand—his broken engagements and his religion.

"Alex." Rich knocked on the door. "Alex!"

She remained silent, wishing he would go away. Why wasn't he showing some restraint? He knew as well as she did that they could never have a relationship. How come she was the only one trying?

"Alex, talk to me. What's wrong?" A strip of light beamed onto the wall when he cracked open the door.

Her tears had come fast and hard, and were gone. Turning away from him, she sniffed and wiped at her cheeks.

"Hey, what happened in there?" He stroked her arm with his hand. His touch turned the tap on again, just enough for one teardrop to form at a time. "Please, Alex, talk to me."

She swallowed. He wasn't going to back off until she spelled it out for him. Didn't he see what was happening?

"Here." He pulled a chair over to her. "Sit down. We're going to talk about this."

She sat down, grateful he hadn't turned on the light.

He flipped a chair around to face hers and when he sat their knees touched.

"Now," he said, taking one of her hands in his, "tell me what's wrong."

Her tears were gone, leaving her skin strained and tight. "I'm not sure how to explain."

"Is there someone back in California? Is that it? I thought Jamie told me you weren't seeing anybody."

"I'm not seeing anybody." She pulled her hand away from his. "But you are."

"Oh, I see," he said slowly, leaning back in his chair.

"But I'm not sure you do see. Not only do you have a girlfriend, or ex-fiancée, or whatever you call her, we're not even the same religion. Doesn't that bother you?"

He rubbed his face with both hands but sidestepped her question. "You must think I'm such a jerk. I shouldn't have kissed you. I'm sorry."

He didn't understand and she couldn't tell him how she felt about him. Her feelings wouldn't change anything anyway.

"I don't think you're a jerk. I wish I did. It would be easier to stay away from you."

"What can I say? I feel so stupid." He got up from the chair. "To be honest, I don't know what I was thinking. I guess only of myself. I didn't mean to hurt you." He turned away. The pain and sincerity in his voice tore at her heart. It was all she could do to stay in her chair and not run to him and throw her arms around him.

"I'm okay," she said.

He turned back around. "This has been really difficult for me," he said. "I can't explain it except . . ." he pulled the chair back, widening the gap between them, and sat down, "I've never met anyone like you. I've never felt so comfortable so quickly with a woman like I have with you."

She knew exactly what he was saying.

"It's almost like I've known you for years. Being with you feels so natural. And this week, while I was gone, I thought about you all the time and wished I could have taken you with me."

He spoke like he was following a script she'd written for him.

"Seeing you today, well, I guess it's pretty obvious how happy I was to see you."

"Rich, you don't have to apologize."

"But I do. I'm the one who overstepped my bounds."

The sliver of light in the room shadowed his pain-creased face.

"It's okay, really," she said. "I overreacted a bit."

"You had every right." He looked at her, direct and unflinching. "I just don't think I realized how much I cared for you."

Had she let it, her chin would have fallen onto her lap. He did feel for her, just like she did for him.

"It's been so nice to have someone to be with, a friend, someone my age, and fun, like you."

"I've enjoyed being with you too, Rich. But you realize we can only be friends, don't you?"

"Yes, of course I do." Then half of his mouth lifted in a smile, "But it sure would help if you were ugly."

She laughed. "I'll see what I can do."

"We are still friends, aren't we?" He stepped in front of her chair and pulled her to her feet.

"Absolutely."

This time their hug was nothing more than a cementing of words, an agreement of feelings. But it left her longing for more. And she realized she'd lied again. She could never be "just friends" with him.

Chapter 21

"I FEEL SO STUPID, TAKING UP A WHOLE COUCH," JAMIE SAID. SHE leaned forward and placed another pillow behind her back.

"Listen, honey, the only way you can attend church today is to stay down. Otherwise you have to go back to your room." Steve draped a lacy afghan over her legs.

"But who's going to help with the music? I don't know anyone else who plays."

"Brother and Sister Correy are back in town. She'll play. Even if she couldn't, it wouldn't matter because you're not getting off this couch."

"Yes, sir."

When Steve turned away to start setting up chairs, Jamie stuck her tongue out at him. Alex clapped her hand over her mouth before her giggle escaped.

"What are you going to do during the meeting, Alex?" Steve unfolded several chairs and clanged them into place.

"I have tons of work to do."

The doorbell rang. Alex jumped up from her chair before she could get stuck in the swarm of members and said, "I'll see you after church." She stopped when she heard Rich's voice.

"Good morning." He walked directly to the couch and kissed Jamie on the cheek. "How's the little mother doing?"

"The little mother's not so little, thank you. But I'm doing fine."

Alex's gaze remained fixed on Rich in his crisp white shirt and charcoal gray suit. He looked so handsome it took her breath away.

"Good morning, Alex. How are you?" He set a stack of books on a folding chair.

"F-Fine, thanks." She gulped. "I was just leaving." With a silly, schoolgirl smile on her face, she took several steps backward until she neared the entry, then turned and scurried up the stairs.

It wasn't the jaunt to the office that had her heart beating up a storm in her chest and had her nerve endings sparking. Handsome didn't describe Rich. He was downright dazzling.

The ringing of the doorbell brought her out of her flustered state. But even through her closed door and amidst the rumble of talking and laughing, her ears picked up Rich's voice like a homing device.

Get to work, you dope. She'd never admit it but had they needed her, she would have stayed and played the piano.

During the next hour she worked on the outline of her next lecture until a tune stumbled from the piano and the group downstairs began to sing. Alex looked up from her reading and listened, cringing when the pianist hit a clinker. Still, it was an improvement over the last time.

A knock sounded on the door.

"Come in." She pushed herself away from the desk.

The door opened and Rich appeared. "Sorry to interrupt."

"You're not."

"Sara was wondering if she could come and see you while we're having Sunday School. She's a little restless from sitting so long."

"Of course. I'd love some company. Send her up."

Rich left the room and returned shortly hand in hand with Sara. It was obvious the little girl adored him.

She twirled a lock of gold curl with her finger. "Hi, Sister McCarty."

"Don't you look pretty today. What a fancy dress."

A smile lifted Sara's round cheeks. "Thank you. It's supposed to be for Easter but Mommy said I could wear it now. I wanted to show it to you."

"I'm glad you did. I really like it."

Rich led Sara over to the desk by Alex. "I'll leave you two girls to your own fun. I need to get back to the meetings. Are you sure you're okay?"

She nodded.

"See you in a bit, then."

"Bye," Sara and Alex said together.

Alex pulled open a folding chair, and Sara sat down beside her. "So, what would you like to do?"

"Let's look at pictures." Sara pointed at the binder of church pictures.

"Do you remember where we were last time?"

Sara nodded and flipped through the pages until she found the one of Jesus' baptism.

Sitting side by side, they went through each picture, usually with Sara narrating.

"I think this is a picture of Lehi." Sara stared at the white-bearded man surrounded by angry-looking people. "He tried to tell everyone how bad they were but they didn't listen."

She turned the next page and continued the story. "He had to take his family and leave."

"And that's Nephi." She pointed to the handsome man with strong arms and a proud look. "He was a good boy. His brothers were naughty."

As if someone had just plugged in her brain, Alex realized these were the names from the Book of Mormon.

"Can I turn to the front of the book for just a minute?" Alex found the table of contents and read the caption for each picture— Lehi Prophesying to the People of Jerusalem, Lehi's Family Leaving Jerusalem. Those were the headings she'd read at the beginning of the chapters in the Book of Mormon.

Sara had a hard time with some of the names she didn't know. But with the help of the table of contents they figured out what each picture was about.

"My mommy and I have a book just like this at home. We look at the pictures all the time. She likes to tell me the stories from the scriptures. Do you like to read the scriptures?"

"I like hearing the stories just like you do."

"This man," Sara pointed to a portrait, "is Joseph Smith. He's the one who found the golden plates."

Alex had heard plenty about Joseph Smith from Jamie and Steve. In fact, the picture of the First Vision was very familiar to her. But instead of denouncing the concept immediately, as she had before, she caught herself thinking, Was it possible to see God? And his son? And then worse, she wondered, What if it were true?

She shook her head to scatter the thoughts.

"Sister McCarty, Sister McCarty?"

Alex rested her hand on the back of Sara's head. "I'm sorry, honey, I was thinking about Joseph Smith."

"Look at these pictures." Sara pointed at the book. "Those are the pioneers."

The following pages were of the Saints leaving Nauvoo and crossing the plains.

What kind of people were these Mormons? Seeing visions, finding golden plates under rocks, volunteering for hardship?

A light tap brought both their heads up, and Sister Beckstead walked in. Her eyes were red-rimmed and puffy.

"Time to go home, sweetie."

"No, Mommy, I want to stay here with Sister McCarty." Sara huddled into Alex's side.

"But church is over. We can come visit another time." Sister Beckstead's voice broke as she finished her sentence. Alex knew she shouldn't pry, but she couldn't sit in silence and watch the woman fall apart in front of her either.

"Sara, why don't you do me a favor?" Alex circled one arm about the child. "Would you mind checking on my sister for me and see if she needs anything? She's not supposed to get off the couch, you know."

"Okay."

Sara slid off the chair and left out of the room.

"Thank you," Sister Beckstead said. "I need a minute to compose myself." She sniffed into a wad of tissues. "I haven't told Sara yet, but her dad and I are getting divorced."

Chapter 22

ALEX WASN'T SURE WHAT TO DO OR SAY. "I'M SO SORRY."

"Even though deep down I knew something had to change in my marriage, I just always hoped it would be for the better, not the worse." Sister Beckstead sighed. "We've grown apart. We just don't have anything in common any more. Except Sara."

"Are you going to be okay?"

The woman nodded. "My emotions are a bit unstable right now—the smallest things can get me crying—but I'll be fine."

"When are you going to tell Sara?"

"I'd like to wait a while, but Donald doesn't seem to want to."

"I see." *What a jerk.*

"I'm sorry. This isn't fair of me to come in and unload all of this on you, especially when we don't even know each other very well."

"Please don't apologize," Alex said. "Sometimes it helps to get your feelings out."

"At least there's one good thing that is coming out of this."

"Oh?" Alex couldn't imagine what.

"For years I've been wanting to take off this extra weight and was even going to ask you to help me with a diet, and now, I've been so upset I haven't been able to eat a thing. I've lost eight pounds."

"You still need to keep up your strength and take care of yourself. Sara needs you, too." For some reason Alex felt like a hypocrite saying those words.

"I know. I'll be careful. My husband used to get so upset at my weight, and now, here he is leaving and I'll finally lose it," her voice quivered, "and it won't even matter." Fresh tears filled her eyes.

"Of course it matters." Alex stepped over and gathered the sobbing woman into her arms.

"Mommy, who are you talking about?"

Sister Beckstead whirled around to see her daughter standing in the doorway.

"No one, sweetie. No one. We'll talk when we get home. Did you find Sister Dixon?"

Sara giggled. "I caught her trying to get off the couch. But I told Brother Rich and he made her lie down again. He's funny. He gave me a piggyback ride."

"I'm glad, sweetie. Well," Sister Beckstead said to Alex, "I need to see Brother Greenwood and Brother Dixon just a minute before we go."

"Are you hungry, Sara?" Alex asked.

"A little."

"Let's go see what's in the kitchen while your mom finishes what she needs to do."

Sara skipped beside her as they headed for the stairs, then counted each step. ". . . Eight, nine, ten. Ten stairs. Did you know I can count to one hundred?"

"That's very good," Alex said.

"Hello, girls." Rich greeted them as they rounded the corner to the kitchen.

"I think Sister Beckstead is looking for you." Alex couldn't believe she was doing the "Brother and Sister" thing. Of course, lately she'd been doing a lot of things she couldn't believe.

"I'll see if I can find her." He touched Sara's nose. She smiled back, a wide grin revealing every tiny tooth in her mouth. Alex wondered if Sara's father realized what a special daughter he had.

"By the way, we missed you on the piano today, *Sister McCarty*," Rich grinned, one eyebrow lifted in a teasing arch.

"Come on Sara, let's find that snack." Sara shot for the kitchen, and Alex looked back over her shoulder at Rich, who was still in the same spot, smiling at her.

Darn that man!

Alex rummaged through the cupboards before she found a package of graham crackers. "Do you like these?"

"Mmmm, yes. Sometimes my mommy puts frosting on them."

"I don't think we have any frosting but I could find you a glass of cold milk to go with them."

"Okay."

Sara perched on a stool at the bar while Alex poured milk into a glass and set the crackers on a plate. "Now, you eat these and I'll go find out what your mom's doing."

Alex walked through the dining room and stopped in the entry. From where she stood she could see Sister Beckstead sitting on a chair, with Rich and Steve behind her, their hands resting on her head. Steve was speaking low and soft. Alex knew they were giving her a blessing. She waited for it to end before she moved.

Instead of shaking Sister Beckstead's hand afterwards, both of the men took turns hugging her. She wiped at her trickling eyes and braved a smile.

"Call if you need anything," Steve said.

After the Becksteads left, Alex joined Jamie on the couch while Steve and Rich put away chairs.

"I feel so bad for her," Alex said. "Does him not being a member have anything to do with them getting a divorce?"

Jamie gathered her legs underneath her and rested her head on the back of the couch. "I imagine most of their trouble stems from that. Colleen talked to me this morning before church. It's not so much that she's LDS and he's not, but that their lifestyles aren't compatible. He drinks and spends a lot of time with his buddies and she's alone, a lot. He won't let her pay tithing. He'll barely let her come to church, and they haven't told Sara but he will absolutely not let her get baptized. When they first got married they loved each other enough to overlook their differences. The years have changed that."

"You talking about Sister Beckstead?" Steve returned to the living room. He removed his suit coat and tie and hung them over the back of a chair.

"Yeah." Alex gathered a few stray hymnbooks and stacked them on the piano. "She's such a nice person. I hope things work out for her."

Carrying his overcoat, Rich came into the room.

"Are you leaving?" Jamie asked.

"Church is over."

"Why don't you stay for lunch? Unless you have other plans."

"No. It's just that I've eaten more meals over here than I have at my own place lately."

"So?" Steve said, rubbing Jamie's feet. "What kind of idiot are you to turn down dinner? Especially on fast Sunday."

"What's fast Sunday?" Alex couldn't remember her father ever talking about it. She found a spot on the love seat, near the warmth of the fireplace.

"We skip two meals the first Sunday of each month, and give the equivalent in money to the Church to help other members in need."

"Except for me," Jamie said. "I can't fast while I'm pregnant." She stretched her stockinged feet out in front of her.

"Maybe they should consider putting some of it toward piano lessons for members," Alex joked.

They all laughed.

"I don't get it. Why don't you just donate the money? What has not eating got to do with it?"

"Fasting isn't something exclusive to Mormons. All through the Old and the New Testament fasting was practiced," Steve explained.

"When we fast we are able to draw closer to the Spirit," Jamie added.

Once again Alex was amazed at the unusual practices Mormons had. There seemed to be no end to their peculiarities. They didn't just have a religion; being a Mormon was a way of life. Their beliefs intruded on every detail of daily life—what you ate, how you dressed, how you acted.

No. She was even more convinced, being a Mormon just wasn't for her.

Chapter 23

WHILE STEVE WATCHED THE NEWS THAT NIGHT, JAMIE AND ALEX lay on Jamie's bed, talking.

"You know, Alex, I've been wanting to talk to you about something."

Alex stiffened, not liking the tone in her sister's voice. Was Jamie going to bug her about not eating again?

"I know Mom has never really forgiven me for joining the Church and she's disappointed because I don't have a wonderful career."

"Jamie—"

"It's true, Alex. I know it is. I just wish . . ." she took a heavy breath, "I wish she didn't have to turn me away because of my beliefs."

Alex thought for a second, knowing to some degree that she herself had been guilty of doing the same thing.

"Has she ever said anything to you about it?" Jamie asked.

Before Alex could answer, Jamie continued, "I mean, I guess that's why she's so detached from me. I'm assuming it's because I joined the Church."

Her mother had said plenty about her feelings on the subject, but Alex didn't see how telling Jamie would improve the situation.

"Jamie, you have to believe that Mom loves you very much. She was disappointed when you joined the Church. She thinks the Mormon religion is very fanatical and that its members are very aggressive. Being around them makes her uncomfortable because . . ."

"We tend to come on a little strong?"

"Uh . . . well, yeah. I guess that's a good way to put it. Plus, I think it scared her when you joined the Church. She's afraid she's going to lose you, too, like she did Dad."

"But that's ridiculous. Dad joining the Church had nothing to do with his death."

Alex stayed silent because she happened to agree with her mother. Even though it was ridiculous to connect the two, somehow they seemed connected.

"He died because some jerk was drinking. Not because he was a Mormon. Do you seriously think Mom believes that?"

Alex shrugged. "I think she believes if Dad hadn't been a Mormon he would've been home with us instead of coming home from church." Alex picked a strand of thread in the bedspread.

"*You* don't think Dad died because he joined the Church, do you?" Jamie rolled onto her side and looked up at her sister.

Alex bit her top lip.

"Well, you don't, do you?"

Alex pulled out the thread. "Not really. But . . ."

"But what?"

A flash of anger loosened her tongue. She threw down the thread. "Okay, yeah. I guess I do feel that way a little bit. That Sunday morning we would've probably been doing something together as a family. But him joining the Church separated our family forever."

After carrying around that idea for years and finally unloading it, Alex would have thought she'd feel better. She didn't.

"Alex." Jamie's tone was soft but firm. "You know that's not true though, don't you?"

"No, I don't know."

Jamie took Alex's hand in hers. "Maybe the Lord had something more important for him to do on the other side."

"What could be more important than raising a family and being with his wife?"

"I'm not saying it was fair, but a lot of times things happen we don't understand. That doesn't mean that they aren't in the Lord's hands."

"I'm sorry but I can't believe that. I can't believe the Lord had something more important for Dad to do than be with us."

"Sometimes we don't understand. But, Alex, I know the Lord is very much aware of us and our needs. He knows our strengths and weaknesses and what we need to help us in this life. Who knows, maybe I would have never looked into the Church and married Steve.

Maybe you wouldn't be the person you are if we hadn't received the growth we did from Dad's death. All I know is the Savior would never ask something of us without preparing a way for us to accomplish it."

"First Nephi, chapter three, verse seven," Alex said.

"What did you say?"

"I said, 'First Nephi, chapter three, verse seven.' It's in the Book of Mormon."

"I know where it is," Jamie said. "But how do *you* know where it is?"

"I happened to read an article in the *Ensign* the other day."

"How about that?" Jamie relaxed against her pillow. "You're just full of surprises."

"Do you really believe it?"

"Believe what? That verse or the Book of Mormon?"

"Either," Alex said. "Both."

"I do, Alex. With all my heart, I believe it. There have been some times lately when I've been so confused. I've wondered why I'm having so many problems having children, when there is nothing I would rather do than be a mom. Especially when I see so many babies born to unwed teenage mothers who can't always take care of those babies. I wonder, why them and not me? I wonder why things with Mom can't be better. I pray constantly that her heart will be softened so she can learn to accept what I've done and not resent me for it.

"But then I read the Book of Mormon, and I feel as if the words were written just for me. And the Spirit is so strong I can barely breathe. You can't feel something like that and deny it, Alex. You just can't."

"What do you mean 'the Spirit'?"

Jamie pushed herself upright so she faced her sister. "It's the Holy Ghost bearing witness of truth. Sometimes when I feel that spirit, prompting me to do something or telling me of the truth of something, I am overwhelmed with the most warm, tingling feeling that fills my chest till I think it will burst. And it leaves me weak and sweaty-palmed."

"You're kidding!" Alex sat up with a start.

"No, why would I kid you about this?"

"That's what it feels like?"

"Well, it's different for everyone and for different things. I remember one time I was trying to get an answer to a problem and I prayed about it constantly. I kept praying for the same thing over and over and over, and not getting an answer. So I finally got down on my knees and told the Lord that I was stumped and that I didn't know what to do. I asked him why he wasn't answering me and what I was supposed to do to get the answer. In my mind I went over the whole problem with him, and then suddenly BINGO! It hit me. The answer was there, plain as day." Jamie lifted her palms and shrugged, then let her hands fall. "I love it when that happens."

Alex bit the inside of her cheek and thought about Jamie's description of "the Spirit."

"Anyway, why do you ask?"

Alex took a deep breath, then said, "If I tell you this, will you please not go wacky on me?"

"Wacky about what? I don't get wacky about things."

"You do too and I'm not in the mood for it."

"Okay," Jamie leaned back and held up her right hand, "I promise, I will remain wackiless."

Alex smiled in spite of herself. "Well, lately I've been having these weird episodes that are a lot like when I get low-blood sugar."

"Yeah?"

"I've tried to pay attention to my eating patterns and energy expenditure, and there really seems to be no explanation for me to have low-blood sugar."

"What are you saying?"

"I'm saying," Alex said slowly, "that I think what you've described is what I've been feeling."

Jamie opened her mouth, then clamped it shut again.

Several seconds passed before Alex said, "You can say something."

"Actually," Jamie tipped her head to the side thoughtfully, "I'm not sure what to say."

"Since when have you ever been speechless?"

"Oh, believe me, I can think of plenty to say. I just want to make sure it's the right thing."

"Just don't tell me that I have to join your church, now that I'm having this happen. I'm not going to. I don't want to. And I don't think Mom could handle it."

"All I'm going to say is that this is between you and the Lord. Obviously he's trying to communicate with you. You need to communicate back. Tell him how you feel about his church and us Mormons and his book. Ask him, not me."

"What do you mean, ask him?"

"Pray, silly. Pour out your heart to him." Jamie stroked her stomach. "Alex, he loves you so much. He wants to help you. But you have to ask."

* * *

That night before Alex climbed into bed she made sure her door was shut and locked. She walked over to her window and looked out at the starlit sky dusting the snow-covered ground with silver shadows. Why was this happening? She had been fine until now. She was a good person, she didn't steal or kill or covet—well, maybe she coveted a little, but hardly ever. And she was no more confused or lost than anyone else. What did this church and the Lord want with her anyway?

She got down on her knees and leaned her head on the edge of the mattress. How could she talk to someone she couldn't see? When others prayed they seemed to know who was listening.

She stayed in that position for another minute, until she shivered from the cold, then got up and climbed into bed. She wasn't ready to pray. She wasn't ready for answers.

Chapter 24

"SISTER MCCARTY, CAN WE GO SLEDDING?"

It was time to put a stop to the "Sister" thing.

"You know what, Sara? You can call me Alex if you want."

"I can?" Sara sat up tall.

Alex had agreed to tend Sara while her mother went to Idaho Falls to meet with her attorney.

"Why don't we make cookies or something?" It was so blasted cold outside.

"I'd rather go sledding. I brought my snowpants." Sara held up a plastic grocery bag filled with books and crayons and, of course, snowpants.

"I guess we could for a little while. I'll have to see if I can find some warm clothes for me to wear." She seriously thought about not looking very hard but the excited look on Sara's face changed her mind. "Let's check in the storage room."

Within minutes they were out in the icy cold of the garage looking for sleds. They found a blue saucer and a red double-man toboggan hanging on the wall. Pulling the equipment behind them, they trudged through the snow around to the back of the house. Above them, Jamie waved and smiled from her window.

They waved back and continued up the hill, dragging themselves through the deep, powdery fluff. The cold stung Alex's cheeks and made her eyes water.

Alex held Sara's hand and pulled her as they neared the top. When they got there they both stopped and panted steam as they caught their breath.

"Wow, I'm pooped," Alex said. "That's hard work."

"I'm pooped, too," Sara said.

Alex noticed Sara had her hands on her waist and her right foot angled slightly forward, standing exactly as she herself was standing.

"Should we go together the first time?"

"That sounds fun."

"Okay, you get in front and I'll sit behind you."

Sara sat down. The plastic toboggan slid forward. "Alex!" she cried.

"Whoa! I gotcha." Alex caught the back end and pulled it onto level ground. "Don't go without me."

"It went all by itself."

Alex sat down behind Sara, flopped her feet onto the sled, and braced herself. Nothing happened.

"Why aren't we going?"

Alex tried to scoot the contraption forward. It sunk deeper into the snow. "I'd better give it just a little push. Hang onto my legs." Sara wrapped her arms tightly around Alex's thighs while Alex pushed against the snow behind them. Without warning, the sled shot forward, throwing them backwards in the toboggan.

They sailed down the hill, trying to sit upright as they bounced their way to the bottom. They were still on their backs when the sled tipped and dumped them into a snowbank.

Alex was convinced half of the snowbank had gone down her back.

"That's not how my dad does it," Sara said, completely covered in snow.

Alex held her comment and got to her feet. "Come on, let's brush off some of this snow and try it again."

Sara rode in the toboggan on the way back up the hill. The frozen air burned Alex's lungs, and she gasped for oxygen, expelling clouds of steam with each breath.

"This time I'll get in first, then you."

Alex planted herself onto the red torpedo and dug her heels into the snow. "Now you."

Sara stepped carefully in front of Alex, then reached out and grabbed the handles tightly.

"Ready?"

Sara nodded.

"Here we gooooo . . ." Alex's voice trailed behind as they plunged down the hill, this time sitting upright. Sprays of snow on each side showered them with ice crystals but the thrill of the ride and whoosh of air set the two girls laughing and screaming. And when they reached the bottom they rolled out of the toboggan onto the snow giggling.

They couldn't get back up the hill fast enough.

Once settled onto the sled, they pushed off and shot down to the bottom again, their voices echoing across the open hillside into the trees.

Alex forgot all about the cold and the wet down her back. Each time they landed at the bottom, their only thoughts were of getting up that hill so they could fly back down.

Sometime around their tenth run, they stopped at the top of the ridge and listened as the roar of an engine approached. Down below, from around the side of Jamie's house, a snowmobile appeared. The rider waved at them and motioned for them to come down.

"Should we go see who it is?" Alex said.

"Okay, I'm getting kind of cold anyway."

Like two bobsledders they nested against each other and crouched over. With one strong shove they tore down the hillside, following the slick path they'd created. Alex pulled up the plastic sides and leaned to her right. The toboggan edged toward the house and floated slowly to a halt ten feet in front of the snowmobiler, who clasped his hands and shook them overhead like a prize fighter.

"I think you guys are ready for the Olympics."

"Hi, Rich." Alex couldn't hide the pleasure from her voice. Her heart played leapfrog with her dancing emotions.

"I wondered if you wanted to go for a ride on one of our new sleds."

"Oh, I— I'm . . ." She didn't want to exclude Sara.

"Could I go in the house while you ride the snowmobile, Alex?" Sara interrupted. "I'm cold."

"Sure, sweetie. You go inside and take off your wet clothes and see if Jamie watched us. I'll be inside in a little while and we'll make some hot chocolate."

"With marshmallows?"

"As many as you want."

"Yippee! I love marshmallows." She turned and skipped away, but stopped. "Brother Rich, when you come in I'll show you a trick Alex taught me."

"A trick, huh? I can't wait."

Alex wished she would have told Sara not to show anyone, to keep it their little secret.

Rich pointed to the top of the hill and said, "Is that blue circle up there yours?"

"We forgot the saucer."

"We'll drive up and bring it back. Here hop on."

Alex threw one leg over the seat, as if she were mounting a low horse, and sidled up behind Rich. One great thing about riding snow-mobiles, it gave her a reason to have her arms around him.

"You ready?" He patted her clasped hands.

The engine sprang to life and lurched forward. Effortlessly it plowed through the powdery snow, winding them up to the top of the ridge and across, then out to the open expanse that lay before them. They traveled to the top of the hill where he brought the machine to a halt. In front of them was a sea of green pines, and beyond that, tall jagged mountain peaks.

Not even the smallest wisp of a cloud interrupted the intense blue of the startling open sky. The white carpet spreading out before them was untouched. The warmth from the bright sun had tree limbs dripping with melting snow and birds chirping happily. They shared the moment with only each other.

It hurt to be with Rich and know they had no chance for a future together. Was this how Colleen Beckstead felt?

"So," he turned around on the seat so they faced each other, "what do you think?"

"About the snowmobile or the view?"

"All of it."

She spoke slowly, "I don't think there's a more beautiful place on earth." She didn't look at him when he took her mittened hand in his.

"Sometimes," he said, "when my head gets clogged, I come out here and absorb the serenity."

They sat motionless. If there was a sound, they didn't hear it. If there was a breeze, they didn't feel it. If there was a fireplace burning, they didn't smell it.

"Is your head clogged now?"

He nodded. And tightened his grip on her hand.

She didn't have any idea what he was talking about, but she found herself saying, "You always seem to know exactly what you want and where you're going. I can't imagine you ever getting confused."

"Sometimes I think I know what I'm doing, but then I realize I haven't got a clue." He leaned back against the handlebars.

"You know what, Rich?"

"No?"

"I sure wish I knew what we were talking about."

He laughed, softly at first, then louder, his voice circling around them. "So do I, Alex, so do I."

"I probably should be getting back," she said.

"Thanks for coming with me. It's funny, isn't it?"

"What is?"

"I feel as though I've known you for years and that I could talk to you about anything."

"I . . ." she started, wondering if she should really say it, "I feel the same way."

It was out. And it felt good. The earth hadn't shattered, she didn't die, and Rich didn't explode or disappear.

"You do?"

She nodded. What was this cruel joke life was playing on them? Why would two people so obviously suited for each other be destined never to be together?

He spoke softly. "I like how unpredictable you are. I'm never sure what you'll do or say next. And I love how you make me laugh, and how happy I feel when I'm with you."

She wanted to say "thank you," but the words lodged in her throat. She dropped her chin, tried to swallow, and felt the orange yarn ball on top of her knit cap flop forward.

Rich pressed down the snow around the snowmobile with his boot. She watched him for a moment, listened to the crunch of the compressing powder, then said, "What are you saying?"

"I don't know." He released her hand. "I don't know," he said again, his voice sounding tired. He shook his head and turned forward.

His abrupt movements and the growl of the starting engine shattered the moment.

Alex held onto him again, knowing when she let go it would be forever.

Chapter 25

SARA MET THEM AT THE DOOR.

"Are you having hot chocolate with us?" she asked.

"Maybe next time. I need to get back to work," Rich said.

"But I wanted to show you my trick."

He looked at Alex. They hadn't spoken on the way back from the ride. Pure willpower kept her from fleeing to her room to cry her eyes out. She looked away and started removing her gloves and hat. "We don't want to keep him if he's in a hurry, Sara."

"Can I just show you my trick?" Sara said. "I've been practicing."

"Okay, munchkin. I'd love to see your trick, then I have to go."

Sara bounded away and climbed up on a bar stool. Rich tugged off his boots and followed her into the kitchen. Alex wished she could hop on the snowmobile and go forever and not look back. She'd gotten over other men before, and she knew eventually she would get over Rich. The trouble was, she didn't want to.

"First I have to rub the spoon like this," Sara said, giving the face of the spoon a few strokes with her thumb, "then I put it on my nose . . ."

Alex stood back and watched Sara balance the spoon on the end of her upturned nose.

The sight of the piece of silverware hanging in the middle of Sara's face brought a smile to Rich's lips. Sara concentrated so hard her eyes crossed. When the spoon stayed balanced, Sara held out her hands and said, "Ta-da!" Rich and Alex both applauded.

"Very good, Sara. That's quite a trick."

"You try, Brother Rich. I bet you can do it. You have a big nose."

Alex choked on a laugh.

Rich reached up and felt his nose. "You think my nose is big?" Although he was asking Sara he looked at Alex.

"Not as big as my daddy's." Alex smiled at Sara's innocent remark.

"I guess I'll try, but if my nose is so big maybe I should have a soup spoon instead."

"No, use this one. I've got it all warmed up for you." Sara handed him the utensil and he placed it on the tip of his nose. It immediately clattered to the floor.

"You need to lean your head back a little." She hopped off the stool and retrieved the spoon.

"This is my last try. I need to get going." Rich rubbed the spoon with his thumb and made another attempt. The spoon hung for several seconds then fell onto the counter.

"That was good." Sara bounced on her seat. "I can't wait to show my friends at school lunch."

"Sara, why don't you go ask Jamie if she wants some hot chocolate," Alex said.

"Okay." The child galloped out of the kitchen and bumped up the stairs.

"Nice trick," Rich said, touching his nose again.

"Sorry about that."

"Yeah, well, nothing like having a five-year-old smash your ego into a million pieces."

"She probably meant it as a compliment. And if it helps, I like your nose very much."

"Thank you." He rubbed his thumb along the edge of the counter. "Listen, Alex, I need to apologize to you. I seem to keep putting you in awkward situations. I'm sorry. I don't know what's wrong with my brain some days."

"Hey," she brushed the air with her hand, "don't apologize. It's okay." She hadn't decided yet if it helped knowing Rich cared for her as much as she cared for him. Would that make it any easier to get over him? Her doubt swallowed the notion.

"I'd better shove off. If Steve calls, tell him I'm on my way back."

"Okay. Thanks for the ride. Those machines are a lot of fun."

"You're welcome to ride one any time you want. Just make sure

Steve or I go with you. With all these trees it would be easy to get lost. I'd hate to lose you."

She knew he was referring to her riding the snowmobile, but his last words circled her brain and spiraled down to wrap themselves around her heart.

* * *

Toward evening Sara fell asleep. Jamie sat in a chair in the office with her feet propped onto another chair while Alex worked on the computer, entering recipes.

"Did you have fun with Rich today?" Jamie pinned together quilt squares while they talked.

"Yeah, it was fun," she said flatly. She wasn't in the mood to discuss Rich.

"He sure seems to like you." Jamie's tone was light, teasing.

Alex shut her eyes and pulled in a deep breath, then released it. "He's nice. But we're just friends."

"Steve says you're all he talks about at work." Jamie continued pinning her fabric. Alex stared blankly at the computer monitor in front of her.

"It's probably because he's lonely," Alex finally said. "He'll be fine when he gets back to Boise and sees his girlfriend again."

"Monica? She's not much of a girlfriend. They never see each other and Steve says she never writes or calls. You'd think if they had something serious going on, he'd talk about it."

"I know she writes because I saw a card from her at the office."

Jamie set her pins down. "Steve says she's really bossy to Rich and always points out his flaws. It's embarrassing for Steve to be around them when she does that."

Alex hoped Rich didn't tolerate Monica's criticism. He didn't deserve it.

Jamie continued, "How could anyone find a thing wrong with that man? He's as handsome as a movie star and has a great personality, don't you think?"

Alex was trying hard *not* to think about it. In fact, she couldn't think about anything at the moment. She was sure the strange sensation she was feeling wasn't the Spirit either. Her vision had blurred, her limbs were weak, and her breath came in shallow puffs.

"Alex?"

She recognized Jamie's voice but it sounded like it was coming through a long tunnel.

"Alex, are you okay?"

She didn't have the strength to answer before she passed out.

When she opened her eyes she saw Dr. Rawlins' face above hers. She sat up with a start.

"No, no, you stay down," he said.

"What's going on? Why are you here?"

Jamie's and Steve's faces appeared above her.

Oh, great!

"You passed out, Alex," Jamie said. "You scared me to death."

"I'd like to speak with Alex alone for a moment if I could," Dr. Rawlins said.

They left her alone with the doctor.

"Your sister tells me you have a history of anorexia."

Alex nodded, diverting her eyes from his gaze.

"Do you feel like you've overcome that problem completely?"

"Yes." She wasn't lying; she didn't feel she had an eating disorder.

"How much do you weigh right now?"

"I'm not sure. I don't really weigh myself that often."

"How about a guess."

"Probably a hundred and five, or so."

"How tall are you?"

Alex hated this inquisition. She was just fine.

"Five seven."

"Do you realize you are at least twenty pounds underweight? If, in fact, you weigh what you say."

Alex didn't reply.

"I'd like to ask you another question. When was your last period?"

Alex looked away.

"Alex?"

"Three months ago."

"Your sister has a scale in the bathroom. I'd like you to weigh yourself."

Anger started to build in Alex's chest. All of this was unnecessary.

She went into the bathroom, stared down at the scale and stepped on. The digital reading bounced from one number to the next. It finally settled on ninety-nine.

Alex gasped.

When had that happened?

Dr. Rawlins greeted her with a raised brow when she joined him.

"Was your guess a little off?"

She nodded.

"Do you even weigh one hundred?"

She shook her head.

"Alex, I know you've been through all the treatment before, so you know how serious anorexia is. You're a nutrition expert; you know how important your health is. As a doctor I feel it is my duty to tell you I think medical intervention is advisable. As your friend I would like to encourage you to consider getting help."

"I can handle this myself," Alex defended herself. "I know what to do. I just can't eat when I'm worried or upset, like I have been with Jamie. But I'll take better care of myself. I know how to do it."

The doctor frowned. "Against my better judgment I'm going to let you do this. But I'm going to check on your progress. I want to see you get your weight to at least one hundred and ten."

Eleven pounds. He was worse than Sandy. She could never gain that much.

"Alex, one hundred and ten, or I will have to make your family aware of the problem and instruct them to admit you to a treatment center."

"Okay, I'll do it," Alex said reluctantly.

For the first time she looked at Dr. Rawlins' face. In his eyes were warmth and concern. He sincerely cared; she couldn't deny that.

He opened the door for the others to join them.

Alex prepared herself for the questions.

* * *

"You don't have to sit and watch me. I'll eat every bite." Alex forced herself to put the spoonful of scrambled egg into her mouth and chew.

"Dr. Rawlins told me that it would be better if we did."

"But, Jamie—"

"No, 'buts,' Alex. I nearly had a heart attack when you passed out yesterday. I'm not about to watch that happen again."

Alex felt guilty for adding to Jamie's concerns, but all this fuss and worry was unnecessary.

"I can't eat another bite." Alex pushed the plate away and forced herself to quit calculating fat grams and calories. She had no choice but to follow through with the doctor's orders. For now.

"I knew you'd lost weight; your face and neck and legs are so thin. But you always wear so many layers of clothes and those big, baggy shirts I didn't realize you were under a hundred pounds until Dr. Rawlins told me."

Alex was annoyed with the doctor for announcing her weight to Steve and Jamie. "I dress like that because it's comfortable, and I'm not used to the cold," she said stiffly.

"Dr. Rawlins says that it's typical for people with too little body fat to be cold all the time."

Alex was tired of talking about her weight. The subject had not only been beaten to death but had been dissected and analyzed under a microscope. She was ready to change the subject, but she wasn't quite finished. She had one last thing to say.

"I'd like to say something else about this issue then I hope we can let it drop."

"Okay."

"I'm twenty-seven years old. I've been lecturing for years to fitness professionals about the importance of proper nutrition and good health. All I'm asking for is a little credit here. I didn't realize my weight had dropped so low and I plan on taking care of it. Okay?"

"You promise?"

"Yes, I promise."

"Thank you." The sisters hugged briefly.

Steve walked into the room as they finished their conversation. Alex thought he'd been sweet about the whole episode and hadn't gone overboard with concern.

"You're just in time," Alex said. "I was going to tell Jamie the exciting news."

"What news?" Jamie looked from Alex's face to Steve's.

"Well," Alex smiled, then said, "Mom's coming Saturday. She's going to stay a whole week."

"How about that, honey?" Steve said, waiting for a reply. "Honey?"

Alex didn't like the distressed look on her sister's face. "Jamie, aren't you excited?"

Jamie's face showed a myriad of emotions, none of which were excitement.

"Honey, what's wrong?"

"I don't want to see . . . my motherrrrrr," she wailed, and ran from the room, crying.

Steve and Alex looked at each other in shock.

"Uh-oh," Alex said. "I think we should have asked her first."

After stewing and pacing and wondering if she'd made a bad situation worse, Alex decided she had no other choice but to go and talk to her sister.

"Jamie?" Alex cracked open the bedroom door and peered inside. The room was dark.

"Yes," her voice came weakly.

"Can I come in?"

"Sure."

Alex walked over to the window and opened the blinds. Hope of spring shone in the clear, sunny day. Boulders along the hillside she'd never seen before peeked through the melting snow.

"Can I come in?"

"I guess so." Jamie rubbed her eyes and tucked her hair behind her ears.

Alex sat in a floral chintz chair near the bed. "You want to talk about it?"

Jamie chewed on the inside of her lip for a moment before answering. "I wish talking about it would make a difference, but it doesn't. Mom acts like you're the only daughter she has. She treats me like a . . ." Jamie hiccupped ". . . a stranger."

"Jamie, c'mon, it's not that bad."

Flaring with anger, Jamie said, "You don't think so? Well, how about this? The only time I hear her voice is when I call and get her answering machine. Oh, except I did catch her home when I called to tell her I was expecting again. But she was on her way to a Broadway opening and couldn't talk. She said she'd call back."

Alex didn't even want to ask. "Did she?"

"No. It's been three and a half months."

Alex wished she had an excuse, some kind of explanation. There was no excuse for her mother to be so unfeeling about Jamie's trials.

Jamie was stony-faced. "Believe me when I tell you, she doesn't think of me as her daughter anymore."

"But I know you're wrong, Jamie. She's told me how concerned she is about you and how excited she is to have a granddaughter."

"You told her we were having a girl?"

"I hope it's okay."

"And she was excited?"

"Jamie, she was thrilled. She started remembering what you looked like as a baby, how darling you were with your curly hair and big eyes."

"Really?"

"She also said she was very excited to come and visit and even admitted that she hadn't been very good at keeping in touch." Alex wanted desperately to say something to help. "It may not make up for all the things she's missed, but she is trying. She really is."

Jamie looked apologetic. "I didn't mean to flip out like I did," she said.

"We should've talked it over with you first."

"No, I just overreacted. These yo-yo hormones of mine are impossible to gauge. I'm up, I'm down, I'm spinning around in circles. I owe you an apology."

"You don't need to apologize for anything, but I hope you'll give her a chance. Maybe this visit is what we need to make some changes so our family can be close again."

Jamie nodded. "I hope so. I'd love that more than anything."

Chapter 26

"Alex, I've got to run to Ashton on business Saturday. Rich said he's got to go to I.F. to pick up paint supplies and would love to take you to the airport."

Alex had made a decision to stay away from Rich. He was on her "avoid at all costs" list. In fact, he was at the top, just above hot fudge cake.

"I don't really think I need anyone to go with me. I'm sure with some directions I can find the airport."

"But Rich has to go there anyway, you might as well go together." Steve had one eyebrow raised.

Alex shook her head. "I'd rather go alone."

"There's supposed to be a big snowstorm," Jamie said. "What if —"

"Please," Alex held up her hand, "it's decided. I'm picking up Mother alone. I don't care how much it snows."

* * *

Early Saturday morning Jamie and Alex sat in the living room watching the snow out the window. The forecast called for eight to twelve inches of snow.

The phone rang.

"It's for you, Alex. It's Sandy."

Alex took the phone from her sister.

"Sandy, how are you?"

As Alex listened, Jamie mouthed, "What does she want?"

"I think I can manage," Alex said into the phone, "but that's awfully soon." She listened for a moment, pulling at the cuticle on her thumbnail with her teeth. "So the tour starts mid-July and we're promoting the cookbook with the video?"

"Wow!" Jamie whispered.

"It does sound great. I just have one request. I want to be in on the scheduling. If we leave it up to Greg he'll have me doing two cities a day." Alex rolled her eyes at Jamie and combed her fingers through her hair. After another moment she laughed and said, "Thanks, but I don't even want to be the next Richard Simmons. I just hope it's a success. I'll send what I have as soon as I can."

She turned off the cordless phone and set it back on the table.

"Sounds like this cookbook could be really big." Jamie reached for her embroidery hoop and started working on a teddy bear's tu-tu.

Alex shrugged. "The market is saturated with cookbooks and exercise videos. One more isn't going to make a difference." She didn't want to get her hopes up.

Jamie smiled encouragingly. "You're well known in the industry. A lot of your sales will come by word of mouth."

"I hope you're right, Jamie. Otherwise you'll be getting one thousand copies of my book and video for your birthday."

Jamie gave Alex a worried look. "Alex, are you sure you don't need to get back home? As much as I want you here with me, I don't want to jeopardize your career."

Alex knew if she went back to California it would be to get away from Rich, not to get back to work.

"My job is holding steady," she reassured Jamie. "I earned some time off after all the conferences I did during the winter. Plus, I need time to work on this crazy cookbook. It's not like I'm Julia Child or anything."

Jamie glanced out the window. "Wow. Look at that snow. Alex, you can't drive in this weather. It's a blizzard out there."

"But Mom's already in the air. I can't just let her land in Idaho Falls and not be there to pick her up."

"We can get word to her. She can stay in a hotel overnight. Believe me, Mom wouldn't want you to risk it."

Alex looked at the snowflakes sifting past the window. They were the size of cotton balls. She hadn't forgotten about her last trip through the snow. Maybe Jamie was right. Maybe she should wait until tomorrow.

Through the blur of white she saw a black vehicle crawl up the drive. Rich's truck.

Her heart beat triple time. She jumped to her feet. "Look, Rich just pulled in."

Alex opened the door before he knocked.

"What are you doing?" She'd never be able to smell the musky fragrance of his cologne again without thinking of him.

"I came to take you to Idaho Falls."

She shut the door behind him and laughed. "Don't be silly, you don't have to drive me to the airport."

"I'm not letting you go by yourself." Had any other man said that she would have told him where to get off. But not Rich. The protective tone in his voice cloaked her heart in its warmth.

"I'm trying to talk her into staying home. Waiting until tomorrow." Jamie went back to her cross-stitch.

"I'm not sure that's a good idea, either. If you wait until morning you may have worse conditions on your hands. The storm's dropping down to the valleys tonight. It could be several days before you can make the trip."

"Several days?" Alex couldn't leave her mother alone for that long.

"If you're going to go, you'd better do it today."

She trusted Rich. He knew how to handle the roads and his truck was equipped to travel in all conditions. But that long ride alone with him in the truck was going to be a killer.

"I just have to grab my purse." She turned to Jamie. "But what about you? Are you going to be here alone?"

"Colleen said she'd come over until Steve gets back at one."

Alex sighed with defeat. She looked at Rich. "I really appreciate you doing this. Especially in such crummy weather."

"Hey, I'm no fair-weather friend. I thought you might be a little concerned about driving in the snow and I was going there anyway."

Jamie spoke up, "I'm relieved to know you'll be with Rich."

"We'll call when we get there," Rich told Jamie.

Alex ran upstairs and grabbed her purse off the dresser. Taking a glance in the mirror she wished she would have taken time to put on a little more make-up, then she shrugged and rushed back downstairs. She couldn't help thinking about what Rich had said about not being a fair-weather friend. There wasn't a doubt in her mind. No matter what kind of storms came into her life, she could ask for Rich's help and he would be there.

"You guys be careful," Jamie called as they stepped into the whirling whiteness.

Rich held the door for Alex while she climbed inside the truck. Being outside in the storm made her realize there was no way she could have made it on her own. Especially in her car with her lack of snow-driving experience.

He climbed in, pulled the door shut, and fastened his seatbelt. Even though the snow didn't seem to be falling heavily, it quickly covered the ground. Rich steered around the ruts and drifts on the long driveway and pulled onto the main road. Soft music came from the speakers. Alex recognized the tune from one of the church meetings.

"I can't remember the name of this song."

He listened for a moment. "It's 'Where Can I Turn for Peace?' We can change it."

"No, I like it. It's soothing."

"When I had challenges on my mission, I would sit and read the words in the hymnbook over and over."

"You like hymns, don't you?"

"My mother led the music in our ward back home for as long as I can remember. We always listened to them or sang them at home. I guess it's just a habit."

She listened to the music, wondering what the words were like, grateful for its calming effect. She needed it, because the storm seemed to worsen with each mile. Her muscles stiffened as her mind replayed her last encounter with icy roads.

"Do you think we should turn around?"

"Alex, you don't think I'd take you if it weren't safe, do you?" His expression looked pained. Something in his eyes, the worried slant of his lifted brows, told her so.

"No, of course not." Had she hurt his feelings?

"I'd never put you in danger." He looked straight ahead. "Ever."

"I know that. I feel safe with you." She reached over and brushed his shoulder with her hand. Before she could pull her arm back, he caught her hand in his and held it.

"Alex, we need to talk."

Oh no! "Rich, please, I don't really want to go over that eating stuff again."

"Actually I wasn't even going to ask you about that, but now that you mention it, I'd like to know how you are."

"I'm fine. I'm great. I've never been better!" She jerked her hand away from his and folded her arms with a huff. What did she have to do to convince these people?

"I didn't mean to upset you. I'm only asking because I care."

She took a deep breath and tried to say apologetically, "I appreciate it, but I'm fine."

"I'd like to ask you something else, if you don't mind."

"Sure," she said, her voice edged with bitterness, "Anything you'd like to know." How much had Steve, Jamie, and Rich discussed her situation when she wasn't around?

"Your sister said you were anorexic in high school."

"Yeah."

"What happened?"

She stared out the window, wishing she could somehow disappear.

"Never mind," Rich said. "It's none of my business. I'm sorry I even asked."

Now she felt like a creep. He wasn't out to lecture her or make her change. He'd merely asked a question and she'd been flat-out rude.

"Rich," she reached for his hand, "I'm sorry."

He gave her hand a squeeze and said, "That's okay, I shouldn't have asked something so personal."

"I'd like to talk about it if you still want to know."

He nodded.

Taking a deep breath, she began after a short pause. "After Dad died, Mom wasn't home much. I was in charge of Jamie and the meals, and pretty much everything at home. Of course I couldn't cook real well, so we ate a lot of Spaghettios and cereal, and peanut butter and jelly. Life was pretty awful back then and food was one thing that gave me some joy and satisfaction. So I ate. A lot.

"By the time I was in junior high I was pretty chubby. I outweighed my friends by thirty pounds. None of the kids would let me forget it either. They teased me constantly; even Jamie and her friends said things that hurt my feelings. My mom was trying to be helpful, by putting me on diets and stuff, but it only made me feel worse."

Alex sighed. She'd pretty much worked through her old feelings long ago with a therapist, but the emotions were still real and painful.

"Then in high school I got really sick one winter; a bad cold turned into pneumonia. I spent almost three weeks out of school and when I got back, the only thing people could say was how great I looked because I'd lost some weight.

"For once I felt good about myself. I was getting positive attention and the kids were acting nice to me. In my mind I figured that if I lost more weight, they would like me and accept me even more.

"So, I stopped eating. And it worked. Suddenly people were paying attention to me. Even teachers. My mom was so happy I was getting thin, she took me out and bought me all these great clothes. I started dating and I had friends."

Rich listened intently as she spoke.

"By then I couldn't stop. I was afraid to eat, because I didn't want to ever be fat again and lose all that I had finally achieved. I kept thinking just a few more pounds then I'll stop. But I didn't know how to level off.

"Finally, it all came to head when I collapsed in gym class. At the doctor's office I was examined and they admitted me immediately into the hospital. I was down to eighty-three pounds. I was dehydrated and my electrolytes were completely out of balance. They released me when I got my weight up to ninety with strict instructions that I continue to gain weight or I'd have to come back in."

"Did you?"

"It took quite a few years and I had a lot of setbacks but I managed to get my weight up to one hundred six and stayed there for quite a while."

"Do you feel like you're better?"

"You mean, do I still have anorexia?"

He looked at her and nodded.

"I think I'll always have a tendency to fall into my old patterns when I'm upset or stressed, but no, I don't still have it, nor am I now anorexic. I do need to gain some weight, and I will. I'm feeling much better."

"I'm glad," he said. "Thanks for telling me."

"So," she said, ready to change the subject. "What was it you wanted to talk to me about?" She knew he wasn't about to say "I'm quitting the church for you" anymore than she was going to say "I'm joining the church for *you*." So what was it?

"This is going to come as a surprise to you. You're the first person I'm telling. I haven't even said anything to Steve and Jamie yet, but I've made a decision."

Alex pressed her back into the seat, shut her eyes, and waited for his announcement. Somehow she doubted this news would brighten her day.

"It looks like I'll be going home sooner than I thought."

"Oh, really?" She hoped the cheerfulness in her voice didn't sound too fake.

"I don't think I'll be coming back."

Her eyelids flew open. She sat up with a start, nearly slicing herself in half with the seatbelt. "What do you mean?"

"I've got a job offer in Boise and I'm going to take it."

Why should she care? Why? She fought for control of her emotions. "But what about your business and Steve and Jamie and your house? Everything you have is here."

She blinked hard just as the wipers streaked across the windshield, and her vision blurred.

"I don't know how to explain it." For the first time since they got on the road he took his eyes off course and looked at her. "It's kind of your fault."

"My fault?!"

"Having you around has made me realize that I'm lonely. I love Island Park and the outdoor business I'm in, but I want to share my life with someone. I'm tired of being alone. You've helped me see that."

She slumped back against the seat. Her scalp felt like it was being cinched tightly on top of her head.

"I'm tired of going home to an empty house."

Alex knew exactly what he was talking about. "I understand," she said slowly.

"You do?"

She nodded and looked down at her knees. A loose thread on the hem of her shirt caught her eye. "Sure I do. I live alone. I cook for one, shop alone, do my laundry alone. Sometimes I turn on the television just to have another voice in the house. I know exactly how you feel."

"Yeah, I guess you do." The road slanted downward. With each mile the snow grew lighter, until only rain fell.

She wasn't sure how much time had passed, but as she looked down she realized she'd undone the whole hem of her shirt and had a finger wrapped in thread.

"What about Monica?"

He cleared his throat. "I guess she has something to do with this, too. She's been calling a lot and writing."

Alex remembered the card at the shop.

"She's anxious to get back together. In fact, her father's the one offering me the job."

Alex didn't like what she was hearing.

"What kind of job?"

"Accounting."

She barely heard what he said, his voice was so soft.

"I didn't know you were an accountant."

"That was my major at school. But I never got my CPA."

"Really?"

He looked over at her again. "Yes, really."

"You want to work in an office and wear a suit all day?" She shifted in her seat, pulled up a foot, and hooked her other knee over it. Then she looked directly at him.

"It was my major. It's not like it's something I'm not even interested in."

"Hey," she held up one hand, "it's your choice. You don't have to justify it with me. I just can't see you sitting in a stuffy old office punching numbers." She unwound the string from her finger.

"He wants me to be a manager. I won't be behind a desk all day."

"An accountant, huh?" She pulled open the little trash container and put the thread inside. "You must really love this girl."

She saw his reaction. It wasn't her imagination. He clenched the steering wheel so tightly his knuckles went white.

"She's a . . . ," he licked his lips and swallowed, ". . . a wonderful girl."

She felt the tension in the air.

He glanced at her. For a moment their gazes locked. His eyes reflected the confusion she felt in her own heart.

Maybe his church didn't have all the answers after all.

Chapter 27

A SEA OF SOGGY CLOUDS HUNG OVER THE SMALL AIRPORT, EAST OF town. Inside the terminal, the faint odor of cigarettes mixed with the aroma of fresh coffee from a nearby refreshment booth. Airport smells. Alex was all too familiar with them and grateful she wasn't about to climb into one of those steel bellies and endure another claustrophobic trip to some strange destination.

Rich volunteered to call Jamie while Alex waited for her mother's plane.

She watched him stroll out of sight then sighed. She'd miss him when he walked out of her life for good.

Around her people swarmed and bustled, boarded and unboarded, but Alex was numb amidst the activity. Even her excitement to see her mother again waned as she tried to cut the emotional ties that held Rich in her heart.

Moments later Rich joined her again and reported that Jamie was fine. No further effort for conversation was made. There was nothing to say.

"You're Alex McCarty!"

Alex jumped and turned to see a young woman behind her, bouncing excitedly.

"Yes, I am."

"I'm so happy to meet you. I attended a conference you spoke at in Salt Lake City. My name's Laurel."

"Nice to meet you, Laurel." Alex extended her hand and the woman clamped on and shook it with vigor.

"After I took your class I changed the way I eat completely. I've lost twenty pounds and three dress sizes."

This was payday for Alex. The Laurels in the world almost made all the work and travel worth it.

"I cut your picture out of a fitness magazine and taped it onto my fridge. Every time I saw how great you looked I put the ice cream back in the freezer. But you look even thinner in person."

Alex couldn't tell if Laurel meant it as a compliment or not. She didn't waste time worrying about it. She got a great idea. "Laurel, would you mind writing me a letter telling me exactly what you just said? I'm working on a cookbook and would love to include your testimonial in it."

"Really?" Laurel clapped her hands to her cheeks. "This is so exciting."

Alex found a business card and a pen to write down Jamie's address.

"This is so neat! My husband won't believe it. And my friend Karen is gonna flip. After your lecture we went on a diet together. I'm a little worried about her though." Laurel spoke more softly. "She's gone a little overboard with it—you know, she works out twice a day, hours at a time, and she's lost so much weight. We both wanted to look like you." Laurel shifted the luggage on her shoulder. "She just can't seem to stop."

Laurel's words stopped Alex cold, the words reverberating in her head: *overboard, wanted to look like you, can't seem to stop.* Had people gotten the wrong message? She wasn't out to tell people to starve themselves. But while she was busy lecturing on health, nutrition, and fitness, was she sending out an unspoken message?

What was she telling people by her appearance alone?

"Oh," Laurel dropped her suitcase, "would you mind if I got a picture of us together?"

"Of course not," Alex mumbled, still worried about all the Karens who tried to starve themselves to look like her.

Laurel produced a small disposable camera, and Rich volunteered to take the picture.

Alex glanced up at the monitor. Her mother's flight number was flashing. The plane had landed.

Smiling, Laurel stood beside Alex and slid an arm around her waist. Alex forced a smile.

"Okay, ladies. Say fat-free cheese."

The light flashed, Alex blinked, and Laurel resumed her exuberance.

"Would you mind if I took a picture of you with your . . ." She glanced from Alex to Rich and back to Alex, ". . . friend?" Laurel asked.

The "fan-fun" was starting to wear off.

Rich stood next to Alex and slid his arm around her waist. Instinctively she did the same.

"One, two, three . . ." The camera flashed. "That was great. You make a handsome couple." She dropped the camera into her purse, "Well, I gotta run. It was wonderful meeting you. I'll send that letter right away."

Rich and Alex stayed arm in arm as Laurel scurried up the ramp toward the exit.

"I think they should name the next hurricane after her," Rich said. His arm fell to his side as he turned to look at Alex. "Hey, are you okay?"

"What have I done?"

Rich's forehead wrinkled with confusion. "What do you mean?"

"I mean, Laurel's friend, losing all that weight. It was because of me."

"You don't tell people to lose weight and be thin, do you?"

"No. But they look to me as some sort of role model."

"Maybe instead of writing a cookbook you should be writing a book telling women that being healthy is more important than being thin. It is, isn't it?"

As she stared at Rich, her thoughts locked onto his suggestion. Maybe she had a more important message to be sharing with people than just good nutrition. Maybe she needed to talk to women about her eating disorder.

"Alex?"

His voice brought her thoughts back to the airport.

"I'm sorry, what did you say?"

He had no time to answer before they heard, "Alex, darling!"

Alex turned and saw an attractive blonde woman, wearing a black leather, thigh-length coat over jeans tucked into black high-heeled boots, hurrying toward her.

"Mother!" Alex stepped forward to meet her. Embracing, they patted each other's backs.

"Let me look at you." Judith McCarty stepped away, then crushed her daughter in another hug.

"It's so wonderful to see you, Mom. You look terrific."

"Thank you, sweetie. So do you. I still picture you as my chubby little girl, but look how thin you are. You could use a little makeup, though."

Alex let the comment pass, hoping Rich hadn't heard.

"I'd like you to meet my friend." Alex gestured toward him. "Rich, this is my mother, Judith McCarty."

Judith released her daughter and turned. "My goodness." She took a step back and gave him a generous smile. "It's so nice to meet you." She turned to Alex and winked.

Judith held out a hand that glittered with gold and diamonds, and Rich shook it.

The three started for the terminal entrance where the baggage claim was located. Judith filled them in on the weather and business of New York.

"You two stay here and I'll get the luggage," Rich said.

When he was out of earshot, Judith turned to her daughter and said, "Alexis McCarty, why haven't you said anything about him before?"

"Mother!"

"If I had a man like that around me, I wouldn't let him out of my sight."

Alex shut her eyes and took a deep breath. "So, Mom, how are you feeling?"

"Quite wretched. But what can you expect after all that turbulence? And that slop they call food!"

"Are you hungry? We could get something to eat."

"No, no, darling." She patted Alex's shoulder. "I'm fine, really. I just can't wait to get to Jamie's house and get settled. So," Judith smiled, "tell me more about Rich."

"Mother, please!"

"All right. We can talk later." Judith looked around the lobby. "I wonder if he's finding everything okay."

"Here he comes." Alex saw his face above a stack of luggage he wheeled around the corner. "Good grief, Mom. How long are you planning on staying?"

"What do you mean?"

"All that luggage."

"Sweetie, besides all my clothes and shoes, I've got some gifts and extra things I brought along. I could have easily brought more, but I ran out of suitcases."

Alex shook her head and sighed. She was happy her mother was here, but her earlier encounter with Laurel had distracted her. She was anxious to get home. She had some serious thinking to do.

With the five suitcases, clothes bag, and carry-on stored in the back under the camper shell, they were back on the freeway, heading north on I-20. Stopping at a drive through, they got a cup of coffee and a sesame bagel with cream cheese for Judith; a whole wheat bagel, plain, and orange juice for Alex, and a double cheeseburger, large fries with fry sauce, and a chocolate milk shake for Rich.

As they munched, they listened to Judith's complaints of the plane ride and Alex worried that Rich would find her mother snooty and arrogant. When she looked over at him, though, he was smiling pleasantly despite having some trouble trying to dip fries and drive at the same time. So Alex reached over and held the plastic container of fry sauce for him.

"Do you like the snow, Mrs. McCarty?"

"Please, call me Judith."

While her mom talked about her recent attraction to snow skiing, Alex assisted Rich with his food, and finally couldn't stand it any longer. She took one of the fries, dunked it, and shoved it into her mouth. The salty crunch with sweet sauce sent her taste buds dancing. She'd loved fries as a kid. She still loved them.

After one more of the crispy potatoes, she wiped her fingers on a napkin then caught sight of Rich's shake and reached for his cup. He looked surprised, but handed it to her. "Have all you want," he invited.

With her eyes shut she drew in a long creamy drink of the thick chocolate. Pure heaven. Nothing tasted better than fries and a shake.

"Your father used to take us to Big Daddy's for french fries and chocolate shakes. Do you remember, Alex?"

Alex remembered. Those memories were some of the pleasant ones, when she was still a normal child.

"He always ordered caramel marshmallow," Judith went on.

Rarely did her mother speak of her father, if ever. The subject was usually so upsetting that the whole family avoided the subject. Alex wasn't used to seeing her mother recall his memory with fondness.

"How could I forget? They made their shakes so thick they stood this far above the rim of the glass." She spread her thumb and finger three inches apart.

"I haven't thought about that place in years." Judith's voice drifted a little as she gazed out the window. The truck climbed toward the mountains, and Alex could see that the rain had turned into snow. She watched as her mother stared out the window, lost in her thoughts, absently twisting one of the rings on her fingers.

Was the past finally catching up with her? Alex wondered if the pain of her father's death was bubbling to the surface after all these years, and if so, why? Had something happened to her mother that she didn't know about?

Alex reached over and circled her fingers around her mother's small hand.

Suddenly her mother seemed small, fragile, and vulnerable. And it scared her.

Chapter 28

Jamie was on the couch in the front room, still working her cross-stitch, when they walked through the front door.

"You made it! I was getting so worried." She threw her sewing onto the coffee table. "Steve," she hollered, "they're here."

She pushed herself to her feet.

Alex watched as mother and daughter met each other in the center of the room.

They didn't embrace immediately, but when Jamie reached out her hand toward her mother, they fell into a hug. Both were teary-eyed when they parted. Alex smiled, hoping this was a new beginning, a chance to put the past behind them and build a close relationship for the future.

Steve bounded down the stairs to greet them. "Judith, nice to see you." He didn't waste time with formalities, just pulled her into a hug, patted her on the back a few times, and said, "Glad you could make it. Come on in where it's warm."

"Not until I get a look at my daughter." Judith's eyes glistened as she grasped Jamie's hands and took a long look. "Seeing you reminds me of myself so many years ago. I can't believe you're really going to make me a grandma."

They hugged again, and Alex couldn't help the excitement she felt seeing them openly show affection. Inviting Judith to visit was the right thing to do. She knew that now without any doubt.

"I think I'll take off," Rich said, as the group moved toward the living room.

"Stay and eat with us. We've already got a place set for you," Jamie said.

"Thanks, but I need to get home. I've got some phone calls to make before it gets too late."

Alex wondered if any of those calls were to Monica and her father.

"Rich," Judith stopped him before he went out the door, "Thank you for bringing Alex to pick me up."

"Happy to do it. Good night." With a wave he stepped outside and was gone.

Alex felt the bang of the door echo in her chest. Every good-bye she said to him brought her closer to the final farewell.

As Steve and Jamie fussed over Judith, Alex found herself drifting in and out of the conversation. They discussed Steve's business and ideas for new ventures. They discussed Jamie's crafts and how things were with the baby. They discussed many things that didn't have to do with religion. And Alex was grateful. She preferred they stayed on safe subjects.

During dinner she picked at her food and finally pushed the plate away.

"Why don't we go upstairs and help you unpack, Mom?" Jamie scooted her chair away from the table. "Come on, Mom, let me show you around."

As they toured the downstairs, Judith used words like "cute," "charming," and "quaint" to describe Jamie's home. Of course, Judith's apartment in New York was professionally decorated and *Lifestyles of the Rich and Famous* elegant. Alex preferred the simplicity and inviting comfort of Jamie's home.

"This is an interesting statue on your piano."

Alex hadn't really studied it before, but the eighteen-inch statue of Christ standing with outstretched hands caught and held her attention. The detail of the expression on his face held her gaze as she focused on the serenity of his smile and the loving expression on his face. For a moment Alex was transfixed. Everything around her was blocked out, every noise and movement went unnoticed.

This was Jesus Christ.

Her heartbeat quickened and a peaceful warmth flushed over her. This was Jesus Christ!

There was such an outpouring of love on his face that Alex felt drawn in and for a moment sensed his presence. He'd never seemed real, never seemed more than just a historical figure from the past. Until now.

"Alex. Alex?" Jamie's voice broke the moment.

Alex shook her head. "Sorry, what were you saying?"

"We're going upstairs. Are you coming?" Jamie started for the stairs.

Alex took one last look at the statue and followed behind her sister and mother. Did Jesus really play a part in her life? Had she been missing something all these years? What would change if she did decide to let him into her world? Would knowing Jesus help her with her problems? If so, how?

Once in her room, Judith tested the mattress and punched at the pillows. Alex couldn't tell if they met her mother's standards or not.

"We'll help you unpack, Mom," Jamie said.

"Thank you, sweetie. But I want you to get off your feet. Alex can lift the bags."

Jamie watched from the bed as Alex and Judith unloaded the suitcases until the drawers and closet bulged.

"Mother, did you bring everything you own?" Alex held a slinky black dress with rhinestones studding the shoulders and wondered where exactly her mother planned on wearing it.

"What's in this last suitcase?" Jamie snapped the latch on a smaller bag.

"Oh," Judith hesitated, "I guess this is as good a time as any to show you this."

"Show us what?" Jamie leaned over and looked closely as Judith lifted the lid.

"First of all, I found the doll you were asking for, Alex." Judith brought out a cardboard container as long as a shoebox but half the width and handed it to her.

It took a second to dig through the tissue paper, but Alex finally found her doll and lifted her carefully out of the box. She'd forgotten how dainty it was.

"I remember when you got that doll," Jamie said. "I kept wanting to play with her but you wouldn't even let me near. I couldn't understand why you'd get a doll you couldn't play with." She reached for the ballerina. "She's in perfect condition. Look at those sweet little shoes."

"You said you wanted to give her to someone?" Judith asked.

Alex thought twice about giving the doll to Sara, but a promise was a promise. "Yes, a little girl I know named Sara."

"You're giving it to Sara?" Jamie handed the doll back to Alex.

"I think she needs it more than I do."

"Is there something wrong? Is the little girl sick?" Judith softly touched the dancer's pink tu-tu.

"Her mother and father are getting divorced. I want to do something to help her."

The three women sat in silence and stared at the doll.

Judith finally broke the quiet. "There's something else I'd like to show you." She pulled a stack of papers and several books out of the suitcase. "These," she took a deep breath, "were your father's."

Jamie and Alex gasped simultaneously.

"I don't understand." Alex immediately took the pile and spread out the contents across the bed.

Up until this time they'd only had faded memories and a few pictures to remember their father by. In front of her lay a photo album, a scrapbook, some scriptures, a journal, and a Book of Remembrance with four-generation chart. Her father had kept a journal!

Alex felt like she'd just won the lottery.

"This is wonderful! Jamie, can you even believe it?"

By now Jamie was bawling. Puddles formed in the corners of Alex's eyes as well. "I didn't know these things even existed," Alex said.

The girls laughed and cried, then hugged each other and the books. Then they laughed and cried some more.

"I'm sorry . . ." Judith said.

Jamie and Alex fell silent.

Judith spoke again. "I'm sorry for waiting to show you these things." Her gold bracelets jingled as she clasped and unclasped her hands. "I just wasn't able to face the memories," she said. "Until now."

The horrid feeling Alex had had about her mother on the way home from the airport returned. Something was wrong, something had happened. She braced herself, knowing she would have to be strong for Jamie.

"What do you mean *now*, Mom?" Jamie traced her finger over their father's name, inscribed on the corner of the journal.

Judith pursed her lips together then gave a weak smile. "Several weeks ago I went in for a routine mammogram."

Alex held her breath. Her grandmother had died of breast cancer.

"They found a suspicious lump, and I had to go in for a biopsy and—if needed—surgery."

Jamie covered her mouth with her hand.

"Thank goodness it wasn't cancerous," Judith said quickly, "but girls . . ." She lost her composure for a moment, fighting hard to hold the tears, then continued. "It was like running smack straight into a brick wall. I've never thought anything would ever happen to me. My career and my friends and of course, you two. It all seems so permanent, so lasting. Then when this happened I realized . . . I could die." Her voice cracked and the tears freely fell. "The thought of leaving you girls alone . . . Darn!" She took a tissue from her pocket and mopped at her eyes. "I've cried so much lately, you'd think I'd dry up by now."

Alex and Jamie remained motionless, watching their mother struggle. Alex's heart ached for the pain her mother felt.

"And right after that happened I got your call, Alex. It seemed like something or someone was trying to tell me that I needed to make some changes in my life. Especially with relationships. So when the day comes that I do die, you won't forget me."

"Mom, we would never forget you," Alex said, alarmed her mother would even think such a thing.

"I know, honey, but I want us to have some fond memories of each other. And there's something else . . ." She dabbed at her eyes again. "Even though remembering is very painful for me, you need to have these memories of your father."

Judith's tears turned into sobs, and Alex took her mother's trembling frame in her arms. She realized with new appreciation how her mother, as a young woman, had met the challenge of dealing with the death of her husband, worked hard to raise her family, and made something of herself. Alex's love and admiration for her mother grew enormously in that moment.

When the wave of emotion subsided, Alex sat back down on the bed with Jamie, who was being unusually quiet.

"Girls," Judith said, "There's something else I'd like to say."

Alex and Jamie looked at each other, then back at their mother.

"I've always felt like I should apologize to you for the way you had to grow up. I didn't like having to leave you alone while I worked so much. I missed you every moment I was away, and I worried about you constantly. I was afraid you'd grow up hating me because I was never home."

"We were young, Mom, but we understood you did what you had to do," Alex said.

Judith braved a smile. "I see what lovely women you've become, both of you so strong, so intelligent, and I realize I can't take any credit for the people you are. I wasn't the one who shaped you."

Alex bolted to her feet. "That's not true. We're the people we are today because of you and Dad."

Judith shook her head. "No. I'm not sure how it happened, but you girls are more wonderful than I could ever have dreamed possible. I am so proud of both of you, and I know your father is proud of you, too."

Her mother's words felt like salve on an open wound, gentle, caring, healing. Alex knew it was hard to delve into issues from the past, but she also knew, all of their pain came from the same source.

"Sometimes I feel like you were raised by angels because I wasn't around enough. Maybe your father had a hand in that. I don't know. But I did the best I could. I really did."

Judith choked on her last word. She drew in a long breath, then said, "I guess that's what I get for holding things in for twenty years."

She clutched her tissue tightly in her hand and continued. "Since I'm getting things off my chest I might as well get it all off." She looked at Jamie and smiled tentatively. Mascara had streaked down her cheeks and her lipstick was gone.

"I think I should leave you two alone." Alex stood.

"No, Alex, I'd like you to stay." Judith's bottom lip trembled. "Jamie, I know I've needed to say this for a long time. I don't really know why I've waited so long to talk to you about this." Judith fingered the bracelets on her wrist for a moment. "I owe you an apology for the way I've acted since you joined the Church."

The room stayed completely silent. Jamie didn't even look at her mother.

"I know I don't deserve your forgiveness, but I would give anything if you would give me another chance. I've spent so much time harboring hurt feelings and in the process nearly destroying our relationship.

"You have to understand, sweetie, in a way I blamed your father's death on the fact that he joined the Mormon church."

Jamie's eyes shifted to Alex's face, then back to the buttons on the front of her blouse.

"I honestly felt when you joined I would lose you, too." Judith wiped at her nose with the crumpled tissue. "I don't understand what it is about this restrictive religion of yours that is so attractive, but I love you. I see how happy you are and what a wonderful husband you have, and that's enough. All I can ask for my daughters is that you have joy in your lives."

This time, when Jamie finally did look up at her mother, tears trailed down her cheeks.

Alex was so proud of her mother. But she didn't expect what happened next.

"I've been waiting a long time to hear that," Jamie said softly.

"I know," Judith sniffed.

"But I think it's too late." Jamie jumped up from the bed and left the room, slamming the door behind her.

Chapter 29

"I HAVEN'T SEEN THIS MUCH SNOW SINCE I WENT TO SWITZERLAND two years ago." Judith let the curtain fall, walked over to the rocker in their bedroom, and sat down. "Do you think we'll be able to make it back to the airport?"

"Mom, I wish you'd reconsider."

Alex had spent the previous night trying to console her mother and helping her repack her suitcases.

"She doesn't want me here and I don't blame her." Judith's tone was even, unemotional. Alex knew there was great pain behind those words, but it was buried in a mountain of guilt and pity. As usual, Alex was caught in the middle.

"I think she just needs some time," Alex said. "She said herself that she's overemotional when she's pregnant."

Judith's voice was cool. "Then the last thing she needs is to have me here upsetting her."

A soft knock on the door startled them.

"Yes," Alex said, walking to the door. She opened it to find a puffy-eyed, crumpled Jamie in the hallway.

"Is Mom awake?"

Jamie didn't know Judith hadn't slept the entire night.

"Yes."

"Do you think she'd talk to me?"

"Why don't you come in and see?"

Alex stepped aside and let her sister enter. She watched as Judith and Jamie stared at each other, their expressions cautious and uncertain.

Then Jamie looked over at the bed where suitcases lay open, stacks of folded clothing and bags of shoes ready to go inside.

"What are you doing?" Her red-rimmed eyes opened wide in alarm.

"I thought it would be best if I went back home."

"But you can't, you just got here."

Judith looked sadly at her youngest daughter, remaining silent.

"I don't want you to go."

Judith's face softened slightly.

"I spent the whole night thinking and praying." Jamie paced to one side of the room. "I told the Lord how I felt about you turning me away when I joined the Church. And that I was still mad because you never even came to visit me when I lost my first two babies. And that you've never even called to thank me for the birthday gifts I've sent you, or just to see—" she choked back a sob, fought for composure "—if I'm okay."

"I'm so sorry, Jamie." Judith twisted a silk t-shirt into a knot.

"I know you are, Mom. I know you are. And I know why you did what you did. I thought about it all night, putting myself in your place. I tried to understand what you went through with Dad's death and my baptism, and I realized I was being very *un*-Christlike by not being forgiving. It was wrong and selfish of me, and I'm sorry."

"Jamie, you don't have to apologize." Judith put down the wadded shirt and waited.

"More than anything, Mom, I want us to be close again. I've missed having you in my life." Jamie looked at her mother pleadingly.

Tears shone in Judith's eyes. "I've missed you, too, honey."

Hesitantly they approached each other, then with outstretched arms they embraced as years of misunderstanding, pain, and anger, melted steadily with the warmth of their love.

Relief filled Alex at the sight of her mother and sister finally coming back together.

"You will stay, won't you Mom?" Jamie asked.

"If you really want me."

"I couldn't bear to see you leave now."

They hugged again, then Judith started laughing. "I guess that means I get to unpack again."

"We'll help," Jamie said, lifting a sweater from the suitcase. "Won't we Alex? Alex?"

Alex blinked, realizing her sister was talking to her. "I'm sorry, what were you saying?"

"Are you okay, Alex?" Jamie handed her the sweater, which Alex absently slid into a drawer.

"I'm fine. I was just thinking about all those things of Dad's you brought."

"We haven't even looked at them," Jamie cried.

"We can unpack later," Judith said. "Let's go through those instead."

"I want to look at the photo album first," Alex said.

Scrunching together on the bed, they opened the photo album to the first page. There was a large baby picture of their father in a diaper, lying on a satin-edged blanket. A roll of curls ran like a Mohawk down the center of his head, and he revealed two tiny front teeth.

"How cute! Is that really Dad?" Jamie asked.

"That picture won first prize in a baby contest at one of the department stores. Wasn't he adorable? You looked a lot like your father when you were a baby, Alex."

They turned the page.

"Look at him on his bike. And in his scout uniform." They examined picture after picture as their mother explained each setting and told stories about their father's childhood and teen years. Stories they'd never heard before.

The next page revealed a picture of him in graduation robes and cap, with a tassel hanging to the side of his face. "Look how handsome he is," Jamie exclaimed.

"That's how your father looked when I met him. I went to my friend's graduation—she was in his class—and I met him at a dance afterward. I think there's a picture of us that first night together."

They flipped the page and there it was, the picture of their mom and dad on the night they met. Jamie was the spitting image of Judith.

"The first thing that attracted me to your father was his eyes. We bumped into each other at the drinking fountain, and when I turned to say 'excuse me' I looked up into his eyes and melted." Judith's gaze wandered to a remote corner of the room, deep in thought.

Alex loved hearing her mother share memories that had been vaulted away for so many years. Each succeeding picture took the story one step further, their courtship, their engagement, their wedding. And then pictures of the girls started. At times Alex's heart ached seeing pictures of them with their father, hanging upside down from a tree limb, dangling spoons off the ends of their noses, splashing in the waves on the shore at Virginia Beach.

The book was half done when they came to the final picture.

"This is your dad on his baptism day. Those are the elders who taught him. That's Elder Thomas and the other is Elder Beckstead."

"Elder Beckstead!" Alex and Jamie said together.

"Couldn't be." Jamie looked closer.

"I wonder?" Alex examined the picture.

"Do you know Elder Beckstead's first name, Mom?" Jamie asked.

"No. I only saw them once at the house. I was very opposed to your father having anything to do with the Church, so he met with them away from the house."

"Does it even look like him?" Alex asked. She'd never seen Colleen's husband before.

"Kind of, but Donald has a beard and is balding on top. It's hard to tell. I doubt it is though. I mean, what are the chances?"

"What are you girls talking about?" Judith asked with exasperation.

"There's a guy in our branch named Beckstead. But I always thought he was a nonmember," Jamie said. "Maybe Steve knows. Steve!" she hollered.

He didn't reply.

"I guess he didn't hear me. I know he's awake. Help me."

"STEVE!" they all called in unison.

They fell back in laughter when they heard heavy footsteps charge through the house and up the stairs.

He burst into the room. "What?" His eyes were wide, his face flushed. "What's wrong?"

Jamie gave her husband a tender look at his concern. "Nothing. I just need to ask you something."

"You scared me to death."

"Sorry, honey. Donald Beckstead isn't a member of the Church, is he?"

He was still breathing heavily. "Not anymore. Why?" He held his hand on his chest.

"Are you saying he was a member once?"

"Yes. He had some trouble after his mission and got excommunicated and never got back into the Church. I think Colleen almost brought him around, but after they got married he slipped into some of his old ways. Why?"

"Do you know where he went on his mission?" Alex tingled at the thought that Colleen's husband could be the same person who taught her father.

"Canada."

"Oh," Alex said with disappointment.

"No, wait. Now that I think of it, he might have gone to Pennsylvania."

"Philadelphia?" Jamie said.

"Yeah, maybe. Why?"

"You're never going to believe this, but I think he was one of the missionaries who baptized my dad," Jamie said.

* * *

"If it's still snowing this much in the spring, what's winter like? I just wish we could've gone shopping in West Yellowstone." Alex leafed through the photo album for the tenth time, unable to get her fill of seeing so many pictures of her father.

The discordant notes of the piano downstairs from the church meeting rattled up through the wall into their room.

"What in the world are they doing down there?" Judith adjusted the band on her watch and paced across the floor. "Guess I'll try and drown out that singing with the television."

Judith left the room. Alex had barely opened her father's journal open when a knock came at the door. Unfolding her legs, she climbed off the bed and opened it.

"Colleen, come in." Alex stepped back and the woman entered. "You've lost more weight, haven't you?"

"I guess so," Colleen said. Her dress hung about her shoulders and sagged in the chest and the back. The weary lines on her face matched her limp, lifeless hair.

"Things must be pretty rough, huh?"

"You could say that." Sister Beckstead collapsed onto the edge of the bed. "I just didn't feel like sitting in a meeting right now. I hope you don't mind me barging in on you like this."

"You're always welcome. Is Sara downstairs?"

"No, she wasn't feeling well. I left her home with her dad."

"That reminds me." Alex pulled out the photograph book. "We were looking at this photo album of my father's and found a picture of the day he got baptized." Alex flipped the pages. "I know this sounds silly but do you recognize either of these missionaries?"

She handed the book to Colleen then sat down beside her as the woman squinted and studied the picture.

"It's Donald," she whispered.

Thoroughly delighted, Alex bounced on the bed. "We had a hunch it was! Can you believe it? Who'd have thought your husband baptized my father?"

Colleen shook her head slowly, as if it took all her energy to engage her muscles.

Alex realized by Colleen's reaction it might not have been such a good idea to spring this on her so quickly. "I hope you don't mind me showing you this. We wondered if it was Donald or not."

"That was so long ago." She touched the picture. "Look how handsome he was." After another moment she shut the book and handed it back to Alex.

"Did you know him when he was on his mission?" Alex asked her.

"No. After. He wasn't a member of the Church any longer. He'd said he wanted to get back into the Church. Of course I believed him, and I think he believed it himself for a time. I married him thinking he'd eventually get his membership back and we'd go to the temple. Boy was I wrong."

Alex had asked Jamie earlier what it meant to get excommunicated, and she thought she understood a little. "I'm sorry" was all she said.

Colleen rested her hand on top of Alex's knuckles. "I am, too."

"Have you two made any decisions?"

"It's funny, now that I've retained an attorney and am trying to make plans for the future, he won't discuss the matter."

"Maybe he's having second thoughts," Alex offered.

"If he is it's because he doesn't want to leave Sara. He's been very possessive of her lately. Of course she's loving the attention, but she doesn't know it's going to end soon."

Alex didn't know what to say.

"I don't want to keep you." Colleen stood and smoothed her dress. "Thanks for listening, Alex. I'm sure going to miss you when you go back to California."

They said good-bye. After a few minutes Alex stepped into the hallway and tiptoed near the stairway, listening as a prayer was being said below. After the "Amen," she lingered in the shadows straining to hear or even see Rich. At last she saw him talking to a tall, thin-faced man who looked like someone out of a Norman Rockwell painting.

"The snow's supposed to let up tonight," Rich was saying, "and we'll spend the next couple of days grooming trails. When you get some free time, come take one of the new sleds for a run."

"I've been meaning to," the man said. "I get some time off next week."

"I'll be out of town then, but Steve can get you set up with anything you need."

"You heading to Boise?"

Rich nodded. "I guess it's not a secret anymore. I've accepted a new job so I'll be moving back there."

Alex's knees went weak.

"Well, I'll be dipped," the man said. "What about the business here?"

"I'm going to sell out to Steve and he'll hire some help. I won't leave until he's covered."

Alex wondered how Steve had taken the news.

"We'll hate to see you go."

"I can't turn down this offer. Plus, I wouldn't mind having a date now and then, maybe even finding a wife. There's not much to choose from around here."

Alex felt a stab in her chest; his words were like daggers.

"Ain't that the truth." The man slapped Rich on the shoulder. "Good luck to you in Boise."

The men walked to the front door and Rich shook his hand in parting. Alex stepped back into the shadows, but Rich turned too quickly and saw her.

"Good morning, Alex."

"Hi." She eased down the stairway. "How was church?"

"We could have used your piano playing."

She smiled. "Yeah, I heard."

"You'll be relieved to know this will be the last time we have to meet here. The building will be ready next Sunday."

"I haven't minded it."

She avoided his eyes.

"There you are, Alex." Steve walked in from the kitchen. "I guess Rich told you the big news?"

"You mean about his job?"

Steve nodded.

"How do you feel about it?" she asked.

"I'd like to cut his legs off and beat him with them, but I understand why he has to go. Still," Steve arched his eyebrows, "that doesn't make it any easier."

"I wish there was some other way," Rich said.

Alex descended the last four stairs and noticed Jamie over on the couch, crying.

"Jamie, what's wrong?" Alex pushed past the men and hurried over to her sister.

She sniffed into a tissue. "I just feel bad Rich is leaving."

Rich walked over to the couch. "Please don't cry. It's hard enough to leave." He knelt down and circled her with a hug.

Jamie rested her forehead on his shoulder. Rich looked up at Alex, like he was asking for help. He'd dropped this bomb. She wasn't about to help him pick up the pieces of rubble he was leaving behind. But that's exactly what she'd get stuck doing. His leaving not only hurt her, but changed Steve and Jamie's lives drastically. Maybe he had to do what he was doing, but she was mad at him for doing it.

Somehow the week passed. Judith helped Alex a great deal on her cookbook. Between the two of them they added a dozen more recipes and had plans to test many more. But Alex's main focus was on the book's foreword where she put into words the darkest times of her life—her struggles with anorexia. Neither her mother nor her sister knew she was adding this; she wasn't quite ready to tell them. All she knew was that she had to do something. No one needed to go through the pain and agony she'd gone through because she'd pinned her worth on the numbers on a scale.

"Sweetie." Judith looked up from the computer where she was

entering recipes. "I've been meaning to talk to you."

"About what, Mom?"

"Well," Judith got up from the chair and came around to Alex's side of the desk, "I guess I spent all of my time patching up things with Jamie and didn't get around to you."

"Around to me? What for? We don't have anything to talk out."

Resting against the edge of the desk, Judith looked her daughter straight in the eye and said, "I think we do, and it has a lot to do with this cookbook and the part your working on."

"What do you mean?"

"I was entering all the soup recipes and came across the foreword you'd written."

"Mom, we don't need to get into a heavy discussion."

"But there are some things I need to say to you. Things I've wanted to say for a long time."

Alex set her notebook down. Inside, she dreaded what was coming. She wasn't in the mood for this conversation.

Judith took a deep breath. "Because you were the oldest, you had much more responsibility than a child your age should have had after your father died. I expected you to babysit, clean, cook, and take care of everything while I worked. That wasn't fair."

Alex looked down at her lap. "I just did what had to be done."

"I never could have done it without you. I leaned on you a lot back then, still do, in some ways. And I know I was hard on you, honey."

Alex wanted to assure her mother that she hadn't, but the fact was, it was true.

"Part of the way I acted was because I had no control over what happened to your father, and I wanted to try my best to keep you girls and your lives in my control. I didn't want anything to happen to you."

Alex knew that was impossible, but she understood why her mother tried.

"I'm sorry I wasn't more understanding when you were younger and struggling with your weight. I know I didn't help you by pointing it out so often."

"I worried that you would only love me if I were thin."

Judith closed her eyes, and her chin dropped forward. "What would make you think such a thing?"

Alex had always wanted to tell her mother how she felt, but had never wanted to cause problems. "The only time I ever got any attention was when I started losing weight. I didn't mean to equate thinness with love, but it seemed to be the only positive reinforcement I ever got," she said. In her head she knew it wasn't logical that her mother would not love her if she weren't thin, but deep down inside it seemed true.

Judith looked at her daughter tearfully. "I can't imagine what you've struggled with all these years."

"It's been hard, but I'm doing better. And I'm more than happy to put all of this in the past."

"How are you doing now, honey? I don't see you eat hardly anything."

"I'm doing fine. I struggle at times, but I've come a long way since high school."

"I'm so proud of you."

"Thanks, Mom, that means a lot to me."

With renewed spirits they hugged. Alex breathed a sigh of relief, grateful the topic had been put to rest.

* * *

Over the next few days the house was a flurry of activity. Judith had enough energy to power the city of Chicago. She put finishing touches on the nursery and cleaned out all the closets in Jamie's house. She even spent time on Steve's computer, finishing her latest project for the magazine and staying in contact with her New York office by fax machine.

On the first clear afternoon Alex and her mother finally ran to West Yellowstone while Jamie worked on Primary materials.

Alex searched everywhere for a present for Rich and had nearly given up when she found the perfect gift—a camera. It had so many gadgets and features it practically took the pictures by itself. It was much more than she had planned on spending but she wanted to give him a going-away gift, or wedding gift—something—to wish him well. And maybe even something to remind him of her.

Judith's purchases filled the trunk and back seat. She bought something for everyone back in her office and in the family. Alex could barely see over the packages in the rearview mirror as they drove back to Island Park.

Every evening, after Jamie went to bed, Alex and her mother did their best to help Jamie by finishing some of her painting projects. As was her tradition for Christmas, the Fourth of July, and Easter, Jamie made little gifts for friends and neighbors. Knowing that it was Jamie's love for crafts and painting that had helped her to survive all the challenges she'd had, Alex didn't feel she could tell her sister to bag the darn Easter gifts. With Jamie in no condition to complete all the crafts she'd started, Alex and Judith decided to surprise Jamie and finish the projects for her. Even though they were fully aware that their skills were no match for Jamie's, they continued to work, hoping their efforts would be good enough. They finished the decorations just in time.

Early one morning Alex overheard Jamie and Steve in the bedroom talking about her unfinished projects. Jamie was obviously upset and Steve tried his best to console her, without much luck. No man alive was a fair match for the hormones of a pregnant woman.

"Excuse me," Alex interrupted as she entered the room. "I couldn't help overhearing. I thought I'd show you this." She held up a bunny, with a string of brightly painted Easter eggs between his paws.

Jamie began crying at the sight of the decoration, a painful reminder that she hadn't been able to finish the gifts. Steve hugged her, raising his eyes heavenward as if to plead for patience and help.

"Mom and I finished them for you."

"You what?" Jamie stopped crying and stared at Alex wide-eyed, her mouth hanging open. She looked at the craft, then at her sister, then at the smiling, toothy rabbit again. "I didn't paint that?"

"No," Alex said, "Don't look too closely though; it's not as good as the one you made, but Mother and I were able to copy it." Alex glanced down at the bunny. "Well, we *tried* to copy it."

"It looks wonderful." Jamie scooted off the bed. Her growing stomach made the hug awkward, especially with one of Alex's hands full, but the girls hugged and Jamie wiped at her tears. "I can't believe you'd do that for me."

Alex smiled, enjoying the warmth spreading over her.

"I don't know how to thank you." Jamie mopped her wet cheeks again.

"You think they're good enough to give away? We weren't real handy with that hot glue gun at first." Alex held up two bandaged fingers to prove it.

With Alex and Judith's help, Steve loaded the decorations and brightly frosted sugar cookies baked that morning into his Blazer to deliver.

Staying busy had helped Alex keep Rich out of her mind for most of the week. Then his name came up at the dinner table.

"Is Rich going to be at church tomorrow?" Jamie asked Steve.

"He's planning on leaving right after church."

This was the first Alex had heard of his definite plans.

"He's sure had a busy week," Jamie said, glancing over at Alex, who quickly looked down at the napkin on her lap.

"I think he's trying to get everything organized before he leaves. Between his work grooming the trails and all the tour groups we've had . . ." Steve stopped and swallowed hard, ". . . I don't know what I'm going to do without him."

"I don't understand," Judith said. "What's this boy's problem anyway? Why in the world does he want to move to Boise?"

"Island Park doesn't have much of a single life, especially for a Mormon bachelor." Steve paused. "And he does have a girlfriend in Boise. I don't think a day's gone by in the last few weeks that she hasn't called. Maybe he's lonely for her. I don't know. But I'm sure she has something to do with it, and the fact that her father offered him a pretty cushy job with an outlandish salary."

"I'm sorry he's leaving, I can see how much you all care for him." Judith's gaze rested upon Alex, who pushed her untouched plate of food away.

"It will be hard to replace him," Steve said.

"No one can ever take Rich's place," Jamie said. "No one."

* * *

Sunday morning Alex and Judith were planning a combined birthday and Easter eve dinner for the next Saturday. Jamie rested upstairs and Steve had gone to the church house for their first big Sunday back in the newly repaired building. The doorbell rang.

"I'll get it." Alex jotted one more item down on the shopping list then walked to the entry.

She swung open the oak door to find Rich standing in front of her, holding a large present in his hands.

"I came to tell you good-bye."

Chapter 30

ALEX'S HEART COLLAPSED. SHE FORCED A SMILE. "I HEARD YOU were leaving today. Come on in." She stepped aside and let him pass.

They entered the living room and sat next to each other on the couch.

"You must be anxious to get home." She leaned forward and straightened the magazines on the coffee table.

"Yeah, I guess so. My brother and his wife are coming in from Chicago. He's going to school there. She's expecting a baby the same time as Jamie."

"That's nice." She still hadn't looked him in the eye. She couldn't. She knew what would happen if she did.

"I haven't seen them for a year and a half."

"That's a long time."

"My mother said Dad's even coming over to be with the family."

She glanced up briefly. "I hope it goes well," she said sincerely.

"Me, too." He slid the package her way. "I brought you a little something."

"Thanks. I have something for you, too." She stepped over to the piano where she'd left his present.

"You didn't have to get me anything." He walked toward her. They met in front of the crackling fireplace.

"I wanted to thank you for all the fun we've had these last couple of weeks and for your friendship. I don't think you'll ever know how much it helped to be able to talk to you." She thrust the package toward him.

"I'll only be a phone call away."

But it would never be the same again.

"Do you want to open the gifts now?"

"You can open yours, but if you don't mind, I think I'd like to wait." Alex didn't trust her emotions for only a half minute longer. It didn't help to have him standing so close.

"Alex?" He placed the box on the mantel then reached toward her. She stepped back, trying to focus her eyes on the buttons of his shirt. Softly, he lifted her chin with his finger until their eyes met.

"I wish I knew what you were thinking."

Her throat constricted. She was glad he didn't know what she was thinking.

He let his hand drop to her shoulder and rest for a moment before turning toward the fireplace. "I'm going to miss you."

She couldn't stop the trembling of her bottom lip.

"I'm going to miss you, too," she whispered.

In one motion he turned and crushed her to his chest. Part of her wanted to vent her anger and pound the life out of him, and the other didn't want to ever let go.

"I wish things were different."

She wanted to tell him she did, too, but she couldn't get herself to say it out loud.

With gentle strokes he smoothed her hair until the intensity of the moment passed. When they parted Alex forced the bravest smile she could muster onto her face.

"Listen," she found the strength to say. "You're doing what's right. Everything will work out for you in Boise, you'll see." Some people would've called what she just said "faith"; she'd call it a lie.

His grin was uneven. "Thanks. I hope you're right."

"Your new job will keep you busy, but I hope you find time to keep painting. You have such a wonderful gift. Promise me you won't stop."

He nodded. "I promise."

She looked him square in the eye. It hurt like the devil but she knew she'd survive. She was getting pretty good at bouncing back. Maybe that would be her next video, *Bouncing Back with Alex McCarty: The Aerobic Way to Get Over a Broken Heart.*

"I better get going while the sun's still shining," he said.

"Looks like you'll have clear weather all the way."

"I hope so."

She swallowed but knew nothing short of a good cry would remove the lump in her throat. "Bye, Rich."

"Good-bye, Alex."

Have a good life.

Alex hadn't exaggerated when she told the rest of the family she needed to go to her room because of a headache. It was true, but the splitting pain in her head was nothing compared to the tearing ache she felt in her heart.

The gift he'd given her sat on the rocking chair across from the bed. No matter what she did or where she looked, her eyes kept coming back to that box covered with red and white striped paper and a simple white ribbon.

She couldn't stand it any longer.

In a flash she whisked up the present and snatched the card. Neatly written on the outside of the envelope was her name. Alex.

She studied Rich's handwriting. The small, even letters slanted to the right and were neatly formed, not quite cursive, not quite printed. She tore open the envelope and pulled out a standard thank-you card. Inside he'd written:

Dear Alex,

> *I couldn't leave without giving you these gifts. I have something else to give you, but I want it to wait until I'm gone. I also want to wish you a happy Easter and pray that you will always have great joy in your life and receive all the blessings you deserve. These last few weeks have been some of the happiest I've known. Thank you for spending time with me.*

> > *Love,*
> > *Rich*

Alex tossed the card onto the bed, then stopped. Love. He'd said, "Love." She read it again. What did he mean when he said that? Did he love her like a sister? A friend? Was it just a formal way of closing his note? When he said "love," did he mean—love? Alex shrugged helplessly. At this point, did it matter?

Without delay she unwrapped two books and a CD. The latter was the same instrumental hymns CD Rich had played in his car when they were driving. The first book was covered with a floral fabric and had her name inscribed on the front, but when she opened it there were only blank lined pages. Then she realized—it was a journal.

How thoughtful. She'd already toyed with the idea of keeping a journal but honestly didn't think her thoughts would be of interest to anyone else. Having a journal sitting there in her hands, with her name on it, made her think otherwise. Maybe she'd give it a try.

The next book was the Book of Mormon. Disappointment filled her. She wasn't sure what she'd been expecting but this certainly wasn't it. Inside the front cover Rich had written,

> *Now don't get mad. I know how you feel about us Mormons, but when I tried to decide what to give you, I knew the best and only gift would be to share with you the most important thing in my life. The gospel. I want you to know that I believe this church is the true church of Jesus Christ because I received a witness, as strong and as sure as the book these words are written in. And if you'd like to have a knowledge of this for yourself, all you have to do is read this great book, then ask the Lord. You can know for yourself that it is true. And once you have this knowledge of the true gospel of Jesus Christ, you can handle everything else this crazy world has to offer.*
>
> *There is a promise in Moroni 10:3-5. Please, for me, read it. And then, for yourself, put it to the test. The Lord will not let you down. I know he loves you. I love you, too. Rich*

She threw the book onto the bed as hot, stinging tears scalded her eyes. It was one thing to say, "love," but the "I love you" completely uncorked her. Why was he saying that to her? Especially when he was in Boise with Monica.

Darn him!

A commotion of voices in the entry caught her attention. Dr. Rawlins had just come in.

Leaving the gifts on her bed, Alex decided to join the group downstairs.

"Let me take your coat and hat," Steve was saying downstairs. "Jamie's on the couch."

"Thank you, Steve." Alex recognized the voice of Jamie's doctor. Alex forced a smile onto her face as she walked into the living room.

"Good evening, Dr. Rawlins," she said.

"How are you, Alex?"

"Fine, thank you." As Alex sat next to her mother on the loveseat, Judith patted her daughter's knee. Her mother seemed to have an unspoken understanding of how Alex was feeling. Her extra hugs and added warmth gave Alex strength and encouragement.

"Doctor," Jamie said, "I'd like you to meet my mother, Judith McCarty."

Judith stood and shook the doctor's hand and they exchanged greetings.

"It's a pleasure to meet you, Dr. Rawlins. Could I get you something warm to drink?" That was Judith, Alex smiled, the consummate host and diplomat.

"No, thank you." He looked at Judith a moment, who smiled. "Well, then again, maybe I will. If you're having something, that is," he added.

"I've got a pot of peppermint tea steeping. I'll be right back," she said pleasantly.

Alex and Jamie exchanged raised eyebrows and smiled at each other. For years they'd wanted their mother to find a nice man her age to share her life with.

"So, how are mother and baby doing this evening?" The doctor sat on the chair Steve had moved near Jamie.

"I feel great. I really think I could be getting up and around a little more now, don't you?"

He checked her pulse and didn't respond for a moment. "I'm certainly glad you're feeling well, but I doubt it would last if you engaged in a lot of activity. I'd like you to continue resting as much of the day as you can."

"What about the dinner next Saturday? It's my mother's birthday. Couldn't I have just one day off? It wouldn't be a huge affair. Just Sara and Colleen Beckstead, you, and a few others."

"I don't know . . ." he said slowly.

"Besides," Jamie looked at him, her eyes wide and imploring, "you're going to be there. What could happen?"

"Oh, all right. As long as you're not standing and cooking all day."

Jamie clapped her hands. "Thank you. That's wonderful news."

"Just don't overdo." He shook his finger at her. "Now, anything else to report? Any bleeding, contractions, unusual aches, and pains?"

"Nothing. I feel super."

"Glad to hear it. We'll wait until our next checkup and examine you again."

"I haven't seen a doctor make a house call in thirty years." Judith entered the room carrying a cloth-covered silver tray with a teapot and cups.

Dr. Rawlins put the equipment back in his bag. "Jamie's a little more special than my other patients, plus she's the only one who lives here in Island Park. The rest come to see me in Idaho Falls the two days I drive to the office."

"You live here in Island Park?"

"Just outside of town."

Judith set the tray down on the coffee table. "Excuse me for a moment. I forgot the banana nut bread. It's fresh from the oven."

"I can't remember the last time I had banana nut bread," Dr. Rawlins said. "Would you mind if I wash my hands?" He smiled warmly at his hostess.

Judith led him to the kitchen, asking him about his background and marital status. Alex and Jamie held their giggles until the two left the room.

"Is it my imagination or was Mom flirting just a little?" Jamie asked.

"I'd say Dr. Rawlins was doing his share, too," Alex smirked.

"Did I miss something?" Steve looked toward the kitchen then back at them. The girls laughed again.

Jamie pushed him with her foot. "It's just nice seeing Mom with a man her own age," she said with a wink.

Before Steve could answer there was a knock at the door. To everyone's surprise Colleen and Sara had come to visit. But they weren't alone. Colleen's husband was with them.

Chapter 31

"I HOPE IT'S NOT TOO LATE TO COME BY," COLLEEN SAID.

At Steve's invitation the Beckstead family filed into the living room. Alex jumped to her feet and caught Sara in a big hug. "I missed seeing you Sunday. Are you feeling better?"

"Oh, yes, lots."

"Alex, Jamie," Colleen said, "I'd like you to meet my husband, Donald. Donald, this is Alex McCarty and Jamie Dixon. You met Jamie's husband at the door."

"Nice to meet you." The bearded man reached and shook Alex's hand, then stepped over and shook Jamie's. Alex had pictured him being rough and wild looking, but his beard was neatly trimmed and his hair carefully combed. Even his plaid shirt and jeans were pressed and tidy. It was hard not to be drawn to his rosy cheeks and the creases around his eyes that made him look like he was smiling even though his mouth wasn't.

Judith and Dr. Rawlins came into the room carrying refreshments. The introductions were made once again.

"Please, sit down." Steve helped locate a place for everyone. Sara sat on Alex's lap.

"It's been quite a while since we last met, hasn't it?" Judith said to Donald.

"Almost twenty years."

Alex was surprised to see him reach for his wife's hand.

"I'm sorry to hear about your husband's passing," he said. "He was a wonderful man. I'd never met anyone like him before."

Alex looked at the two people, nearly strangers, who shared a common bond.

"He thought a lot of you and your companion," Judith spoke quietly. "He talked about you after you left our town."

"My daddy was a missionary," Sara said proudly. "Did he really baptize your daddy?"

"Yes, Sara," Alex said. "He did. Isn't that something?"

"Mommy said you have a picture. Can I see it?"

"Sure you can. Why don't you come help me get it?" Alex and Sara held hands as they walked out of the room and up the stairs. Alex hoped she could find out from Sara what was going on between her mom and dad.

When they got into Alex's room, she said, "I'm sure glad your father came to visit us tonight."

"Do you miss your daddy?" Sara asked.

"Very much."

"I hope my daddy never has to go live in heaven. We aren't a forever family yet."

"A forever family?" Alex looked into Sara's clear eyes, full of innocence, and sensed the conviction of her words.

"If we don't go to the temple we can't be together forever. I asked my daddy today if he would take our family to the temple so I don't lose him when we get to heaven."

"What did he say?"

"He didn't say anything. But he held me on his lap for a long time and we listened to pretty music. And do you know what?" Sara motioned with her finger for Alex to come close. "I think he cried because I felt little drops on top of my head. My mommy said that even dads cry."

"Yes, I'm sure they do." How a father could leave an angel like Sara and a devoted wife like Colleen, Alex would never know. "Let's take the book downstairs, okay?"

Sara carried the album to her parents. Alex helped them find the picture.

"Look at that," Donald said. "I had hair."

"Now you have hair on your chin, instead of your head, Daddy." Sara's comment brought a round of laughter from the group.

"Sure is a small world, isn't it?" Donald looked at Judith.

"Yes, it is. You know," Judith said thoughtfully, "that was the happiest and saddest day of my husband's life. Joining the church and getting baptized was very important to him, but he knew I was dead set against it."

"Our mission president almost didn't allow it to happen," Donald said. "He was concerned about the impact it would have on your family. But I'd never seen anyone more prepared to accept the gospel than your husband was. Each time we taught him the lessons it was as if something inside of him lit up. He told us he felt he was hearing things he already knew, things that were familiar to him." Donald looked at Judith, his face shadowed with empathy. "He struggled a great deal with the fact that you didn't want him to get baptized."

"Well, it's over now," Judith said, almost cutting off Donald's last word. "How would you all like some banana nut bread and herb tea?"

Dr. Rawlins stood and said, "I think I'd better get going. I've got to get up early and drive to the clinic in the morning"

"I'll walk you to the door," Judith said.

Just before he turned to leave, he pointed to Jamie and said, "You—rest. And you—" he pointed to Alex, "—eat."

Alex and Jamie nodded their heads and laughed. Alex wished everyone would just let the issue drop. She was fine and there really was no reason for them to worry about her.

"Mommy said you were having a party next week." Sara looked up at Jamie.

"That's right. We want you to bring your mommy and your daddy and come," Jamie said.

"Can we, Daddy? Can we?"

Alex held her breath, hoping he didn't feel pressured.

"Of course, Sara. We wouldn't miss it." He looked over his shoulder toward the front door, then back at Alex. "I hope I didn't upset your mother by talking about your father like that."

"Actually," Jamie said, "each new thing she learns about him seems to help take away some of the pain."

Alex tried to reassure him with a smile.

"I think we'd better get going," Colleen said as Sara's face became one wide yawn. "We were out for a drive and decided to stop and say hi."

Donald helped Colleen to her feet. He rested his hand at the small of her back while they said their good-byes.

The men talked basketball as they made their way to the door.

Colleen turned to Judith and said, "I appreciate you talking to us about your husband. Baptizing him was the highlight of Donald's mission. He said he never forgot Brother McCarty and was quite upset when I told him about your husband's death. In fact, he hasn't been the same since I told him the news."

As soon as the family was bundled up and gone, Jamie and Alex both erupted.

"Can you believe that?" Jamie said.

"What's going on?" Alex asked.

"You'd think those two were newlyweds. He couldn't leave her alone." Jamie sat up and swung her legs to the floor.

"He wasn't at all like I pictured him to be." Alex gathered cups and napkins.

"All I can say is *that* isn't the same Donald Beckstead I ran into down at the service station a month ago," Steve said. "He wouldn't say more than two words to me then."

"People can change," Jamie said, "especially when someone's prayed and fasted as hard as she has."

Judith looked away. She picked up the tea tray and left the room. *People do change*, Alex agreed. *Sometimes even when they don't want to.*

* * *

That night, holed up in the study, Alex sat cross-legged in Steve's leather office chair, with her father's journal open in her lap. She'd also brought the books and CD Rich had given her. They all seemed to go together, spiritual materials from the men in her past.

With anticipation and a little dread, Alex turned the first page and read the beginning entry in her father's journal.

April 30, 1978 - I am so filled with the Spirit I can barely write, but I cannot let this day pass without recording the most wonderful experience of my life. The only thing that compares to the joy I feel right now would be the birth of my beautiful daughters, Alexis Marie and Jamie Christine. How I would love to share this moment with them. If I could give them but one thing in this life it would be to give them the gospel of Jesus Christ.

Alex's heart seemed to expand. How similar his words were to Rich's.

I had no idea that one conversation with a friend at work would lead me to this day, but it has changed my life forever. Nothing is the same anymore.

My friend Ed, in the next office, is a Mormon. I've always admired his integrity and courage. He puts up with a lot of teasing from co-workers here at National Insurance. But to know Ed is to know what peace and true happiness really is. Nothing is more important to him than his church and his family. And now, today, I can honestly say I feel the same way.

A few months ago I casually asked Ed what made his religion different from all the others. He opened his desk drawer and brought out a book called The Book of Mormon. "This," he said. "You'll learn more about the Savior and his divine mission by reading this than from any other book." He then handed me the book and told me to read some scriptures in Moroni, chapter ten, verses three through five.

I let the book sit in my briefcase for several days. Then one night, after my family had gone to bed I opened it and read the reference. I was so overcome with feelings of peace and love that I was brought to tears. And I knew I had to find out more.

Ed introduced me to the missionaries, two humble, young men who had devoted two years of their lives to sharing the gospel. I met with them in Ed's home and there I was taught the truth. Each time I met with them I felt that same sweet feeling that they explained to me was the

Spirit of the Holy Ghost witnessing to me the truth of what they were saying. And, as if I'd heard their teachings long ago, I learned of this gospel, this restored gospel of Jesus Christ and knew without a doubt that it indeed was true and that no matter what the sacrifice, I had to become a member.

Alex shut the book. She was touched by her father's testimony. He had no reason to lie. These were his private thoughts and his most sincere feelings. How she longed to see him again, hear him speak to her, feel his arms around her.

She read further in the journal about the challenge he had going against his wife's wishes and that no other pain on earth could hurt as badly as knowing that she had no desire to share in his joy.

Somehow, someday, I continually pray that I will be able to touch Judith's life and help her see that the gospel gives us freedom and purpose. Not just joy for this life, but for eternity. I also pray that I might be able to share this with my sweet daughters. That would be my one wish in life, for them to have the same happiness the gospel brings to my life. And to share this together, forever, would be heaven.

Forever. A forever family. Her father had wanted it, too, just like Sara.

Jamie and Steve had tried to tell her, Rich had tried to tell her, and now her father was trying to tell her. She could know for herself one way or the other if their church was true. If what she was feeling was indeed the Lord's spirit, then maybe the Lord himself was trying to reach her.

A hymnbook, lying among the papers, magazines, and other books on top of Steve's desk, caught her eye. She thought of the song Rich told her about, "Where Can I Turn for Peace?" The tune that played occasionally in the back of her mind, the one she caught herself humming at quiet times of the day.

Looking through the index, she located the title and corresponding hymn number, then thumbed through the book until she found the song. Settling back into the chair she read each word of the three verses, slowly, carefully.

The song told her that there was no other source to find peace except through the Savior, her friend. Then she read the last line of the last verse again. "Constant he is and kind, Love without end."

Love without end. What a beautiful thought.

Power, comfort, and hope—this quiet hymn provided this and more. She had to admit, everything about the Mormon church seemed to be geared toward learning about Jesus Christ. *He must seem so real to them.* Perhaps there was more to Christ than just Christmas and Easter.

Letting her body follow her heart, she slipped from the chair on to her knees, clasped her hands and took a deep breath.

It was time to know.

Chapter 32

"FATHER IN HEAVEN," SHE SAID, "I APOLOGIZE THAT I DON'T REALLY know what I'm doing or the correct way to pray. I'm sure I'll get my Thee's and Thou's mixed up, but there's something I need to ask You—I mean, Thee.

"Is this church, this Mormon church, really true? And I don't just mean, a nice religion with good people, I mean *true*. It seems like this is all I'm hearing about lately. From the living and from the dead.

"Why does it matter so much to be a member of the 'true church'? I'm a good person, I follow the commandments, and the golden rule. What is such a big deal about belonging to this church?

"And another thing, while I'm down here, what was the point of bringing Rich into my life? Was it just to get another person to talk to me about the Church or something? Could Thou, or Thee, help me to be happy for him? I miss him and I even think I love him, but he's going to marry Monica.

"Either way, whatever Rich does, I need to find out for myself, once and for all, about the Mormon church. Everyone tells me if I ask, You'll answer." She paused for a moment. "Well, I'm asking."

Following the way Steve and Jamie closed their prayers, she added, "In the name of Jesus Christ, Amen."

She sat for a moment on her heels and listened as the clock above her ticked a steady rhythm. Nothing. Wasn't something supposed to happen?

Finally, she stood up and sat back down in the chair. Her gaze rested on the Book of Mormon. Maybe she'd start with reading the promise in Moroni. She flipped through the pages until she found it at the very end.

Beginning at verse three she read until she came to the part that said, *". . . and if ye shall ask with a sincere heart, with real intent, having faith in Christ, he will manifest the truth of it unto you, by the power of the Holy Ghost. And by the power of the Holy Ghost ye may know the truth of all things."*

She'd be willing to settle for just knowing the truth of a few things.

"Well, here goes nothin'." With a flutter of pages she turned to the front of the book and started reading.

* * *

"Alex, what are you doing in here? I've been looking all over for you." It took a moment for Alex to recognize Jamie's voice and blurry face. "Jamie?"

"Did you sleep in this chair all night?"

Alex nodded.

"You look awful. Why didn't you go to bed?"

Once the fog in Alex's mind started to clear, she realized she had stayed up almost the entire night. It hadn't been a dream—the feelings she felt, the experience she'd had, really happened.

"Oh, Jamie." Alex shook the sleep from her head, sat up, and looked clearly at her sister. She rested her fingertips on her trembling lips, her eyes filled with tears. "It happened. You said it would and it did. I know it's true."

"What's true? What are you talking about?"

"This book, your church, Joseph Smith. It's all true, what you've been trying to tell me." Stiff from sleeping in the chair, Alex pushed herself up onto her feet and practically collapsed into Jamie's arms.

"I don't understand." Jamie held her sister's arms tightly and pushed her away in order to see her face more clearly. "Are you saying what I think you're saying?"

"Yes. I stayed up all night reading this book." She held up the Book of Mormon. "And Jamie, it happened. Somewhere between Omni and the Words of Mormon, when I was starting to doze, something happened inside of me." She placed her hand on her chest. "And the feeling grew and grew until I thought I would burst. And everything I was reading became as visual to me as if it were a movie being played on a huge movie screen. For a moment, I thought I could hear Dad's voice telling me it was true, and then . . . ," she gulped, "this warm, powerful feeling came over me, and I felt Jesus' love, or the Holy Ghost, I'm not sure who's who yet. But this gentle kind of peace—I don't know how to explain it—washed over me, starting at my head then trickling down the rest of my body. I couldn't hear or see anything, but I knew, almost as if the feeling could talk to my mind, that I had just received my answer, that the Book of Mormon is true. And if it's true, then that means Joseph Smith really did see Heavenly Father and Jesus Christ, doesn't it?"

Jamie nodded.

"And if he saw them, then it must mean that he really did restore the true church upon the earth." She looked at Jamie's tear-filled eyes. "Right?"

Jamie nodded again.

"Say something, will you?"

"I just can't believe you're telling me this." Jamie could barely speak through her emotions. "I'm so happy."

Tears streamed down both their faces as Jamie pulled her sister into a hug, both of them switching from tears to laughter, and back to tears again.

"Happy about what?" Alex and Jamie turned to find their mother standing in the doorway.

* * *

Judith continued to cry as they helped her downstairs to the couch where Steve was reading the morning paper.

"What happened?" He jumped to his feet and helped guide her to a cushion. "Jamie, what's wrong with your mom?"

"Alex told me some wonderful news this morning. But for Mother, it's not quite so wonderful."

Steve looked at Alex. "I don't get it. How could good news upset your mother so much?"

"The news is about your church." Alex sat on the arm of the couch near her mother. She felt like a first-class heel. For years she'd been upset with Jamie for hurting their mom by joining the Church.

Now she finally understood what courage it had taken Jamie to go ahead, even though her mother had so strongly disapproved.

"First of all I can't believe I'm even saying this, but after what happened last night, I know I can't deny it. Just like Joseph Smith, he couldn't deny what he saw." She looked straight at Steve and said, "I believe the Book of Mormon is true."

In one leap Steve had Alex on her feet and in his arms. "This is wonderful. I can't believe it!" He danced her around in a circle and said, "This is wonderful," about six more times. Then he stopped and looked at Judith. Her tears had dried but her face was long, her chin heavy, her eyes drooping and red.

"I think I understand now." He dropped on one knee in front of Judith. "Judith, I don't know what to say."

Judith finally looked up at Alex. Mother and daughter didn't speak.

"Mom," Alex said. "I didn't have any intention of this happening. Believe me, no one tried harder than me not to let it happen. But it did. The feeling I had last night still warms my whole soul. I was touched by something heavenly, something wonderful, something greater than I am. I feel more joy and more peace than I have ever felt in my life. Please, Mom, don't be sad. Be happy for me."

Judith lifted the corners of her mouth in a worried smile that didn't quite reach her eyes. Still, she reached out her arms to her daughter, and Alex took her hands, pulling her mother into a hug.

"I'm sorry if this hurts you," Alex said.

"At least, your father would be happy." She sighed. "I just never thought you'd—" She choked back a cry behind a crumpled tissue. "Excuse me," she said, standing up. They watched silently as Judith left the room.

"Now what do I do?"

"She needs some time. You need to do what is right for you, what feels right in your heart."

Did it feel right in her heart? Yes, it did. But did she have to choose between the Church and her mother?

"Would you like to learn more about the Church and the other principles of the gospel?" Steve asked.

"Yes." Alex didn't want to do anything else but learn about this person Jesus Christ who had changed her life. If only it didn't hurt her mother so badly.

"Then you'll want to visit with the missionaries. They will teach you and answer any questions you might have."

"Can't you do that?"

"Sure, but this is their special calling. And Jamie and I will be right there with you."

"You will?"

Jamie took her hand. "You'd better believe it."

"I feel so bad for Mom." Tears filled Alex's eyes.

"I know," Jamie said, "Me too."

* * *

During the next three days Alex met with the missionaries three times. She finished the Book of Mormon, cried all the way through the video "The First Vision," and asked hundreds of questions. She wanted to know about the temple, the prophet, about tithing, missions, and church callings; she even wanted to include the Word of Wisdom in her cookbook. Everything it contained she endorsed wholeheartedly.

"There's one more thing I'd like to suggest you do, aside from your scripture reading," Elder Babcock said. He was half the size of his Tongan companion, Elder Tinefa, but he knew everything in the scriptures from Genesis to Abraham and Alex admired his knowledge. "It would be a good idea to keep a journal, record your thoughts and feelings especially your spiritual experiences. That way, when you have doubts or wonder about the decision you've made, you'll be able to go back and read the accounts that brought you to the gospel."

Jamie nodded and gave her hand a squeeze.

Alex thought of the journal Rich had given her. "Thank you, Elder Babcock. I think that's a great idea."

That night after writing in her journal, while Alex was saying her prayers, she had to stop and pause. Rich's face seemed to materialize in her mind and distract her thoughts so much she couldn't continue.

"Heavenly Father," she prayed silently, "I've tried to keep my mind off Rich, and it hasn't been very easy. It helps having him gone. I think I'm to the point where I can actually express my gratitude for having him in my life for such a short time. I'd like to ask Thee to please bless him, too. He's a good man and he deserves to be happy. He helped me have the courage to seek after the truth, even if he is marrying what's-her-name. Okay, I really do know her name, Monica. Bless them to be happy. But please help me find another man just like him."

Chapter 33

SPICY, SWEET SMELLS DANCED IN THE AIR WITH CHEERFUL NOTES from an old Johnny Mathis album playing on the stereo as Alex dusted the living room and watered the tulips from Rich. The party was tonight.

Every inch of counter space was occupied with baked goods and treats, and a turkey and a ham roasted in the oven. The aroma of freshly baked pies swirled around Alex's nose until she thought she'd be lifted off her feet.

"When do we eat? I'm starved!" Steve shut the door behind him with a bang. He hung his coat and hat on hooks, then kicked his boots onto a mat.

"Mmm." He sniffed the air, eyed the pies, then walked up behind Jamie to give her and the unborn baby a hug. "You know, you have enough food here to feed the entire western hemisphere." He stuck a finger into the cream she was whipping and licked it clean.

"You can have the beaters when I'm finished," Jamie promised.

"When's everyone supposed to get here for dinner?" He snitched one last taste and received a smack on his hand.

"We're eating early, around five. Why don't you go see if there's a ball game on or something."

"I'll bring you a mug of tea," Alex said as he left the room, hanging his head in defeat.

"He's been so bored lately with Rich gone," Jamie said. "I'm going to have to find him another playmate."

"I'll take him some of these chocolate chip cookies. That'll cheer him up." Alex filled a mug and took a plateful of cookies into her brother-in-law.

"Ooooh, thank you." Gingerly Steve sipped the tea then set it on a coaster and took one of the cookies.

Alex rested on the arm of the couch and looked at the TV. "What'cha watchin'?" she asked.

"Not much on right now. Oh, I forgot, there was a letter for you in the mail." He reached into his shirt pocket and pulled out an envelope.

For a second Alex wondered if Rich had written, but she didn't recognize the handwriting.

She tore it open and found a folded note and two pictures. It was from Laurel, the girl at the airport. Clicking on the lamp next to her, Alex read the testimonial and high praises that Laurel wrote. She thought that parts of the letter would be a nice addition to the cookbook. She wondered about soliciting some more quotes from other fans. She decided to talk to Sandy about it.

Next she picked up the pictures. And gasped. Bringing the picture within inches of her face, she stared closely at the woman standing next to Laurel. That person in the picture couldn't be her.

Every morning Alex looked in the mirror. She knew what she looked like. At least she thought she did. There was no way that person in the picture was her.

How? Where? When had this happened?

She looked at the picture again. Her cheekbones jutted sharply above hollow cheeks. Her eyes looked like two dark sinkholes in her head.

I don't look like that. The light must have been bad.

She got up and went into the bathroom and shut the door.

Studying her reflection in the mirror she compared what she saw to the face in the picture. She decided she didn't look as awful as the person in the photographs.

She gave a small sigh of relief and promised herself to try harder to eat more—even to gain a few pounds—as she returned to the couch. Everything was going to be fine. She just needed to get a grip on her eating. Sure. She just needed to do what the doctor said. Putting on a few pounds wouldn't be so tough. Especially with all that food in the kitchen.

She felt much better. She could do this. She was fine.

Steve woke when she sat down.

"Oh, hi." He covered a yawn.

"Sorry. I didn't mean to wake you."

"No problem." He noticed the pictures in her hands. "What are those?"

She handed Steve the photos, wondering if he'd react to her image like she had.

He looked at each of them, then back to her.

"You two look good together. For what it's worth, I think Rich is making a big mistake."

So did she.

"He's never going to be happy with her. I tried to talk him out of leaving; we even got in an argument about it. But his mind's made up."

Alex couldn't talk.

"You okay?"

She shrugged.

"I know how you feel." He dropped the pictures onto the coffee table.

If anyone knew, Steve did.

Reaching for her hand, he pulled her next to him on the couch. After a healing hug, they sat and watched cartoons together.

Around five o'clock, Dr. Rawlins, the first of the guests, arrived. He was carrying a gift as well as a cellophane-wrapped basket of fruit in his arms.

"Happy birthday," he called as he walked through the front door that had a "Please come in" sign on it.

Judith hadn't wanted anyone to fuss over her birthday, or for that matter, even remember it. But it was an excuse to entertain. She loved to throw parties and entertain guests, and wasn't about to miss a chance to do both.

Hugs and greetings were exchanged, and Judith beamed with pleasure as he complimented her on her ensemble of cream stretch pants, cream turtleneck, and deep red wool blazer. Judith smiled with pleasure as she led him into the kitchen for soft drinks and pre-dinner snacks.

The Becksteads arrived soon after, and a huge fuss was made over Sara's pink satin dress. Sara's hair was a mass of curls fastened on top with a matching bow. Colleen herself looked stunning in a new moss-green pantsuit made of soft fabric that showed off her trim new figure. She'd also been to the beauty shop and received a fresh cut and perm. Alex couldn't believe she was the same woman she'd talked to less than a month ago.

Standing next to his wife was Donald. His eyes were full of love and affection as he looked proudly at his daughter and wife.

The missionaries arrived right on the Becksteads' heels. Elder Tinefa filled the doorway with his broad shoulders and the room with his laugh. In no time he had Sara giggling.

Elder Babcock shook Alex's hand, something she was getting used to, then followed his companion into the living room, where everyone had gathered around the bright fire. Standing up, Steve cleared his throat.

"Jamie and I are overwhelmed tonight to have you here with us. How wonderful to share dinner and remember the importance of Easter Sunday with people we love. We're also celebrating my mother-in-law's birthday. I know there are plenty of mother-in-law jokes around, but none of them apply to her. She's great. And if you don't believe me, take a look at her daughters."

Judith smiled proudly at her son-in-law.

"Dr. Rawlins, Brother and Sister Beckstead and Sara, we've known you folks since we moved here to Island Park. You're like family to us and we are thankful you could be here tonight.

"And Elder Babcock and Elder Tinefa. Having you here to tonight helps us remember the true meaning of Easter and we're grateful you would spend this time with us.

"Now, without further ado, I think we should have a prayer on this food that has been so lovingly prepared."

The group folded their arms, bowed their heads, and listened as Elder Babcock asked a blessing on the food and invited the Lord's spirit to be with them and help them reflect on the resurrection of the Savior.

This time when the warmth filled her chest, Alex knew exactly what it was, and she added a small, silent prayer of thanks for the sweet spirit stirring her soul.

Dinner was a feast for kings. Elder Tinefa managed to fill his plate four times, and still there was tons of food left in the kitchen. Alex was so busy serving the others that she didn't have time to fill a plate for herself. But she made an extra effort to take a bite of something every chance she got.

After the last round of helpings, everyone sat in their chairs, groaning with agony.

"Anyone for pie?" Judith said brightly. Another groan and a laugh came from the group.

"Why don't we go into the living room?" Jamie said. "It's a little more comfortable in there."

Chairs scooted, dishes were gathered out of the way, and the bunch waddled their way to the couches and chairs.

"We don't really have a program planned," Jamie said. "But we thought it might be nice to sing a couple of Easter songs and read from the Bible."

They sang two songs from the hymnbook, "He Is Risen" and "Christ the Lord Is Risen Today." Sara's sweet voice beside Alex made it difficult at times to read the notes.

After the second song ended, no one spoke. Somehow in her twenty-seven years Alex had missed this part of Easter. The celebrations she'd attended had nothing to do with peace, love, or Christ.

Steve had asked Donald if he would read the story of Easter, so Donald stood and began reading from the New Testament. His deep voice, low and soothing, lent itself to the reverence of the words. Vividly the image of the Garden of Gethsemane opened to Alex's mind. The pictures Sara had shown her in the binder that first Sunday sprang to life—Christ kneeling to pray, then later, hanging on the cross; Mary at the tomb; and the resurrected Jesus Christ in all his glory.

Alex had heard the story before, but never like this. Never with her heart.

Donald was barely able to whisper the last verse. Obviously touched, he closed the book carefully and held it to his chest as he took the seat next to his wife.

No one wanted to break the spell, but finally Steve stood and thanked Donald for the story. The hour was getting late and the missionaries mentioned they needed to be getting back home.

"Before you go please take some of this food home with you," Judith said. She hustled the two missionaries and Dr. Rawlins into the kitchen to load them with goodies.

The Becksteads stood to leave but Alex stopped them. "Before you go I'd like to give Sara a special gift, if that's okay."

Donald and Colleen looked at her, their expressions puzzled.

Alex placed a long, thin, gift-wrapped box in Sara's lap.

"For me?" Sara said.

Alex nodded.

Ever so carefully Sara lifted each piece of tape and removed the paper from the box. Then she raised the lid, handed it to her mother, and sorted through the tissue. When she revealed the doll, she cried, "Oh, Mommy look!"

She looked up at Alex in wonder. "Is she really mine?" Alex nodded and smiled.

"She's the most beautiful doll in the world." Sara's eyes couldn't have been wider. She reached out a tentative finger to trace the doll's costume, then stopped and ran toward Alex. Wrapping her arms around Alex, Sara held her tightly, then, to Alex's surprise, Sara started to cry.

"Honey, what's wrong?" Alex tried to pull her away to look at her, but the little girl clung tightly to her neck. Wondering what she had done to provoke this unexpected reaction, Alex looked at Colleen apologetically. Colleen looked at her husband, who was near tears himself, then back at Alex. Donald knelt down beside Sara and gently lifting her arm, pulled her to his chest. She clung tightly to his neck and hid her head in his shoulder.

"She's just tired," Colleen said.

As Steve went to get coats, Donald whispered to his daughter, "Are you okay now?" Sara nodded and lifted her head. "Why don't you sit here by Mommy and I'll go warm up the car." He kissed her forehead and sat the child gently on the couch next to his wife.

Alex knelt down beside them. "You aren't sad about the doll, are you, Sara?"

"Oh no, I love her. I didn't mean to cry."

"It's okay to cry happy tears. I'm glad you like her." Alex lifted the doll for Sara to see. "She has hair just the color of yours and look, her eyes are blue."

"Just like mine," Sara said softly.

"Let's put her in the box and you can take her home." Alex laid the doll gently inside the box and let Sara replace the lid.

"Thank you, Alex. I love you." Sara's little arms lifted and Alex gave her a hug.

"I love you, too," Alex said, her voice thick with emotion.

"Can I tell Dr. Rawlins good-bye, Mommy?"

"Of course, sweetie." Colleen blinked away the moisture in her eyes. Colleen and Alex watched her skip out of the room.

"I'm sorry," Colleen said. "She's been very sensitive lately."

"I don't mean to pry, but are you two working things out?"

"Alex, it's like a miracle. Donald and I have never been closer. I have prayed and fasted harder for this than for anything in my whole life. Then when you found that picture of him, and I told him about your father . . . All I can say is it was a miracle. Things have never been better. I feel like I did when we first got married."

"I'm so happy for you two, and for Sara."

"It wasn't just Donald, I had some changing to do, too. Once I stopped thinking of myself and my needs and feeling sorry for myself, it all started turning around. He's even talking about going to church Sunday. And did you see him talking to the missionaries? I think they really hit it off. And the fact that it's Easter makes it even more significant because we truly are having a new beginning, a chance to start over."

Donald came back inside. "Brrr, it's cold out there."

Steve helped them find their coats and loaded them with plates full of food. They called their good-byes and were off in the night.

"I'd better shove off," Dr. Rawlins said, coming from the kitchen. "I'm driving to Idaho Falls in the morning to see my son and his family."

"Don't forget this." Judith held up a bag of food.

"Alex," the doctor said, accepting the food, "Could I have a moment with you?"

She walked the doctor to door. "What is it, Dr. Rawlins."

"I checked on some of the outpatient programs through the hospital in Idaho Falls, and I'd like to have you get in touch with one of the counselors there."

"For what?!"

"Alex, I can tell just by looking at you that you haven't put on any weight, and judging by the dark circles under your eyes, I'd bet you've lost another pound or two."

Alex tried to keep her breathing even. Right now was not the time to get the family upset over her weight loss. Jamie seemed to be doing fine, and Alex didn't want to give her any reason to worry. "I'm fine," she said. "I've just been under a lot of strain lately. I'm eating, I promise. I don't need to talk to a counselor."

Dr. Rawlins gave her a long, somber look. "Please be careful, Alex,"

"I'm okay, really," she promised. "I'm doing better."

They didn't continue the discussion and Dr. Rawlins soon left. Alex knew she wasn't fooling him, but she really was fine. And once she got back to California, she could get her life back together.

"Now that was a great party," Judith said, joining Alex and slipping an arm around her daughter's waist as they walked back to the living room. "What a nice group of people."

Alex noticed her sister's pale face and drawn features. "Jamie, are you okay?"

"I'm fine, just tired, that's all. Would you mind if I turn in early? It's been a long day."

Alex watched as Steve helped Jamie up the stairs to their room. She didn't voice her fears but worry filled her.

That night before going to bed, Alex stood at her window and looked out at the glistening path of moonlight through the trees. Change. Life seemed to follow one straight road, then without warning, it turned and twisted and branched into different paths leaving you wondering which way to go.

She didn't doubt that the feelings she felt were real. The Holy Ghost had borne witness to her of the truth. But that didn't make it easy to detour off that familiar road, onto an unknown path.

A star, brighter than the others, caught her eye. *Heavenly Father, thank you for this wonderful night, for the Becksteads and little Sara. Thank you for helping me learn the truth and to learn about the sacrifice of Thy Son.*

Please bless Jamie and her baby. Please help me to be strong and make the changes I need to make. And please help me get better control of my eating.

I'm scared.

Chapter 34

EARLY THE NEXT MORNING A KNOCK SOUNDED ON THE BEDROOM door just as Alex was changing her clothes to go downstairs.

Before Alex could cover herself, Jamie poked her head inside, "Good morn— Alex! Oh my gosh, Alex!" Jamie's mouth fell open and her eyes were wide as she stood there.

"What?" Alex looked around, expecting to see a tarantula-sized spider hanging above her head.

"I . . . You . . ." Jamie continued to stare at her.

"What is it, Jamie?" Now Alex was scared. What was going on?

Jamie walked slowly to her sister, her eyes traveling the length of Alex's body from feet to head. "You're nothing but skin and bones."

Embarrassed, Alex grabbed for her robe but Jamie stopped her. "What have you done to yourself, Alex?"

"I haven't done anything to myself." Alex jerked her arm from her sister's grasp and pulled on the robe.

"I had no idea you'd lost so much weight."

"I haven't lost that much weight." Alex shoved her feet into her slippers and headed for the door.

"Alex, *stop.*"

Alex stopped.

"Look at me." Jamie waited for her sister to turn around. "Alex, please."

Alex turned and looked at her sister.

Jamie's voice quavered. "You look just like you did in high school."

Alex remained silent.

"Why are you doing this? What's going on?"

Alex tried to keep her voice steady. "Jamie, I told you, nothing's going on. I've just been upset lately, and I don't eat well when I'm upset. I'm working with Dr. Rawlins though, and he's helping me. Everything's okay, honest."

Jamie slowly shook her head, as if she still couldn't believe her eyes. "Do you even weigh ninety pounds?"

"Of course I do."

Jamie's expression was filled with doubt.

"Dr. Rawlins is keeping track of my weight," Alex said, knowing full well she was stretching the truth. But she achieved the desired effect; Jamie's shoulders slumped in relief. "He's even got a name for a counselor he wants me to contact," she added, although she had no intention of doing so.

"A counselor," Jamie repeated. "I think that's a good idea."

"I just didn't want you or Mom to worry for no reason. Okay?"

With a trembling smile, Jamie said, "Okay. It's just that you always wear so many layers of clothes, and big shirts and stuff, I didn't realize until now how thin you are. You're an absolute skeleton."

"Not for long. Dr. Rawlins is going to get me fattened up in no time. You'll see. Now, let me get changed and I'll be right down to give Mom her birthday presents."

Jamie gave her a hug. "I'd die if anything happened to you, Alex. Please take care of yourself."

"Don't worry, Jamie, please. I've got everything under control." How many times had she said that recently? Alex wondered.

With one last smile, Jamie left the room.

Alex shut her eyes and exhaled slowly. She kept saying she had everything under control. She did, didn't she?

Steve was stacking logs in the fireplace when Alex finally came downstairs. Judith was in the kitchen rattling dishes and pans and humming cheerfully.

Halfway into the living room, Alex stopped. Standing next to the piano was an easel. Propped up on the easel was a wrapped, flat rectangle with a huge blue bow. Her name was scrawled across the front in Rich's handwriting.

"I can't believe this." Alex rested her hand on the top of the easel and shut her eyes for a moment. She missed him so much!

"Mom," Jamie called. "Alex is ready to open Rich's gift."

Wiping her hands on a dish cloth, Judith joined them.

Snapping back to the moment, Alex said, "Happy Birthday, Mom, although it seems weird for me to be getting a gift."

Carefully she tilted the package forward and tore the paper apart in the back. Then, setting the picture upright, she unveiled a beautiful watercolor landscape of the valley viewed from the ridge behind Jamie's house just as the blush of spring grew into summer.

Alex immediately fell in love with it.

"Did Rich paint this?" Judith left her chair hurriedly and examined the painting closely. Then she looked at the other picture hanging in the front room. "He must have done that painting also, and the ones in your bedroom."

"Alex," Steve said, "you ought to know that's Rich's favorite painting. He's been hanging onto it for a long time. I kept telling him to sell, but he wouldn't part with it. I even offered to buy it."

Alex was stunned speechless. Why had he given her this?

"He's very talented," Judith said. "This is beautiful. I wouldn't mind having one for my house. Are you sure he won't sell his paintings?"

"He may give you one, but he won't sell them," Steve came over and studied the watercolor. "It's amazing how he can capture every branch and blade of grass."

Alex turned to her mother. "Just don't get any ideas about taking my painting," she said.

Judith laughed. "You read my mind. I was going to offer to store it for you at my apartment for a while."

Soon Judith was sitting on the couch beside a stack of presents. She opened each one slowly, enjoying every moment. She loved the soft leather gloves, the perfume, the scarf, and sunflower pin. In the last box she found the jacket from her daughters.

"Girls, it's beautiful," she gasped with delight. "The pattern and colors are just perfect."

Quickly she stood and tried it on. The fit was just right and Judith happily rattled off the different ensembles she had at home that would match it, and the many functions and activities where she could wear it.

During the opening of the presents, Jamie had shown less and less enthusiasm. As soon as the last package was open, she excused herself quietly and left the room. As Alex was helping Steve flatten boxes and wad up the wrapping paper, she had a strange feeling and went to find her sister.

Not finding Jamie on the lower level, Alex went up to her sister's bedroom. The bedroom was empty, but the bathroom door was closed. Alex tapped on the door lightly.

"Jamie, are you okay?" she called.

There was no answer. Alex knocked harder, but there was still no reply. She tried the knob, but it was locked. The uncomfortable feeling she'd had earlier settled into a knot of fear in her stomach.

"Steve!" she called down the stairs. "Come here, quick!"

She started pounding on the door as if her life depended on it. "Jamie!" she screamed. "Jamie!"

Steve didn't wait for an explanation. He tested the doorknob and when it wouldn't open, he held it firm and rammed his shoulder into the wood. The door didn't budge.

"Find something to stick in the lock," he told Alex.

Alex searched frantically. By that time Judith was also in the room and had joined the search. Finally, Alex ripped one of Rich's pictures off the wall and pulled out the nail it had been hanging on.

"Try this."

He inserted the nail and wiggled it around. Finally the knob popped. With a turn he was inside. "Oh, Jamie," he moaned. She lay on the floor, unconscious. Even worse, a puddle of blood-tinged liquid was slowly spreading on the floor beneath her.

Thirty minutes later they met the helicopter at the West Yellowstone Clinic, ready to fly her to Idaho Falls.

"Dr. Rawlins will meet you at the hospital," Steve told the pilot and EMT in charge.

"You folks drive carefully," the pilot said. "We don't want to have to come back for you."

Jamie was still unconscious, and her blood pressure was low. Steve kissed her forehead quickly before they loaded her inside.

"Let's go," Steve said. He ran back to the car before the helicopter blades even started spinning.

"I think you should let Alex drive," Judith said.

"I— I . . ." He wiped furiously at his eyes. "Okay, whatever. Let's just get going."

The waiting room in the hospital smelled like stale cigarettes and coffee. Steve had gone directly to the labor and delivery area when they arrived, but Judith and Alex were asked to wait outside. Not knowing what was happening nearly killed them.

Television had never irritated Alex more than it did at that time. Every smiling face, every cheerful commercial seemed to intensify the sickening ache in her stomach. Had she'd caused her sister to go into premature labor? Jamie had been pretty upset by the discovery of Alex's drastic weight loss that morning. Alex was almost ill with fear and guilt.

She sat down on the brown vinyl couch next to her mother. "Mom?"

Judith opened her eyes and raised her head.

"I didn't mean to wake you."

"You didn't, honey."

"I know that my interest in the Mormon church is hard for you, but I wondered if you would join me in a prayer."

"Alex, I've been praying since we found Jamie this morning."

Alex rubbed her mother's forearm. "I know, me too. But I think it would help her and make us feel better if we did something constructive. What do you think?"

"Sure, sweetie, why not. It's better than sitting here listening to this infernal elevator music."

"Let's find a private spot."

Around the corner from the waiting room they located a small room with narrow bed, a sink and mirror, and a vinyl chair in the corner.

Pulling the door shut behind them, they knelt in the shadowed light from the tiny window.

"I'm not sure I know how to do this correctly," Alex said.

"Just say what's in your heart," her mother said.

With bowed heads and clasped hands, Alex offered up a prayer in Jamie's behalf. She asked for a blessing to be with the doctors and nurses. She prayed for Jamie's strength and health and for Katelyn's life. She pled for help and understanding for them all, that the Lord's will would be done, and that they might have the strength to endure whatever came to pass.

Both women were sniffing and wiping at tears when Alex closed in the Savior's name. Embracing, still on their knees, they drew on each other's strength and knew they had to hold fast for Jamie and the baby's sake.

Urgency seized Alex as they hurried back to the waiting room, hoping they hadn't missed Steve or the doctor. Steve sat slumped over on the edge of a chair, elbows propped on his knees, with his head in his hands.

"Steve!" Alex ran to him and put her arms around him. Looking up, he let Alex hug him, but he didn't speak.

"How is she?" Alex finally broke the silence.

"They can't stop the contractions," he whispered. Alex saw the pain in his eyes. He didn't have to say any more.

From somewhere down the corridor a woman's voice said, "Steve, honey, we're here."

The three turned and saw Steve's parents racing toward them. Mrs. Dixon stood on tip-toe to wrap her arms around her son's chest as she patted the center of his back. She smelled like lilacs and sported a hairdo designed for a bee colony.

"Judith, nice to see you again." Mrs. Dixon pressed her pink powdered cheek to Judith's. Absentmindedly Judith brushed her face with her hand when they parted.

"Son." Mr. Dixon had stood back to let his wife embrace their son. Now he shook Steve's hand, then pulled him into a brief hug.

"How is she? What's the doctor saying?" Mrs. Dixon asked.

Steve's face was ashen. "She's in labor. The baby's chances are slim to none this early in the pregnancy."

"Do they know what's causing her body to do this?" Mrs. Dixon asked.

Steve shook his head. "All Dr. Rawlins said is that for some reason, from the very beginning, her body has fought this pregnancy. In some cases the patient responds to medication and labor stops. Jamie's body isn't responding."

So maybe she wasn't responsible for putting Jamie in the hospital, Alex thought.

"Have you given Jamie a blessing?" Mr. Dixon asked.

"I wanted to wait for you, Dad. I'll check to see if this is a good time for us to come in."

Steve disappeared through a doorway, and returned a few moments later.

"Dr. Rawlins is with Jamie and says we should hurry. They've given her some anesthetic for the contractions. She's sleeping right now."

"You're welcome to come, too," Steve invited his mother, Alex, and Judith.

Judith stepped back uncomfortably, but Alex answered, "Thank you, we'd like to be with Jamie if we could."

The women stood at the foot of the bed while Steve and his father placed drops of consecrated oil on Jamie's head. The commotion of the birthing room seemed to fade as Mr. Dixon placed his hands on Jamie's head and sealed the oil. Then Steve began the blessing.

Alex had expected Steve to command the powers of heaven to stop the contractions and save his unborn child. Instead, he humbly thanked the Lord for their abundant blessings and prayed for greater understanding and strength to endure the challenge they were facing. He even quoted a scripture, saying that "after much tribulation come the blessings of the Lord."

He choked up as he placed their baby's future in the Lord's hands and asked that His will be done.

During the prayer Alex opened her eyes to peek at Jamie, laying helplessly on the bed, with various tubes and bands hooked up to her arm and stomach. This was one thing about God she didn't understand. Why did he allow so much suffering to go on? What good, if any, could come from Jamie losing another baby? Jamie, the most humble, Christlike person Alex knew. Why did she have to endure *this* of all challenges? The only thing Jamie wanted out of life was to be a wife and a mother. God sent millions of children to unfit homes all the time. Why couldn't God give a decent loving couple some of those children?

"Amen" was murmured and the group tightened the circle about her bed. Judith rested her hand on her daughter's arm.

Jamie had slept through the blessing but at least the needle had stopped bouncing on the contraction monitor. Maybe the labor had stopped, Alex prayed. Her mother had received a miracle when she'd had a lump in her breast. Donald Beckstead had received a miracle when he'd realized the importance of his family and the Church. Surely Jamie's situation merited a miracle.

"Why don't we let her get some rest?" Dr. Rawlins said. One by one they moved toward the door. Judith bent over and kissed her daughter's forehead, smoothing Jamie's hair back away from her face, then left the room crying.

"Mom," Alex called after her.

Outside in the hallway Alex found her mother leaning against a wall, drying her face with a tissue.

"It's so hard," she said. "I would give anything to be in her place and spare her all of this pain."

"I know," Alex said. "I know." *Is this how Heavenly Father felt when he watched his son in Gethsemane?*

"I feel so helpless, just like I did when we found out you had anorexia and the doctors told me how close we'd come to losing you." Judith stroked Alex's hair. "I couldn't bear to lose one of you. Alex," Judith stood back from Alex and looked her in the eye, "you have to promise me that you'll take care of yourself. Don't ever take your health for granted."

For once Alex's reaction wasn't anger. Her defenses were down. She realized how fragile Jamie's life, Katelyn's life, and even her life was.

"I won't, Mom."

Still crying, Judith excused herself to go find the ladies room, leaving Alex to ponder her conversation with her mother. She wasn't deliberately starving herself, but, in all honesty, she had to admit she was nevertheless. And she didn't know how to stop.

Hours passed and Jamie's condition didn't change. She slept off and on between contractions, but there was no improvement.

Although the Dixons invited Alex and Judith to come to their home and spend the night, they both declined. If something happened, good or bad, they wanted to be there for Jamie and Steve.

"Please call the minute you hear anything," Mrs. Dixon said.

"Don't know why we're going home, we won't get any sleep," Mr. Dixon said. He pulled on his coat and gloves and helped his wife on with hers.

"You two try to get some rest anyway," Judith said. "Who knows what tomorrow will bring?"

The kink on the left side of Alex's neck knotted as she lifted her head off the back of the couch and looked around. The hospital was dim and quiet where they were. Judith was curled up next to her, a thin hospital blanket clutched to her neck. Alex reached over and tucked the blanket around her mother's feet and stood to stretch. The clock read two-thirty.

Dr. Rawlins had gone to the doctors' lounge for some food and sleep while Steve kept vigil at his wife's bedside.

Alex walked down the hallway, smiling at the night nurse and wondering how anyone could get used to the antiseptic smell that drenched the air.

In the restroom she splashed water on her face and neck and let the blower dry her skin, then applied a thin coat of lotion from a tube in her purse. As she put the lotion back she found a container of Carmex. Tears filled her eyes as she applied the balm to her lips. Right now she could use some of Rich's strength and faith, as a healing balm for her pain. Most of her heart was breaking for Jamie, but a small corner still ached for Rich.

The reminder was too painful. She tossed the Carmex in the trash and tissued off her lips.

On her way out of the restroom she checked the clock again. How slowly the time passed. It was now two-forty and she had nothing else to do. She'd read all the magazines on the floor, walked every inch of space, and looked glumly out the windows located on each end of the hallway.

She walked past the nursery where three newborns were cocooned in clear plastic bassinets. Would Katelyn make it this far?

Down the hallway Alex noticed a scale. Her first impulse was to walk away, then she stopped. She needed to face reality. Something she should've done long before now.

She moved the weights to one hundred, but the arrow still wasn't lined up. She tapped it down to ninety-nine, then ninety-eight. It balanced.

Her breath caught in her throat. Only fifteen pounds from the weight she was in high school when she was hospitalized.

Tears began to fall. She needed help. As strong as she thought she was, she couldn't do it alone.

She was scared and she was ready.

It was time to get the counselor's name from Dr. Rawlins.

* * *

Her mother had shifted positions while she was gone and the blanket had twisted around her legs. Alex studied her mother's face while she slept. Her makeup had rubbed off long ago and her hair tangled from sleep. Judith, who kept up such an independent, brave front, had shown a vulnerable side today.

Alex wondered just how happy her mother was. If Alex had felt loneliness and longing in her life, didn't Judith? No matter how many friends and colleagues she had at work, like Alex, Judith still went home to an empty house.

Then she had an idea. Maybe it was time to relocate, move back to New York so she could be near her mother. Certainly she would have no trouble furthering her career there. It didn't really matter where she lived, as long as she had access to an airport. Her job was wherever the next convention or workshop was. And even though she enjoyed the sun and fun of California, she could get excited about the hum and fast pace of the city, as well as the chance to bury Rich's face in the crowds.

Her attention shifted when she noticed a blinking light beeping at the nurses' station. The nurse picked up the phone and nodded her head, then hung up that extension and picked up a different phone to place another call. Seconds later Alex heard Dr. Rawlins' name being paged.

"Mom." Alex reached down and touched her mother's shoulder.

"What? Is something wrong?" Judith threw the blanket off and sprang to her feet.

"They just paged Dr. Rawlins, I think something's . . ."

A cry from Jamie's room sent them running. They stopped outside her door.

Judith covered her ears and buried her head on Alex's chest. From inside the room Jamie's cries seemed to echo through the door and down the hall.

Alex prayed with every ounce of faith she had.

Seconds ticked like hours on the clock. Each agony-filled moan tore at Alex's heart.

Then the cries stopped and a calm hushed over them like a silent wave. Judith lifted her head and they both froze. And waited.

And waited.

Inside the room she heard muffled voices. The words weren't clear but the urgent tone kept her straining to pick out anything audible to indicate what was happening behind that door.

Clanging metal and deep voices competed in Alex's ears. What was going on?

Judith nearly had the strap of her purse twisted off when Dr. Rawlins finally stepped out of the room, peeling off a surgical mask. Alex looked over his shoulder. The nurses collected machines and instruments, wadded up blue pads and bedding, and amidst their cleaning she saw Steve hunched over the bed.

She looked at Dr. Rawlins' drawn expression and saw tears in his eyes.

"I'm sorry. We've lost the baby," he said. "There was nothing we could do."

Judith crumbled into Alex's arms.

It was over.

Chapter 35

"Do you want to take this tray up to Jamie, Mom?"

Judith put down her magazine. Her red-rimmed eyes and lack of mascara reflected the constant agony she felt for her daughter's loss. The whole family walked around in a daze, day after day, looking like they'd taken a beating. Feeling like there was something more to do, but not knowing what.

Alex's heart ached for the pain her mother felt and she was concerned as well about Steve. The poor man barely spoke. When he did, it was as if his mind wasn't engaged. He listened to conversations but didn't hear anything. He was there in body, but his spirit was elsewhere.

But her biggest concern was for Jamie, who'd confined herself to her bedroom, blinds shut, door closed, entombed in silence.

"I'll take the food to her," Judith said, "but I know she won't eat it." Her voice caught in her throat. "I'm so worried about her. What are we going to do?"

Alex sat the tray on the coffee table and pulled her mother into a hug. Then, pulling a few tissues from one of the many boxes scattered throughout the house, they wiped their faces dry, an exercise they performed dozens of times each day.

"All we can do is be strong for her and pray."

Judith nodded, drew in a long breath, and picked up the tray of food.

Alex shut her eyes, praying for strength to keep herself and everyone else going. She desperately hoped that if they carried on as normal, then everything would be normal.

Except that nothing would ever be the same again.

How she needed a shoulder to cry on, someone to hold her. She'd felt some comfort in her prayers and scripture reading. But it wasn't coming fast enough. She wanted all of this to be over, in the past.

She needed Rich.

He hadn't been able to return for the funeral service. He had taken off with his brothers on a three-day cross-country ski trip to their cabin and couldn't be reached in time.

Why had this happened? Why couldn't everything be the same as it was when Rich was here?

As the family had stood at Katelyn's graveside, watching the tiny casket being lowered into the frozen earth, Alex had known.

Nothing *could* ever be the same again.

Just when she'd thought she'd gotten a handle on this faith, prayer, and fasting thing, it had failed. The Lord had let her down. Hadn't he said he would always be there?

The overcast, blurry day matched the cloudiness in her heart and mind. A storm was building. And just as the turmoil in the skies outside grew stronger, the turmoil inside Alex's heart did the same. The next thing she knew, she'd slipped on enough layers of snow clothes and protective gear to survive the Arctic, then headed outside.

The snowmobile her brother-in-law had been riding before he went to work that morning was parked in the driveway. How many times had he offered to let Alex take it for a ride?

Without another thought Alex climbed on the machine and turned on the engine. Any fear or doubt she'd had about maneuvering the sled was squelched by her need to both vent her anger and physically wrestle with her emotions.

Alex twisted the handle and with a lunge and a roar, the snowmobile shot forward. She dodged the garbage can and woodpile with only inches to spare. After negotiating several more obstacles, including the clothesline and the wooden fence, she emerged onto the open hillside.

Grateful for the hood and goggles protecting her face from the biting cold, Alex angled the snowmobile faster and further up the hill. The path she traveled wound through woods where armies of trees stood at attention, bearing their burdens of snow with broad pine shoulders. The power she felt beneath her and the freedom of flying on the machine gave wings to her emotions. With soaring energy she continued, her destination not a place, but a feeling. Craving peace, she longed to somehow make sense of all the "whys" in her world. Lost in her surroundings, everything, even time, seemed frozen and still.

As the snowmobile chugged up another hill, it began to sputter and cough. Ten yards from the top, it died completely. With the storm of emotion still roiling inside her, she climbed off and trudged up the hill, each step becoming more forceful until she broke into a hampered run. As the snow sunk beneath her, every stride ripped at her muscles and tore at her lungs.

Even when exhaustion took over, she pushed, commanding herself to go on, to run. She pushed onward until the burning in her chest reignited her anger. At the top of the ridge she raised her fists to the sky, looked up, and yelled, "WHY?"

Collapsing to the ground, she heard her echoed voice fade into the treetops. Great heaving sobs gushed like lava from an erupting volcano. With fists pounding the icy snow, she released her anger, asking over and over the question: "Why?"

Soon snow began to fall, but Alex continued to sob, numb to the cold but not the pain in her heart. One short month ago her life had been free and easy, with few worries, and no trauma.

Now, on top of the pain of falling in love with and losing Rich, she had to face anew the memory of her father's death, watch her sister's anguish at losing her baby, and know the heartache her mother felt because now both her daughters had embraced the same church that had killed her husband.

The more Alex thought about it, the harder she cried. And cried. And cried.

Then, when there was nothing left inside, as she lay collapsed in an exhausted heap, panting and gasping, Alex listened to the stillness. Like a drain unplugging, the anger seeped away, leaving her calm, weak, and light.

The snow stopped. And so did her despair. As she lay wrapped in silence, peace came.

She lifted her head, looking around, then pushed herself onto her heels and brushed away the layer of feathery flakes. She felt better, but she was still confused. Jamie had carried this baby longer than any of the others. It was so close this time.

Why did Katelyn have to die?

Through a break in the clouds, low on the horizon, a channel of sun beamed onto a section of trees in the forest. The small circle of color shed light into the black and white world.

A strand of hope.

Then something she'd heard Steve say in Jamie's blessing flashed in her memory. *For after much tribulation come the blessings.*

Did that mean that somehow they would be blessed for enduring such a painful loss?

After much tribulation.

Was the Lord aware of all that had happened?

The peace and warmth in her chest didn't explain why Katelyn wasn't home sleeping in a bassinet, but it did calm her heart and tell her—the Lord was aware.

Where was that scripture? She'd read it before.

She had to get back to the house and find it. For herself and for Jamie.

But when she viewed her surroundings, she realized she didn't have a clue where she was.

Follow the snowmobile path home.

The thought came as clear as spring water.

She charged down the sloping hillside to the sled and hopped on. But her attempts to start the engine were futile. She looked at the gas indicator. Empty.

There was no telling how far she'd traveled, but she could tell by the setting sun that she didn't have time to sit and wonder or berate herself for not checking the gauge earlier. And as if that wasn't enough, a light snow was falling like sifted powdered sugar.

Without signs of human life anywhere, Alex felt small and insignificant amidst the wide expanse of snow-covered rolling hills and towering pines. But she didn't feel alone. In her heart, she knew the Lord was just a prayer away, and she remained calm as she followed the rut left by the snowmobile path back toward home.

But soon darkness closed in and the snowfall grew denser. Hard as she tried, she couldn't stop fear from rooting inside her stomach. Each step grew more painful as her frozen feet slogged through the deep snow.

By now she couldn't see the outline of the trees and the snowmobile path had started to fill with the fresh snow. *Why didn't I tell someone where I was going?*

Rich had warned her not to go off on her own; he'd even told her he didn't want to lose her. Well, he had lost her. In more ways than one.

Peering into the darkness for some pinpoint of light, Alex held her breath, straining to see. Nothing. The wet kiss of snowflakes covered her cheeks and chin, adding to the numbing cold. Then it struck her.

There was absolutely no way she could survive all night outdoors. If no one found her she would die.

They wouldn't even know where to begin looking.

I'm going to die.

A giant sob tore from her throat, *"Noooooo!"* but the heavy falling snow absorbed her cry. This wasn't how she was supposed to die, with so much still to accomplish and so many people still needing her. Just when she'd decided to make so many changes in her life. Her family didn't need, didn't deserve, another tragedy.

Keep moving.

She didn't want to keep moving. She wanted to sit down and cry. She'd never been so cold or scared in her life.

Keep moving!

"How can I keep moving when I can't see the path?" she muttered in annoyance. "I hate the snow!" She tried to stomp her feet but couldn't feel them anymore. As tired as she was, she forced herself to keep moving, noticing that her feet had started to throb and ache with each step as blood seared through her icy extremities.

"I'm not going to die like this."

She had too much to live for to give up without a fight—overcoming her eating disorder, setting a baptismal date with the missionaries. But there was one more thing she was holding out for—the hope that Rich would change his mind about Monica.

Stumbling, she forged ahead, not knowing where she was going or if she would make it. But she wasn't going to stop. The Lord knew what was happening. Her life was in his hands now.

Chapter 36

ALEX DIDN'T KNOW THE NIGHT COULD GET SO BLACK. OR COLD. At least the snow had stopped.

The minute she got back to Jamie and Steve's she was going back to California where she'd never complain about the heat again. Maybe she'd take a steaming shower first and get something to eat. Then maybe get some sleep. Then she'd go home.

She was so tired. Lead-heavy and exhausted, she struggled to put one frozen foot in front of the other, stumbling, dragging, staggering.

Through the blur in her head she imagined the sound of engines and shouts, but no visual proof appeared.

Father in Heaven, is this really it? Now that I've found the gospel and the purpose of life, I'm going to die?

Her legs refused to go on. Focusing on the starlit sky, she pleaded once more for the Lord to sustain her life, to let her live. Then she collapsed to her knees and wept.

* * *

Roaring engines shook Alex from sleep. She fought the noise, reasoning that her mind was playing tricks on her again. Within the frozen shell of numbness, she was prepared to sleep again and most likely never awaken. She'd decided that as dying went, freezing to death wasn't as awful as other ways to go. So, she curled up tighter and waited for sleep to come. But the noise continued.

Lifting her head, her vision foggy, she was blinded by a brilliant light. Was this it? Heaven's door opening?

Unable to rise she remained curled up in the snow as she squinted into the light, waiting for what would happen next. From within the column of light, several figures approached, reached down, and pulled her up. Her legs couldn't straighten, her bones wouldn't give.

"Alex," a voice hollered. "Alex, can you hear me?"

Were these angels?

She opened her cracked, bleeding lips but couldn't speak.

As arms circled and lifted her, a fit of shivers overtook her, shaking her frame. "I've got you. You're going to be okay," she heard. She could have sworn it was Rich's voice she was hearing.

What was he doing in heaven?

Even with the warm blanket wrapped around her, she trembled and quaked.

"That's it, keep shaking. Fight, Alex. I need you. Please don't give up."

It *was* Rich's voice. He was with her now. Telling her to fight.

She was too tired to fight. She'd fight later. In Rich's arms she was finally safe.

* * *

Again, the sound of voices awoke her.

Her feet throbbed, and her toes felt like they were being pinched and burned.

Rich? Where was he? Had she been dreaming or had he really been with her?

"Rich?"

She heard scuffling, then, "I'm here, Alex."

Her vision focused on the most wonderful face she'd ever seen. Rich's face. Filled with worry and love.

"I wasn't dreaming?"

"No, Alex. We found you just in time." He leaned down and kissed her forehead.

"But you were in Boise."

"I came back to see you."

The hospital door opened, and Jamie burst inside, followed by Steve and Judith.

"You're awake. Look, Alex is awake." Jamie flew to Alex's bedside and embraced her.

"Hey, sis." The movement of her bed sent renewed pain to her feet and hands.

"Do you know how lucky you are? The doctors are still wondering how you survived." Jamie wiped at her tears. "Why did you take off on the snowmobile like that?"

"I'm sorry. I didn't mean to scare you."

Judith sniffed into a handful of tissue while Steve kept a protective arm around her.

"I wanted . . ." Alex swallowed. "I wanted some answers. I was confused."

"Did you find what you were looking for?" Rich asked.

Jamie stood next to her husband. Alex looked up at the four loving faces surrounding her. Her heart filled with gratitude for them and their love for her. She was so blessed.

Blessed! She was starting to sound like her sister.

Gathering her strength, she said, "Yes." Her voice trembled, but she continued, "My prayers were answered. I realized that the Lord loves us and is aware of us. I still don't understand why Katelyn had to leave us, but I know she's with him. Steve, I kept thinking of that scripture you used in the blessing you gave Jamie in the hospital."

"I don't remember much about what I said in the blessing. What scripture?"

"It was about tribulation and blessings."

"Oh," Rich said, "I think I know the one you're talking about. I've got my scriptures in the car. I can go get them."

"Would you, Rich?"

"Of course," he said. "Anything."

A nurse came in to check Alex's vitals.

"I'll be right back," Rich said.

The nurse attended to her duties while the family stood back quietly and watched. Rich returned, breathless, just as the nurse was leaving.

He ruffled through the pages for a moment. "Here it is: 'For verily I say unto you, blessed is he that keepeth my commandments, whether in life or in death; and he that is faithful in tribulation, the reward of the same is greater in the kingdom of heaven.

"'Ye cannot behold with your natural eyes, for the present time, the design of your God concerning those things which shall come hereafter, and the glory which shall follow after much tribulation.

"'For after much tribulation come the blessings. Wherefore the day cometh that ye shall be crowned with much glory; the hour is not yet, but is nigh at hand.'"

Tears streamed down Jamie's face. She nodded slightly like she understood.

"Even though getting lost out there was really stupid, I feel like I've learned for myself that prayer really works and that the Lord really is there. And I guess, if something good can come out of what happened, then I'm grateful for it."

"Sweetie," Judith leaned toward her daughter, "how are you feeling?"

"I'm tired, and my feet and hands hurt, and my lips, too. I could use some Carmex." She tried to look down at her lips but only succeeded in pulling a face, which made everyone laugh.

"Dr. Rawlins said it was a good thing you dressed so warmly and kept moving as long as you did. You were just minutes away from hypothermia," Judith told her.

Alex knew it was a miracle she survived. She shivered just thinking about being out there alone in the dark and snow. But there was no doubt in her mind, she was spared because there was much more for her to do here on the earth.

"I think we ought to let you get some sleep," Judith said. "Dave—I mean Dr. Rawlins—said you could leave the clinic tomorrow if you feel up to it."

Her mother kissed her cheek and hugged her gently. Steve followed her lead.

"You okay, Jamie?" Alex hated seeing the weariness of worry on her sister's face. Jamie had been through so much lately. Feelings of guilt pricked at her heart for adding to her sister's burden.

Jamie nodded. "I never would have imagined that you would be the one giving me spiritual strength and guidance from the scriptures."

Alex had to laugh. "Me either."

Jamie's voice dropped to a whisper. "I don't know what I would have done if we'd lost you, too."

"I'm sorry I scared you."

"I'm just glad you're all right."

Alex reached toward her sister with a bandaged hand. "Before you go I need to tell you something." She had no choice. She had to make the announcement, especially after the feelings she'd received up on the frozen mountain. "I've decided to get baptized."

Jamie's excited cry summoned the others. The hugs that followed nearly killed Alex, but the pain dimmed when compared to the great joy she felt with her decision. She tried to decipher the expression on her mother's face.

Finally Judith spoke, "Honey, if this makes you happy then that's all that matters to me."

"Thanks, Mom."

Rich remained after the others left. He put the side-rail down on her bed and sat on the edge, facing her. "I'm not hurting you, am I?"

"I like having you close," she said softly.

Again there was silence. Alex had so much to say, so much to ask, but for some reason didn't know how or where to start.

"That was some announcement you just made," he said.

Alex chuckled. "I bet you never thought those words would come out of my mouth."

"I'm just glad I was here when you said them." His warm smile helped thaw the cold in her bones. "Jamie and Steve told me you'd been meeting with the missionaries."

Their gazes locked. This man had grown to mean so much to her. Somehow she had to tell him how she felt.

Finally, whispering to keep control of her emotions, Alex said, "I couldn't believe it when you found me, Rich. I thought you were an angel from heaven."

"They'd been searching for several hours before I got back in town and found out you were missing."

"I should've listened better. You told me not to go out alone."

"I was going crazy with worry. I couldn't sit and wait. I had to get out there and look for you myself."

His finger traced a line on her arm, above her bandaged hand.

"I have to tell you, Alex, it was almost as if I was guided straight to you. Even with the snowfall, I could still make out traces of the path you took. You were only fifteen minutes from the house when we found you."

Follow the snowmobile path home. Keep moving. She *had* received help from above.

"When I saw you, snow-covered and curled up like that"—tears filled his eyes—"you didn't move or look up or anything when we first spotted you. I thought we were too late." A sob caught in his throat and he looked away. "Alex, I can't stand the thought of not being with you. That's why I came back early. I had to catch you before you went back to California because I . . . well, because I love you."

Alex caught her breath. "I love you, too, Rich." She reached toward him with gauze-wrapped hands, and he enveloped her in a gentle hug. His love and physical touch were more therapeutic than any salve or pain medication the hospital could offer.

"So," she said, when he released his hold on her, "Are you going to tell me what happened in Boise or not?"

He smiled slyly and said nothing.

"Well?" Alex insisted.

"Okay, the bottom line is, it's over between me and Monica. I knew the minute I got home and saw her that I couldn't spend the rest of my life with her, let alone eternity."

Alex's heart thumped triple time.

"Everything about Monica bugged me—her laugh, her perfectly manicured nails, her clothes, the way she didn't want to go outside in the wind because she'd mess up her hair, or go to the gym and work out because she didn't want to sweat. And I guess the biggest problem with her was that . . ." he cleared his throat, ". . . she wasn't you."

"Oh, Rich," Alex said softly.

Rich held her bandaged hand carefully, then leaned forward and pressed a gentle kiss on her forehead. "It looks like you've got me, whether you want me or not."

"Oh, I want you all right," Alex assured him.

"I probably ought to warn you, though," he confessed. "I'm not very good with relationships."

She didn't tell him she already knew about his broken engagements.

He increased the distance between them and rubbed at his chin thoughtfully. She could tell he wanted to talk but was searching for the right words. Finally he said, "It wasn't until I went home last week that I figured out why I've struggled with relationships."

He stood, put his hands in his pockets, and jangled the change inside. "It scared me so much when my parents broke up after my mission. All my life I thought they had a wonderful marriage. The next thing I know they were divorced. I guess I figured the only way to prevent that from happening in my own life was to make everything as perfect as it could be."

Pacing from the sink to the closet door, he continued, "But I've learned over the years that no relationship is perfect. We're all human." He stopped pacing. "I talked to my parents while I was in Boise. I needed to know why their marriage broke up, and you know what they told me?"

Alex shook her head.

"They told me that the problem wasn't because they wanted perfection from each other. My father went through some kind of midlife crisis, feeling frustrated with his job, with himself, with his marriage. My mom admitted she was at fault, too. They both could have tried harder to make things work, talked more, spent more time together, been more active in the Church together." He walked over to the bed and sat down next to her. "I wish I would've had this talk with them sooner. I've wasted so much time trying to guess how to create some sort of marriage guarantee."

Alex looked at him thoughtfully. "Rich, your time wasn't wasted. I'm sure you've learned a lot about yourself and what you want out of life and marriage. Maybe you weren't ready to understand until now," she continued. "That's how I was with the Church. I've known about it for a long time, but for some reason I couldn't really see the gospel for how wonderful it is. Then suddenly, it was like a veil was lifted from my eyes and I understood what the gospel was about." She looked straight at him. "I want you to know your testimony helped me a lot."

The worry lines in his forehead relaxed. "It did?"

"The words you wrote in the Book of Mormon gave me the courage to at least find out one way or the other. And now I finally realize what my life's been lacking all this time. How even with a great career, fame, and fortune," she stopped and looked outside her window, "it still wasn't enough. Now I know why. Because it's the gospel that comes first, then everything else."

"You're really something, you know that." Brushing a strand of hair away from her eyes, he said, "When I was in Boise, all I could think about was coming back here. To you." He cleared his throat. "You can't go back to California, yet. Please stay."

"I'm not going anywhere, Rich."

"I prayed so hard you'd still be here when I came back."

"Really?"

He smiled. "Really."

"You prayed for me?"

"Alex, I've prayed for you since the day I pulled you from your car."

That felt good, Alex thought. No, that felt *great*. She loved having someone care enough to pray for her. "I think your prayers have been answered," she said. "I know mine have."

"I don't ever want to risk losing you again."

After the trial of your faith come the blessings. Alex couldn't get over just how many blessings were coming to her.

He leaned toward her. "I need you in my life, Alex."

"And I need you in mine."

"Can you be patient with me while I try and sort through some things?"

"I've got some of my own sorting to do. I start meeting with an eating disorder counselor down in Idaho Falls next week." She watched his eyes for signs that he'd changed his mind. "Does that bother you?"

"Of course not. I'll support you any way I can. I'm proud of you for having the courage to change your life for the better. That's what I'm trying to do."

"Speaking of change, remind me to call my manager, Sandy, and thank her."

"What are you thanking her for?"

Alex closed her eyes. The medication was kicking in, taking the edge off her pain. "She was the one who insisted I take time off work and come to Island Park." She sighed. "Just think, if I hadn't come, I wouldn't have been here to help Jamie, and I would've never found the Church. I also might never have realized I needed to get my eating under control." She shifted to a more comfortable position. When she had settled herself, Rich smoothed the covers for her.

"It scares me to think I almost didn't come to Idaho, because Rich—I would have never met you." She looked into his eyes that were filled with love and warmth. "I never expected to find you. And now that I have, I can't imagine life without you."

Rich nodded in understanding. "And I never expected to find you." His face drew nearer to hers; their breath blended together. "So, what do we do next?"

"We need to set a date so you can baptize me." Her muscles relaxed with the dulling of her pain. Her head felt heavy.

Rich was startled. "You want me to do it?"

It was all she could do to keep her eyelids open. "I wouldn't dream of having anyone else."

"I'm honored that you would ask," he said humbly.

"Then . . . I should go back . . . to California sometime . . . for work . . ." Alex mumbled, drifting off.

"It will only be for a year," Rich said softly, stroking her arm. "I suppose we're just going to have to rack up some frequent flyer miles between now and then."

"A year?" Alex forced herself to open her eyes and look at him. Her mouth felt like it had been shot with novocaine. Her words were starting to run together. "What's a year got to do with anything?"

"You have to wait a year to get your temple recommend."

"Temple recommend?" Why did she need a temple recommend? She couldn't keep her eyes open any longer. She was so tired. Then it hit her.

"Rich!" Her eyelids flew open. "Are you saying what I think you're saying?"

He chuckled at her sudden alertness. "Yes. I'm talking about spending the rest of eternity together."

Her hug was weak, but Rich wrapped his strong arms securely around her and held her close. Alex couldn't think of anything in the whole world she wanted more than to spend eternity with the man who was holding her in his arms.

He eased her gently back onto her pillow. "Now you need to get your beauty sleep," he said, standing up.

Alex looked up at him. "A year is going to seem like eternity. So much . . . could happen . . . in a . . ." She couldn't fight the effects of the medication any longer and her voice trailed off.

He smoothed her hair back with his hand and placed a soft kiss on her brow. "Don't you worry," he said softly. "Look at all we've been through already." He brushed one corner of her mouth with his. "Nothing will happen. We belong together."

He kissed the other side of her mouth. The nerves in her fingers and toes tingled pleasantly with his touch.

"Yes," she murmured. "Together . . ."

"Forever."

Her voice was barely a whisper. "Forever . . ."

Rich leaned over her tenderly. "Go to sleep now, sweetheart. I'll be here when you wake up. Just rest and get better." He brushed her lips with his. "Sweet dreams."

Alex smiled faintly. She liked the idea that she and Rich would someday be together.

Forever.

ABOUT THE AUTHOR

The issue of anorexia has great personal relevance to Michele Ashman Bell, who says, "Working with young women has given me an appreciation for the pressures our youth feel to be, act, and look a certain way. Having watched an older sister deal with anorexia and its long-term effects for more than twenty-five years, I am well aware of the impact an eating disorder can have, not only on an individual but on an entire family."

Michele says she also wanted to write a book from a nonmember's point of view with "the character's perceptions, thoughts, and feelings about members of the Church and how she viewed the gospel and its teachings." She adds that it was important to her "to write a story that the reader could enjoy but would also be inspirational, especially as Alex McCarty, the heroine, gains a testimony of the gospel."

As a nationally certified aerobics instructor herself, Michele enjoyed writing about a character involved in the fitness industry. She also enjoys tennis, water skiing, and biking as well as remodeling her home, spending time with family, and traveling both inside and outside of the United States. "Aside from writing in my spare time," she says, "I spend most of my time encouraging, supporting, and driving my children to lessons, sports events, and recitals." Michele finds pleasure in designing and sewing costumes for her daughter Kendyl, who is a competitive ice skater.

She served a mission to Frankfurt, Germany and San Jose, California, and has served in both the Relief Society and Young Women organizations. She currently serves as president for the Young Women in her ward.

Michele and her husband, Gary, are the parents of three children: Weston, Kendyl, and Andrea. They currently make their home in Sandy, Utah.

Michele welcomes readers' comments and questions. You can write her at P.O. Box 901513, Sandy, Utah 84090.

NOTE: Eating disorders affect more than 5 million Americans, mostly women; about 1000 will die each year. Approximately 80% of those with eating disorders respond well to treatment. The National Association of Anorexia Nervosa and Associated Disorders provides hot-line counseling, information packets, newsletters, and referrals to support groups and health-care professionals; all services are free. For more information, call (847) 831-3438 or write to Box 7, Highland Park, IL 60035. You can also send email to *anad20@aol.com*.